SINNERS

SE JAKES

This is a work of fiction. Names, characters, places and incidents are the
product of the author's imagination or are used fictitiously. Any resemblance
to actual persons, living or dead, business establishments, events or locales is
entirely coincidental or has been used in a fictional manner.

*Sometimes a broken man ends up stronger than he ever was—
and far more dangerous...*

Travis Smith is a grifter who's wanted by both the Russian Mob and the FBI. He's got the means and motive to stay hidden—until he's picked up by Lochlan "Loch" Black, a CIA operative who threatens to unravel all Travis's secrets.

Loch has enough secrets of his own, and they all lead back to the man he and the CIA have been hunting for years. And when Loch realizes Travis might be the key to that op, he and longtime friend and fellow agent, Tarquin "Tar" Simons, have no choice but to keep Travis under their protection.

But no one's able to protect them all from the man who's been hunting them back for years. Jabez Snow is a former CIA operative who didn't stop his experiments when he disappeared.

And when Travis, Loch and Tar get involved, it triggers a chain of events none of them could foresee, and it threatens all their futures, unless they can hunt down Snow...before he finds them.

For MS...can't ever thank you enough for listening.

CHAPTER ONE

THE DOOR to the bedroom slammed open with a shout, followed quickly in turn by a heart-stopping, unexpectedly loud-as-fuck bang and a flash of blinding light that Travis swore he could see behind closed eyelids, all of which immediately disoriented him, leaving him to struggle out of the bed and blindly find the door.

Smoke and popping sounds filled the air, accompanied by yells of panic. Travis resisted the urge to panic, even when he realized he couldn't see or hear very well.

Later, he'd find out that the SWAT Team assisting the FBI had thrown in flash-bang grenades ahead of their bust, but all he knew in the moment was pure fear and total confusion.

He'd been nearly naked, in bed, and suddenly he was being dragged by strong arms that wouldn't let go no matter how hard he'd struggled. Whether this was a kidnapping or an attempted takeover by another Russian mob family, he hadn't been able to differentiate...not until he heard, "You're under arrest. On the floor on your stomach, hands behind your back."

Travis complied, freezing against the concrete. The metal cuffs clicked tightly on his wrists, he was unceremoniously hauled up, and a blanket was roughly shoved over his shoulders.

"Name?"

"Travis Smith," was all he'd give them. They kept asking him, over and over, what his connection with the Russian mob was until he finally said, "I fuck Serge. That's all. I have no idea about anything else you're talking about."

Which was a partial truth—he knew Sergei was Russian mafia and he fucked him anyway. Partially because he wanted to, but mainly because Travis was grifting Sergei, and had been over the past eight months.

Finally, the feds shoved him into the van, already packed with Russians Travis had seen at one time or another in Sergei's house, now all handcuffed and chained together.

Across from him, Sergei mouthed, "One word and you're dead," and Travis nodded because he wasn't stupid. He didn't want anything to do with the police at all.

But the law had other plans for him. And even after he lawyered up, it didn't seem to matter because all decisions seem to have been made about the best way to handle him. Apparently, it was an end run to force him into testifying, and his public defender didn't seem too familiar with the concept of defending. Because his pathetic choices boiled down to snitch or prison, which, translated, equaled dead or dead.

He heard a cage door slam open and then there was blessed silence in the retreat. He didn't recall anything more until waking in the middle of a police interrogation room, looking down at a paper he'd signed agreeing to turn against Sergei. The cage door slammed shut and Travis understood what he needed to do, why the paper had been signed. He could play along, since he'd been given his escape route.

He was always grateful for that cage door.

He let the marshals get him settled in a safe location, but they weren't about to give him twenty-four seven protection. Instead, he got new identification and some pocket money and had to check in several times a day. And he did that for several days, merely running on survival mode, because he was damned good at surviving. He wanted nothing more than to get the hell out from under the government's stranglehold and go back to what he did best: grifting. Maybe he'd stay away from sleeping with the men he grifted and maybe he wouldn't. But the money he'd earned over the years was tucked away safe and sound, from both the government and other criminals, in an overseas account.

He had no fear of the marshals, the law, authority figures in general. The latter were all he'd known growing up, and he'd spent his twenty-three years learning to thwart, escape, defy and embarrass them.

Granted, Sergei ended up playing a crucial role in this escape—especially when Travis had passed a message through his lawyer about how best to help him get out from under the marshal's watchful eye, which would in turn let him escape the feds and their insistence on his testimony. It involved a chain of people to keep names far removed from Sergei and his reach, but it had been worth it, especially because it would put Travis back with Dodge.

Dodge was mid-forties, handsome as fuck—a silver fox

who was also a master thief with a penchant for helping guys in need get back on their feet. He'd told Travis when they'd first met that someone long ago had helped him get off the streets, and even though he ended up continuing to work them for several more years, it was under his own control, not anyone else's. He charged rent but he didn't care how you earned your money, as long as you kept yourself, and the rest of the house, safe. And if you couldn't figure out how to earn, he'd help you with that too.

Dodge wasn't a monk or a saint, but he was the closest thing to the latter that Travis had met so far.

Now, after leaving behind everything the marshals had given him, he walked along the edge of the highway for half a mile and found Dodge waiting for him, his car running as if he'd just pulled over to take a few minutes rest.

He got into the front seat of Doge's car and breathed a sigh of relief. "It's been a while. Thanks for taking the 911."

"I told you that I always would." Dodge pulled the car back onto the highway smoothly.

The stop was pretty full, mainly truckers and drivers, all of whom were sleepy and distracted enough that they'd believe Travis came out of the bathrooms and hadn't walked up the highway.

If they did, and if the FBI questioned them, he and Dodge would be long gone anyway, Dodge's black car ready to ghost through the night. Travis had no doubt the FBI would be searching for him after this. "You can just drop me off at the nearest train station. I don't want to bring trouble for you."

Dodge threw a smile in his direction. "I won't lie— deciding to help you is causing us all to relocate, but it was time. Things got too comfortable, and with comfort comes mistakes."

"Where to now?"

"I think you'll like it. Upstate New York—not too big, not too small. Close enough to the city but not too close."

"Middle of nowhere. Middle of everywhere." Travis closed his eyes and leaned back against the seat, letting a few moments of safety lull him into relaxation. "Best place to be."

CHAPTER TWO

LOCHLAN WOKE with the smell of fire in his nose and the splitting pain of a hangover pounding through his skull, like a demand. The dream—the same fucking nightmare that had threatened every night for the past eight months and then made good on its promise—wasn't deterred by the whiskey. In fact, the whiskey might make it worse, but Loch preferred to wake numb.

Tonight, the ringing phone threatened to change all of that.

He picked it up anyway.

Dodge had recommended that Travis stay inside and out of trouble for at least a week, and he provided him with the space to do so—a third-floor apartment in the large house he'd rented. But after three days, which in his mind was more than enough time, he decided to test the waters, if for no other reason than a pressing need to slip into his new life and try it on for size.

Dodge didn't bother arguing about the timetable, telling him instead, "Looking to hook up? Go to The Wall. Looking to grift or hook, go high end and hit Tally's. It won't look like it, but you'll find what you need there," in some alternative universe version of normal parent / son life.

Travis wasn't sure what the hell he needed. He had a full bank account under an assumed name, he was bored, and in hiding from the mob and the feds.

Maybe he'd go for just sex tonight. Maybe he'd do the picking up, not for money or scamming, but just for pure goddamned pleasure.

He realized he had no idea what that must feel like.

Maybe tonight he'd actually find out.

In deference to the fact that he was still a wanted man—and with the help of one of Dodge's other charges—he'd cut his hair shorter and took his natural brown to a lighter color. It made his blue eyes look brighter. Made him look like a different guy, which he supposed was the point.

Inside, he still felt exactly the same, and because of that, or in spite of it, he went to Tally's. Even though he was simply looking to hook up, he didn't have to slum for it.

The bar/restaurant was big inside—dark and cool and expensive looking. He got quite a few looks from both sexes, since it was a mixed crowd, but it only took him a couple of minutes to figure out that this was mostly a place for gay and bi men. There was definitely a lot of grifting he could do here, and easily, but instead he laser-focused on one man. The guy was all dark hair, classic, chiseled cheekbones, albeit in a rough-honed kind of way—an irresistible mixture of aristocrat and street. A combination Travis had never been able to resist.

This time, there was no reason to even try. Besides, the guy had laser-focused on him in return.

It was crowded, but he slid into the space the guy made for him and suddenly they were close. So motherfucking, dick-hardeningly close.

"Hey," Travis murmured.

"Hey," the man echoed with a raise of his eyebrow, a flirting mock before the appraisal. From the flare of heat in his eyes, it was apparent he liked what he saw. "Name?"

"Travis."

"Scotch, Travis?" He pointed to his own glass of single malt, neat.

"I'll take a soda—a Coke," Travis countered. His 'no drinking, no drugs' rules was merely survival for him—it had been so when he was actively tricking, and it would still serve him well picking up guys for pleasure.

The soda arrived quickly. Travis picked it up and clinked it against the man's. "Thanks."

"Since you're not drinking, let's get out of here. My place is a few blocks away," the man told him, his voice deep and husky and dammit, Travis had only spoken a single word before it had been assumed that he could be bought. Handsome, rich men, like he assumed this one to be, always did. Maybe it was because power did make everything better.

It did for him, because even though the client rarely realized it, Travis was always the one holding the power. But tonight, the hum in his brain kept pulling him to be led...and he couldn't shake that. Not when he felt a shift of power, an imbalance—and not in his favor—like never before.

You're just freaked because of the arrest. Temporarily off your game.

Still, he didn't scare easily and wasn't about to start now, so sliding back into rent boy/grifting mode and shutting down all other feelings was the quickest way to settle his worries and bring back his confidence. "Someone's in a rush."

"I know what I want. I have no patience with wasting time."

Travis's dick went hard. Hard-*er*. But he still asked, "What's your name?" to level the playing field somewhat before he agreed to just walk off with the guy.

"Lochlan, but people call me Loch." He pronounced it like *lock*.

"That's different."

"Yes, it is." Loch gave Travis a slow, lazy smile that made Travis shift. Loch gave a small laugh, like he knew. "I've never seen you at Tally's before."

"I'm new to the area." Hell, it was the truth. Loch nodded, and when he didn't question Travis further, Travis felt the playing field level slightly. "Let's go." He finished his coke, icy sugar giving him a tiny sliver of the rush he'd soon encounter. A warning. A highlight. Then he met Loch's eyes before turning to lead the way out of the bar and into the cool temperatures of the city streets.

It was a Thursday, with most people behaving like Friday didn't count. Travis followed the man to his car, a black Range Rover, parked a few spaces down from the bar.

"I live in Park Ridge," Loch explained.

It was a gated community, Travis knew, thanks to Dodge, which meant Loch had money. "Works for me." He got into the passenger's side and Loch started the car and pulled away from the curb at an easy pace.

Less than five minutes later, Loch pulled into a long driveway and then into the attached garage. The house was big—elegant-looking. Intimidating even, and that was only the outside. Once he followed Loch in, it was even more so, sleek and masculine and modern.

"You're thinking too hard," Loch told him, a rough palm sliding along the back of his neck. "Second thoughts?"

"No."

"Then what?"

"Your place is great."

"So what? Why am I paying for it?" Loch asked, taking away any doubt that this was a rent boy situation. Travis shrugged. "You've never had another client like me? You seem high end."

True, Travis had never specialized in typical rough trade situations, not because of the risks, but because the pay was shit, and he'd never worked for any kind of service either. He'd relied on his gut instincts, with a little help from Dodge from time to time. "I haven't done this in a while," he finally admitted.

Loch's brows lifted. "So why me?"

"I like a challenge."

"I propositioned you."

"I'm talking about in bed."

The corner of Loch's mouth curled, the hint of a smile, the first he'd seen all night. "So do I."

"What else do you like?" Travis asked.

"For tonight, your name is Liam," Loch told him.

Liam. So this guy was in mourning for someone. That

wasn't an unusual reason for him to pick up someone, and it made sense.

Didn't mean Travis had to like it, though. "Vocal?" he asked, because Loch was under some kind of spell as he stroked Travis's hair.

"Vocal," Loch confirmed. Then his eyes narrowed, and he murmured, "Trouble."

Travis didn't know if that was good or bad, because he liked trouble, and he couldn't tell by the tone of Loch's voice if the man agreed. But when Loch leaned in to kiss him, with a hand behind Travis's neck to hold him in place, to take him, Travis felt a slam of desire with an underlay of fear.

He couldn't remember the last time a client had ever kissed him this much. He'd never had an issue with it, had never thought it too intimate until now. He was feeling and that confused him. He didn't want anything but a pleasant numbness, but Loch seemed determined not to allow that.

Travis felt a chill rush through him as the kisses got more intense, Loch tongue-fucking him, and tried not to shudder. But Loch noticed, and a smile ghosted across his lips. Travis assumed that his response reminded Loch of his precious Liam, and why he was so pissed about playing the role of the dead lover when he'd done much worse?

Don't go there.

Instead, Travis pulled back slightly and stripped off his T-shirt, trying desperately to retain a slight bit of control. His own, maybe. And, in return, Loch ran a hand over the sugar skull tattoo on Travis's chest. It was an elaborate tattoo in grayscale that always got a lot of attention, as did the ever-growing sleeve on his arm.

"Where did you get these?"

"I didn't," Travis said without thinking, then laughed. "I'm not sure. I mean, I didn't get them in the same place."

Loch just went with it and continued his exploration, walking them into the bedroom and pushing Travis back onto the king-sized bed. Loch took off his own shirt and then reached down to unzip Travis's jeans and strip him before climbing into the bed and sliding next to him.

Travis's bare cock rubbed against the soft fabric of Loch's pants, and he couldn't help but arch his hips up to prolong the sensation. He could feel Loch's hardness pressing his as he stroked his hands down Travis's back and ass, kissing him deeply—licking, biting, and Travis hoped he'd have the marks for days after this. He let Loch twist and suck his nipples as he arched and cried out Loch's name, held Loch's broad shoulders, clinging to him like a goddamned virgin.

It was all too much. He closed his eyes against the onslaught of emotions but his body refused to stop feeling, wanting—and worse?

Obeying.

He only bottomed for clients and topped for pleasure. And even though he'd switched to client mindset, his body was fighting it, hard, every step of the way. Then he got lost in the feel of Loch's body against his and because Loch was the kind guy who didn't have to pay for it.

So why did he?

Power. Control. Because it was easier to fuck without hopes of commitment.

Yeah, Travis was your dream man if you were into that sort of thing.

But he gave up fighting it and watched as Loch shed his own pants and rolled on a condom. Travis spent a few seconds staring at the man's body. Chiseled abs, cut muscles and a long, thick cock made Travis's ass ache just looking at him, and then Loch's body was covering his, Loch's hands skimming along his ribs, tongue and teeth alternately caressing and biting his skin along his neck and shoulders.

Once he was moaning Loch's name and slick with sweat, Loch turned and pressed him flat against the mattress on his belly. His fingers were slicked with lube when they entered him and Travis was rutting the sheets, pressing his ass back and fucking himself on Loch's fingers.

"Good, that's good, Liam. You look beautiful," Loch murmured and Travis didn't want to stop being Liam if he could feel like this.

But hell, it was for sure a mindfuck. Because Travis was pretending to be this guy's old lover, and he was following Loch's lead, acting like this wasn't the first time they were together. Except Loch didn't appear to be acting. Instead, his hands roamed Travis's body, bringing pleasure to places he didn't even know turned him on.

Because in the past, it'd never been about him. His orgasm? He had to try to remain on guard during it—that was always when he was at his most vulnerable and he was usually with a stranger. Beyond that, it was literally only a part of the show. This time? It would be real, and Travis was about to lose his mind because of it.

Loch murmured, "Just like that, baby."

Baby. It'd never sounded so fucking sincere or so hot. Because Travis was answering, "Yeah, come on. More. Please hurry."

A beg. This guy had him reduced to begging to be fucked, on his hands and knees, ass in the air and really, truly waiting to be filled. Fucked. Used hard. And he realized all of that was spilling out of his mouth, telling Loch exactly what he wanted...

And Loch was complying, his covered cock sliding inside of Travis's ass, and even though he'd been opened, it still burned. But he took it, wanted it, pressed back even when Loch tried to go slowly.

"Come on—can't wait, Loch. Need it now," he commanded and finally, Loch did what he wanted, pressing so he was fully seated inside of Travis, his balls against Travis's ass. "That's it. Move. Please fucking move..."

"Hold on, baby. I will." Loch began to rock back and forth, and a keening moan escaped Travis as Loch rode him, biting the back of his neck the way Travis had seen stallions do to their mates during mating. It was a way to keep them in place, to remind them of it. A mark, a claim, which led to the biggest orgasms Travis ever remembered having...and one of the few he'd ever had without the use of his own hand.

And when the roar in his ears turned slightly duller, he heard Lock murmur, "We're not done, Liam." And Travis desperately wanted to remain Liam for as long as Loch would have him. Loch roughly turned him over and licked the come from his belly, his cock, as Travis watched helplessly.

Loch watched him as well.

"God, Loch," he practically screamed when Loch slid his half-hard and overstimulated cock inside his hot mouth. Travis bucked up—tried to, anyway, but Loch's hold was strong...and surprisingly gentle. Travis couldn't fight it, so he gave in to every pleasurable sensation he could sink into. Let himself shudder as Loch's talented mouth worked him hard again and then let Loch sink into him.

Let himself wrap around Loch and hold him like he'd never let go.

"Tell me," Loch instructed.

Vocal. That's what he wanted but Travis couldn't control what was coming out of his mouth, dammit. He bit out, "Fucking do it hard," and then, before he could stop himself, "Make me forget..."

Loch's head snapped up and, for a second, Loch was looking at him—Travis, not Liam. "Forget what?"

"Everything else," slipped out before he could stop himself. And Loch nodded, murmuring promises about spending the rest of the night doing just that as they became a tangle of arms, legs, mouths and tongues. Hours flew by as Loch's hands teased and taunted him, getting him hard again when Travis was pretty sure he was spent for the night.

Just as the sun began to rise, Loch was inside of him again, murmuring a different name over and over again into his ear, so quietly that he couldn't quite make it out. Travis didn't care what Loch called him, was torn between wanting to come and wanting to hold onto this feeling forever, because coming meant ending. And as he struggled to keep it together, Loch was doing his best to pull him apart, dismantle any last vestige of control Travis might have.

"Let it go, baby. I know you can," Loch murmured, half plea but mainly command.

The moans drummed up in Travis's throat and he remained incoherent for the rest of the fuck. His mind, his body, one big mass of sensation, his heart in his cock, his body a giant heartbeat of climax as he spurted thick ropes of come between them and he begged, "Loch, please...don't."

"Don't what, Travis?"

Travis. Not Liam. "Don't let go." He was horrified to hear himself say, but it was the truth, because when Loch held him tight, he came again, so unexpectedly that all he could do was stare at Loch helplessly as his body jackknifed with pleasure.

In the aftermath, he almost couldn't look Loch in the eye, instead allowing him to remain holding him, reminding himself harshly over and over that this was a goddamned job as he slammed back down to earth. Or tried to. Loch apparently was attempting to block his re-entry with the press of his hard cock against Travis's ass.

At that moment, Travis let Loch win.

CHAPTER THREE

YOU'RE NOT IN MOURNING—YOU'RE wallowing.

Those had been Tarquin "Tar" Simon's—final words to him the last time they'd spoken, nearly a year ago. Tar hadn't been wrong, but that hadn't stopped Loch from telling his one-time best friend to go fuck himself before diving headfirst into an endless bottle of scotch without looking back. Not until the call, the favor he owed from what now seemed like a lifetime ago, when he'd traded them on the reg with the FBI for even a mere glimpse of Snow's men.

Fine. So Loch had agreed to do the goddamned favor.

Even in his numbed state, he'd known that being that out of it on a job would be fucking dumb. In his profession, in his life, he had enemies. So he'd swum out of the bottle just long enough to take the job, albeit with a small glass of scotch to stop the shakes. It should've been simple—an old bureau friend calling in a chip. A honeypot deal. A witness recapture, pure and simple.

But the man breathing deeply next to him in bed was

anything but simple. From the second Loch had seen him walking into Tally's, he'd wanted to force Travis to his knees and take some of that attitude away, make him moan.

And he'd done just that. Then he'd lain, wide-awake in the dark, biding his time until Travis had woken from his sex-drugged sleep and gone home with the money Loch left for him on his jacket.

Now? It was time to call Tar.

Simple, my ass.

Just the idea of what he was going back into, what he'd discovered in bed in the early morning hours before the dawn nearly convinced Loch to drink the entire bottle of scotch on his night table. He knew he was sobering up when he started to actually feel, and that feeling had started last night when he'd called Travis by his real name while they were fucking... and then he'd felt the marks and tried to convince himself he was hallucinating.

Now he unscrewed the cap and inhaled deeply, breathing it in like the scent of an old lover. He could nearly taste it that way, and for now, that had to be enough. He got up and poured the rest of the liquid down the sink and threw the bottle away. Now was the time to prep for the DTs. By tomorrow he'd be in decent enough shape to see Travis again. He'd done the short road to detox before, even had the meds to make it easier on himself. But he didn't want easy. Didn't deserve it.

This would just be more penance...because there would never be enough of it, evidenced by his discovery in the early morning hours of fucking Travis into the mattress over and over again.

His crescent moon-shaped scars were well hidden—Loch's fingers had brushed over them a few times as he'd rimmed Travis, but he didn't check them then, for obvious reasons. Finally, when he was able to, he pulled back and let his fingertips trace subtly on both sides as he looked and almost froze at the sight of them.

Loch automatically looked for them in every man he'd fucked. He'd seen Tar's, not during sex, but out of necessity, and he'd felt them too because sometimes he had to use his fingertips and not his eyes in the dark. He remembered Tar's sharp intake of breath when he'd run his fingers across the grooves cut deep into his upper thighs, right into the creases of his ass cheeks. It hadn't been sexual in any way, but it had been magnetic. Solidifying. Bonding in a way he'd never bonded with any other man before.

He should be mine, Loch remembered thinking to himself. And Tar was his, his best friend, partner in crime. There was no way Loch was going to ruin it for a fuck.

Instead, they'd started to share men—not the Snow case men, but other men they picked up. It was a way to keep them both safe, in case the man they were fucking was an enemy. So Loch couldn't remember having sex without Tar watching...until Liam. And that's when everything had gone bad.

Dammit. He dialed Tar before he talked himself out of it.

Tar picked up on the first ring, causing Loch to ask, "Were you waiting by the phone?"

"Like a lovesick girl," Tar told him unashamedly.

"You knew."

"I didn't orchestrate it, but yes." Tar never lied—not to

Loch. Tar was a damned good liar, but it always reassured Loch to never be in the receiving end of it. Their friendship had been built on better—the best and the worst either had ever dealt with. There was no room for deceit. "So...you've made contact."

"If you know, then why ask?" Loch closed his eyes, pictured his best friend, guilt flooding him for so many damned reasons.

"Because I wanted contact with you that didn't involve a text," Tar told him. "I figured Skype would be moving too fast for your delicate sensibilities."

"Fuck you." Loch laughed though, and so did Tar, and just like that they were back on the road to recovery. "Does Jasper know?"

"Jasper knows everything. He's annoying as fuck," Tar said irritably. "You okay to keep going on this one?"

Loch bit back a curse—because Tar was right to ask. He figured ripping off the bandaid was the best way to go. "Travis looks a bit like Liam."

A pause on Tar's end wasn't a surprise, especially given the fact that Liam had been the start of the schism that widened to a major fault line after he'd been killed. Finally, Tar said quietly, almost kindly, "That's Snow's type, Loch."

Why hadn't Loch seen that before? Because Tar could also pass for Liam and Travis's brother. And that made something unidentifiable and yet familiar stir deep in Loch's belly before he shoved it back down, which he did with any and all feelings he didn't want to deal with. "Yeah, so, I'll get Travis back here and move out with him."

"He's not with you?"

"No. And I know what the fuck I'm doing," Loch said sharply.

"You can't lose him." Tar tried to keep the urgency out of his voice and mostly failed. "Let me do this one. You're—"

"Too close to it?" He laughed darkly. Painfully. Saw Liam's broken body lying in the parking lot, the blood spilt on the asphalt creating a dark halo around his lover's head...the betrayals too many to count. "I've got this one."

"You've slept with Travis, then?" It wasn't a judgment, just a question.

Loch bristled anyway. "Yes. Many times. That's how I know he'll come back."

"Touché," Tar said quietly. "I'll ask again—are you okay to see it through?"

"You'd do it."

"I'm not suicidal."

"Really?"

"You have to admit you're way closer to the ledge than I am."

Loch nodded at that admission, as if that—and the silence —would transfer over the phone.

It did. "When's he coming back?"

"I was thinking tomorrow night. I can't push it yet."

"You're going to have to. Both the feds and the Russians will be able to track him sooner than later—hell, if you weren't so good I'd say Parks already made you. It's a good thing we're already watching." As Tar spoke, a browser opened on Loch's screen. An apartment.

Travis's apartment.

"You're already here," Loch said.

"Define here." Tar paused. "I had a feeling on this. Look, I was already following the kid—"

"He's not a kid."

"Fine, I was following the very adult young man because I suspected he was Snow's. Before I could grab him, he was swept up in the mob bust and Parks called you for the favor."

"And you figured..."

"Two birds, one stone."

"And no warning from you."

Tar snorted. "You wouldn't have taken a warning—or the job, not if you knew I was involved."

Maybe Tar was right. Loch couldn't be sure. But, now that he was in it, the noose tightened and there wasn't a viable means of escape. Not until they'd gotten Travis off the streets. "Tomorrow."

"You always did like the catch more flies with honey approach," Tar muttered.

"Fucking caveman," Loch shot back.

"Yeah, good to have you back, brother. Really good.... but it's got to be tonight."

Loch refused to say he'd be too shaky. He'd never done down and out well and wasn't about to admit his weakness to Tar. "Fine, but you need to come up with a reason for him to trust me."

"I'll make sure that he thinks the Russians found him."

"When?"

"After midnight. The footage will load from the live feed."

"And where will you be?"

"Close enough to help when needed."

"If."

"If and when," Tar countered, cutting the line to ensure getting the last word.

"Child," Loch muttered into the silence. He hung up on his end and brooded. Tar was already securing safe houses, he knew and Loch was more worried about seeing him than he was dealing with Travis.

He looked down at his hands. He could still feel Travis's skin under his fingertips, and he shifted to let himself feel the nail scrapes that Travis had made down his back when they'd both been coming.

Fuck. Loch had to swallow the lump back in his throat. To distract himself further, he clicked on the feed Tar had messaged him and found himself looking at Travis's apartment.

It was on the third floor of Dodge's house, a notorious fix-it man himself. Combined with the fact that Travis knew him, that Dodge was willing to take him in was very telling.

But Travis had come in looking to fuck, not to grift or hook. Loch had surprised him, which threw Travis off his game.

Good. That's what Loch did best...except he'd thrown himself off his game as well in the process.

Travis was the first guy since Liam that Loch actually tried to pretend was Liam... and couldn't. Not after Travis came through, loud and clear...and Loch hadn't minded.

"Fuck." He raked a hand through his hair as he pretended to focus on the pile of random magazines and newspapers on Travis's night table.

But his attention soon turned to Travis arriving home, stripping as he walked through the apartment. His shirt was off and Loch texted him before he could go farther with, *Free tonight?*

Because he wanted to see Travis's face when he did it—wanted to see the purest reaction.

He heard Travis's phone ding and watched him glance at it and smile. Not a 'got him' smile, but a real, small, soft smile.

The kind of smile you let happen when you're unguarded, when you know you're safe and no one's watching.

That was almost enough for Loch to turn off the live feed. Almost. Instead, he waited until Travis texted him back. Travis waited just long enough to not look too eager...and he typed and erased a few times before Loch got his message.

Sure thing. Eight o'clock okay?

Perfect. You'll be just in time for my shakes, Loch wanted to text, but instead, he texted back, *See you at eight*, and swallowed some of the pills to get him through.

Maybe it was better if Travis saw him not feeling well. Maybe that would bring out a side of him that Loch needed to see—either a conscience or a predator who knew to feed on the weak.

Before he could think on that more, Travis resumed his strip show, walking slowly toward the bathroom, like he somehow knew he was being watched. Which was ridiculous, but still made for a damned good show.

The jeans went one way, the boxer briefs another, and Travis was bare-ass naked under the bathroom lights. The shower thankfully didn't have a curtain, and the water and steam engulfed Travis when he walked inside the enclosure.

The first thing Travis did was grab his cock. Loch did the same, pushing down his sweats, already hard. He kept his eyes focused on Travis as, cock in hand, he pushed back from the desk and stroked himself to the rhythm Travis set.

Travis threw his head back under the spray, then leaned forward, clutching the wall as he spurted against the tiles, even as Loch murmured, "Travis," and came all over his own hand.

Under the hot spray, Travis caught his breath as he pressed a palm to the tile wall for support and murmured, "Loch," as he came.

Lochlan had to know he was watching this, and there was no way Tar was switching his screen off. He palmed his dick, knowing Loch was doing the same—which made it all that much harder—and he stared at the screen, at the young man in the shower.

Travis's back was muscled, rangy, with some scars that Tar would bet were a combo of a shitty childhood, Snow's camps, and life-on-the-street badges of honor. If he zeroed in on them, he'd bet he'd find a few that matched his own.

He shook that off, continuing his assessment of Travis's body. He had several tattoos, according to the official fed rap sheet (and now Tar could concur with firsthand knowledge), and his dick was elegant and his lips were full. And even alone in his shower, he knew how to put on a hell of a show.

Tar pictured Travis with Loch—Loch fucking him, Travis's mouth rounding to the surprised O it just did...and then he pictured himself riding Travis to orgasm, pumping into him hard enough to make Travis scream.

Yeah, that would definitely happen. Travis was the best way for Loch and Tar to get back on their horse...together.

Tar had waited for nearly a year for Liam to get the hell out of his best friend's life, and then another eight months for Loch to come to his senses and get back in the game... and thankfully, Park had needed a favor right about the time Tar was ready to march into Loch's life and shake him until he woke the fuck up. During the time they'd been apart, he knew Loch had been drinking too much, a bad fucking habit he'd had since he'd been a teen, and he'd been ignoring his own personal safety. Tar bet it was hours before he'd even considered checking Travis for the marks.

Now, he stared at the screen—at Travis, who laid down on the bed, naked—then sighed. They'd be in deep with this one—he could feel it. A Snow connection was rare, and while not unwanted, it brought with it a ton of new complications.

He knew he'd never be free of Snow—the marks on his own body proved that a thousand times over—but Travis? He was young. New.

Complicated.

Tar hadn't gotten the best shake in life, but hell, he hadn't gotten the shittiest either. And he'd seen some pretty shitty shakes in his thirty-three years. He'd been to hell and back several times, and he was pretty sure the trips wouldn't stop. As long as they weren't one way, he could deal.

What Travis's had been like? Well, he and Loch were about to find out. But even though Tar was only mere blocks away from Loch now, it didn't feel close enough. A chill ran through Tar as he wondered how close Snow would actually let himself come to his two most favorite—most hated—prodigies in order to grab Travis?

He guessed it depended on what category Travis fell into. And Travis's story had checked out—somewhat. He'd been sleeping with Sergei, a Russian mobster, for months. He wasn't living with him, but he'd been staying at the main house/hangout the night of the raid. He pulled up the footage he'd obtained from Park onto a split screen so he could view it and keep an eye on Travis in real time.

According to Park's footage, it looked like the flash-bang had predictable effects on all of them, maybe more so on Travis, which was odd, in light of the torture he'd have received at the hands of Snow and his men.

"There," he murmured, and focused in on the spot where Sergei had leaned in to mouth something to Travis. Tar couldn't make out the words, but whatever it had been...the effect it had on Travis seemed intense. Travis's eyes closed for a long moment, and when they reopened, his entire countenance seemed to change.

Ah, fuck. Tar closed the screen with the old footage, continued watching Travis prepare for bed, and began to make preparations of his own to move the hell out.

The man who was a huge part of his own past—and Loch's—was also part of Travis's as well, and whether or not he actively remembered it now, he would, no doubt at the worst possible time.

It'd been years since Tar had met a new escapee...five, to be exact, and that was a man they'd actively hunted down. Travis was a brand-new conquest who'd come up out of the blue.

Tar texted Jasper, his supervisor at the CIA, and even

though technically Tar and Loch didn't exist, Jasper answered immediately.

Whatever you need. Just bring him in safely.

He hesitated before texting Jasper back, *Looks like Loch's back in.*

About time, was all Jasper added.

CHAPTER FOUR

TAR CALLED him a couple of hours later—and fifteen minutes before Travis was due to arrive. Loch thought about ignoring the call but picked up anyway. "I know what I'm doing."

"I know that. I just wanted to reassure you that I've got his shower jerk-off on tape if you need a repeat."

"Dammit," he muttered. He stretched, his muscles loosened though slightly sore from last night's activities. He'd begun to think of himself as a hardened mess of scar tissue where a soul should be...at least until Liam had walked into his life.

So when he'd seen Liam's ghost walking into the bar last night, all of the scars seemed to dissolve. He'd felt his mouth curve into a smile, so ready to raise his hand and say, "Liam, over here."

And then, Liam had made eye contact, and no, it wasn't his baby, but the man had Liam's eyes. His looks. They weren't twins, more like brothers, except now that he'd fucked Travis, he realized the two were nothing alike.

Paying to fuck was nothing new. He'd done it for years—pre-and post-Liam.

This? *Was* different. Felt different from the start, but Loch was good at pretending nothing was wrong.

"Were you watching in real time?" Tar inquired.

"Maybe."

Tar snorted. "Guess it was like old times."

It was, but that sharing was all pre-Liam. Because Liam knew about it, didn't want anything to do with Tar and didn't want Loch to be with him either. It made for some tense moments, but over two years, things softened between Liam and Tar.

And then Liam had been killed and Loch realized that he hadn't spent enough time watching Liam.... not the way he watched Tar.

Liam never knew about what Tar had been though...what Loch had as well. Why? Because then Loch would have to admit shit to him he'd never wanted to. "I know what I'm doing," he repeated.

"Yeah, I know. But still," Tar reasoned. "What exactly are you gong to tell him?"

Loch sighed and realized he hadn't thought this through completely. He glanced at Travis's now empty apartment and said, "Let's go with me being a merc who just wants to know what Travis knows about the Russians. I'll tell him I'm saving him from them and from testifying, and if he tells me I'll give him a new identity."

"And he'll believe you why?"

"Because he wants to—either because he's scared of the mob or the Russians...or because he's Snow's and he knows about me."

"Do you think he knows?"

"No," Loch said honestly. "Or if he does, he has no idea that I'm familiar with the situation." Which was why he needed to take his time and vet Travis, a very dangerous prospect.

First, it was about assessing if Snow had sent him in to hurt Loch or Tar. Or spy on them. Or worse, kill them. Most likely, Travis didn't even know who—or what—he was.

Anyone who'd spent time in Snow's torture camp was dangerous as hell. Most were assassin-level dangerous, but so much more deadly. The experiments inflicted on them trained them not to worry about pain or having a conscience. They had triggers that would force them to finish a job, even if the job was to kill their own family members.

"Okay, so let's go over the steps," Tar said.

"First figure out if he know who and what he is," Loch said, more out of habit than anything. His checklist to vet was ingrained, but he and Tar still went over the steps every single time. Part superstition, part reminder to never forget, to never let their guard down.

"He's been grifting the Russian mob, so I'm guessing he's retained a lot of skills," Tar added. "Plus, he escaped the marshals."

Loch sighed. "He seemed...surprised. Almost pissed that I assumed he was a rent boy."

Tar frowned. "Anything else?"

"It's been years. Where the hell's he been?"

He could hear the guilt in Tar's answer. "I wish I knew."

Travis was going back for more, against all his better judgment and all the encouragement from Dodge. The money from last night, tucked in his pocket so he could tuck it back into one of Loch's drawers when he wasn't looking.

He didn't want the money. It ruined everything, made him feel used, for the first time ever. He might've sold Loch on the fantasy, but Loch did the exact same thing to him. And seeing Loch's text? His relief had swirled, mixing with panic and anger.

He'd replied *yes* anyway.

Now, as he headed up the front steps of Loch's house, Loch opened the door with that same hungry look from last night on his face. And it pushed a fire through Travis's veins as he strutted toward the open door and directly into Loch's arms, situating himself against Loch's body as though he'd never belonged anywhere else.

But he waited then, for Loch's direction. Because there were rules. Rules that had him bottoming when he hadn't done so in years.

That's what's fucking you up. He knew that, even as he tried to pretend he hadn't enjoyed it.

He'd never been one to lie to himself. "Happy to see me?"

Loch gave a slow, lazy smile, then ground his pelvis against Travis's. "Does that seem happy to you?"

He didn't give Travis a chance to answer, dipping his head down for a long, hard kiss. Travis responded by twining his hands in Loch's hair, letting Loch's tongue play along his, fucking his mouth.

"You're wearing too many clothes," Loch told him when he broke the kiss.

Travis took a step back, which meant disengaging, and his

body already missed the contact. But the heat in Loch's eyes when he stripped down was worth it, especially when Loch followed suit and made fast work of his shirt and unzipped his jeans.

Then he motioned for Travis to follow him into the living area, where Loch settled into a large leather recliner and encouraged Travis to climb onto him.

Travis didn't need to be told twice. He covered Loch's body and began riding Loch's leg, unashamedly, nuzzling the man's neck as Loch watched him, an arm tucked behind his head, a small smile on his lips.

"God, you're beautiful," Loch murmured. "Could watch you do this all night. Keep going. Make yourself come. I want to see it."

That wasn't going to be difficult. Travis forced himself to sit up, palm on his cock, stroking, tugging, until he came, seconds later, all over his belly and chest, hitting his collarbone. He leaned his forehead against Loch's stomach and just breathed, his body trembling from the force of his orgasm and hell, what was Loch doing to him?

He didn't tell you that you were Liam tonight.

Loch was easing him off, waking him into the bedroom, where he had Travis lay down. Then he wiped his belly and chest off before turning him over and putting him on his hands and knees. He heard the zipper on Loch's jeans and braced as Loch's fingers ran along the seam of his ass.

God, Loch's sheets smelled like them still, which meant he hadn't rushed to change them.

He was down on his elbows, ass in the air. And he whimpered—*whimpered*, for Christ's sake—as Loch's tongue ran along his ass cheek before running down along the same seam. And then Loch was parting his ass cheeks, tonguing him, burying his face in Travis's ass and Travis heard the moans overtaking him. And he was rock hard again, held open, with Loch's thumbs pressing into him, pulling him apart...allowing Loch's tongue to take him in a way that was insanely intimate and completely humiliating at the same time. And all Travis could do was beg for more. And so he did.

And that's what Loch gave him. One big, intimate mind-fuck of a circle.

"Blushing," Loch asked as Travis buried his face into the pillow. "Ah, I like making you blush. Making you beg. So do you."

Fuck you—I don't. "Yeah," he heard himself sigh his agreement from that part of him that rarely got to roam free. That part was too wild, too feral, needy and angry for anyone to handle.

Except for Loch.

Because he's paying. But if Loch was paying, he shouldn't have to do the work of assuaging the wild feral child who came out when Travis felt threatened or uncertain.

And Loch was working, actively, systematically, to break Travis's cage. Travis wanted to know why. Needed to. Because whatever was happening here, sex and lust, was wrapped up in something darker...and Travis hadn't survived years on the streets without instincts.

Travis hadn't caught his breath when Loch pressed his cock inside of him. It was slick with lube but still, Loch was big and Travis was sore from the night before. It hurt so goddamned good, so much so he pushed back into his cock, forcing Loch deep inside him.

"C'mon, Loch—ride me hard," he urged and Loch groaned and grabbed his hips, doing just that. "God, that's good. Fuck me. Fill me."

"Jesus, Travis," he heard Loch groan as his hips stuttered and Loch began to lose control. Travis felt extraordinary pride in making that happen.

Loch knew he was never getting back what he'd lost, and truth be told, he didn't want it back anyway. The guilt he felt at breaking up with Liam, only to have Liam get murdered by a car bomb a month later was still fresh as anything. Pretending with Travis helped only enough to make him remember that what he and Liam had had? Wasn't enough for him, no matter how hard he'd tried to make it be so.

After Liam's death, throwing himself back into work hadn't been his remedy of choice. Sex? Definitely. He looked at the men who'd shared his bed since all as means to an end. If it gave him pleasure as well, so be it.

The fact that this particular job looked like Liam? He'd definitely taken advantage of it because that would make his seduction—and what lay beyond that—an easier sell.

Typically, he and Tar didn't like turning witnesses over to the FBI, but in this case, they'd been told that Travis had sensitive intel that could solidify their RICO case against the Russians. He and Tar couldn't deny the benefits of that since they had no interest in seeing the Russian mob thrive.

He and Tar didn't hurt innocents. Neither had tolerance for that kind of crap. And Travis had literally gotten into bed with the mob. He wasn't even close to an innocent...but if he'd been tortured by Jabez Snow? Then Loch and Tar owed it to Travis to help him.

As if Travis could hear the wheels in Loch's head turning, Travis stirred, casting a sleepy eye at Loch, almost an accusing one. "Time is it?"

"After two in the morning."

"Shit—sorry."

"I'm not," he hissed as Travis's cock brushed his thigh. He waited for Travis to say, "Cost you more for the night," but as he rubbed his cock along Travis's ass crack, all Travis did was groan and lean his head back against Loch shoulder.

Like they were lovers.

Like this was the job of a lifetime. If they had awards for this shit, Loch would give him an Oscar, at the very least, because his dick didn't care about the veracity of the performance. It only wanted to bury inside that tight hole again and find its pleasure.

Out of the blue, Travis shifted and then flipped him, so Loch was flat on his back, Travis straddling him. But instead of freezing, wondering if Travis was triggered to kill him, Loch reached over to the nightstand to grab a condom. "Put this on me, Travis, and then ride my cock."

Travis tilted his head, then gave a smirk. He reached out and tweaked Loch's nipple hard—one, then the other—and Loch wasn't sure he was going to comply. He forced his breathing under control—it wasn't the time to panic. He wasn't completely vulnerable, but hell, he couldn't deny that this was a turn-on.

Finally, Travis leaned forward and stroked Loch's cock a few times before easing himself down on it, hissing when Loch was fully seated inside of him.

"Yeah, Loch—that's good," he murmured, his eyes glazing as he rocked.

Loch pushed his hips up—hard— and Travis smiled wickedly, an expression Loch hadn't seen before. "You like that, baby?"

Travis pushed his tongue out between his teeth, raised his brows. Loch grabbed his hips and slammed up into him and finally, the smirk was gone from Travis's face, replaced by a groan and a tight expression.

"Harder, Loch," Travis told him, his voice husky, demanding and Loch held Travis's hips down hard, refusing to let him move. Travis, obviously frustrated, stared at Loch, but complied.

"Get yourself off. If you don't come when I say, you're not coming," Loch told him and Travis nodded. Loch eased off on his grip and let Travis do most of the work, riding him, taking Loch's length deep inside of him and grinding his hips to make it press his prostate, groaning in pleasure each and every time.

Fuck, Loch wasn't going to be able to hold on much longer, not after watching Travis's debauched performance, his mouth red and swollen, cheeks flushed with pleasure, eyes heavy-lidded.

"Now, Travis," he ground out as he came hard and Travis yelled, almost howled as he came, spurting between them. Loch wasn't far behind, his orgasm taking him over. He closed his eyes, laying himself bare to the man biting along his neck. It was a rush in the sickest way possible. Would he cheat death, or would he get his in the end?

Would it be penance for pushing Liam away? For getting him killed?

Loch had all but forgotten what fucking without being drunk was like, and he'd also realized it was odd fucking someone sober without having Tar there.

But the danger factor with Travis, the possibility that he was one of Snow's trained assassins—and the notion that he was leaving himself vulnerable in front of a trained killer equal to or possibly greater than him or Tar? Was fucking hot. Travis wasn't restrained, and Loch knew how vulnerable a man was when he was coming. Talk about letting your guard down...ultimate test of trust, and there was zero trust built between him and Travis.

But still, somehow, Travis trusted him, almost against his will. And still, something was stirring there, a realization of some sort and Loch was thrusting inside of him, with Travis holding on.

Soon enough, it would be time for business over pleasure.

CHAPTER FIVE

TRAVIS WOKE, disoriented and angry, in Loch's bed. According to the clock it was nearly four in the morning, and he was alone under the covers. The door to the bedroom was open, and there was a light on in another room down the hall.

He stood, grabbed for his jeans and shirt and pulled both on before padding down the hall to find Loch, all the while wondering why he was so out of sorts.

Christ, the guy let you sleep—that's not a crime.

Loch had been seducing him. Again, not a crime...except it'd gone too far. Loch had hit the tripwire without meaning to, which took things to a whole new level. And it left Travis far too vulnerable to be remotely comfortable.

Since when did you become a victim?

"What's wrong?" Loch asked, and Travis realized he'd been standing in the doorway of Loch's office. Loch was sitting behind a desk, with his laptop and a cup of coffee. "Was I supposed to not let you sleep?"

"Why would you?"

Loch shrugged and looked unconcerned. "I have

nowhere to be. I'll pay you for all your time. Besides that, I asked you if you needed me to wake you and you said no."

Travis frowned. "Bullshit."

"I guess that last round of sex gave you amnesia."

Shit. *Shit.* Travis crossed his arms and changed the subject. "Who are you?"

"What do you mean?"

"This isn't a normal client relationship."

"I know," Loch said, and a weird flutter of hope shifted inside Travis's cage, trying to escape. It voluntarily went back in when Loch told him, "This time, neither of us are clients."

"What are you talking about?"

Loch shifted the computer so Travis could see the screen. "They've found you."

"What do you mean, *they've* found me?" Travis demanded. "Who's they?"

"Don't play dumb, Travis. It doesn't suit you." Loch motioned him over to the computer and clicked a few buttons to a spit screen, showing eight different views like the street outside Travis's apartment. The alley. The hallway leading into his apartment and...

"That's my fucking apartment." Travis pointed, then leaned in more closely. "Who the fuck is that?"

"I guess your Russian friend didn't believe you'd keep your mouth shut," Loch said mildly.

"So he's there to..."

"Kill you," Loch told him bluntly. "Do you recognize him?"

Travis went cold. "Not sure." But he was—and very—that it was Vadim—Sergei's main bodyguard, and a giant son of a bitch who enjoyed slitting the throats of anyone who looked at Sergei the wrong way. "Who the hell are you? Because our meeting wasn't a coincidence."

"Based on your MO—and Dodge's—I figured it was only a matter of time you'd head out to Tally's," Loch agreed. "And I'm the guy who's going to save your ass."

"So you were just pretending." He wasn't sure if he was asking if Loch had been pretending to be a john, if he'd been pretending to have lost someone named Liam, or if he'd been pretending to be into Travis...and into the fuck...

"Weren't you?" Loch asked mildly. "Last I checked, you were a grifter. Or did you miss your rent boy past so much you wanted to give it one last spin?"

Travis ignored the jab, because his past was what had kept him alive and mainly off the streets. It might not have been pleasant, but it beat a lot of the alternatives. "Who do you work for?"

"I'm not with the FBI or the Russian mob. So right now, that makes me the person least likely to kill you...and most likely to save your life."

"And what do I need to do to earn that honor?"

"You ran from the FBI."

"Because I'm not snitching. That's why I left Witness Protection," Travis told him. "You and I both know I'm expendable to them. And there's no guarantee my testimony will mean shit."

Loch didn't argue. "We'll discuss the next steps."

"Next steps? Like what? Run? Because that would be my next step."

"No, you're staying here."

"And then what? You get me a new identity or something?"

"Or something."

"There's no way I'm testifying," Travis told him. Loch wasn't touching him, and yet Travis had the feeling that he was in some kind of steel trap that had just shut hard.

Breathe, Travis. Use some of that charm that's gotten you this far. "So you're going to get me a new identity...out of the goodness of your heart?"

"Of course not—but the information you'll give me will help me. And then—"

"You won't need me anymore," Travis finished. "I'm expendable to you as well as the feds. How convenient."

Loch smirked and put a packet on the table between them. Travis looked down and saw the passport and driver's license through the clear plastic baggie...the license already had his picture on it. "Here's what you get out of it. I have no interest in killing you or turning you in. Give me intel, and a few days to bear it out and then I'll drop you at the nearest airport or train station and you'll start living your new life."

"How long?" Travis pressed.

"Depends on what you tell me."

"They'll all know I talked."

"Yes. But the Russians won't live long enough to know that," Loch shot back...and Travis believed him. But that didn't make him any less leery about the choices facing him.

Because if he refused to give intel...

Fuck. He couldn't afford that. Something told him trusting Loch was the best way out of this situation, although the rattling in his head got louder. So he raised his voice to talk above it, even thought Loch frowned when he shouted, "Fine. Let's talk now—or I'm gone."

"I'm not ready to talk. And you're not going anywhere."

Travis sighed. "What're you going to do — imprison me?" He blinked and suddenly, Loch was on him, stronger than the steel trap Travis had envisioned earlier and way more lethal. He had Travis pinned to the wall, handcuffed and was dragging him into the next room (easily, no matter how hard Travis fought) and shoved him on his back onto the bed.

"Better than jail, right?" Loch asked mildly.

"Remains to be seen," Travis said through clenched teeth as Loch dragged his arms over his head and bound them there by the wrists, with new cuffs that came out of nowhere. Travis immediately began to tug and realized it would take a hell of a lot to get free—and the bed was metal so he couldn't simply hope to break it. "You can't do this, Loch."

"But I have." Loch's gaze raked over him, and Travis willed himself not to get hard because this wasn't some kind of sex game—this was his life. "I could've made it far more uncomfortable for you, so if you'd prefer that, just—"

"Fuck you," he spat. "Let me run."

"Sorry. My job is to keep you safe."

"Right. Said that already," he stared up at the ceiling. "Don't forget the fact that you're using me."

"How long are you planning on keeping me?"

"Why? Do you need to get paid for your time?" Loch sniped.

Asshole. "As a matter of fact, yes. Because I'm losing valuable work time. Not all of us are blessed with unlimited money."

Loch stared at him, not answering. Travis yanked at the cuffs again, uselessly, because there was nothing else he could physically do.

Finally, Loch said, "If I pay you, I expect you to perform a service."

"You bastard—that's blackmail. Especially considering how you're keeping me here against my will."

"I never claimed to be a moral man. Take it or leave it. Money will be deposited in an account under the new name you'll no doubt need post-trial."

"And I'm just supposed to believe you?"

"I paid you on our first night...and I left money for you this morning."

"Fuck." Travis blew out a breath. There were no good options, but making money? That was survival and he needed to be practical.

Fucking Loch for money? Obviously Loch thought that's what'd been happening. *Since he already thinks you're a whore, you might as well go all the way and own it.* Because Travis had been deluding himself in thinking that something more was happening between them. "Fine. Offer accepted."

Loch nodded, a strange expression crossing his face. "Obviously, you're on called twenty-four seven. Because what else is there for you to do?"

Travis bit back a curse and accepted his challenge. "I'm used to working in undesirable conditions."

A flicker of something flashed across Loch's face that Travis took perverse pleasure in before Loch said, "Right then. You'll be the first to know when—"

"Flat fee. For that day," Travis continued. "Whether we're fucking or not. Plus showers whenever I want and whatever food I want. And TV and movies, unlimited."

"Naked, at my choice," Loch shot back.

Travis grit his teeth. "Fine. And limits on the sex—"

"No still means no here," Loch said quietly, not letting him finish. "Your safe word will always work, same way it always did."

"I didn't want to be tied like this all the time."

"I'll make some kind of arrangement where you'll have more freedom, but a part of you will be bound in some fashion."

Travis shuddered involuntarily and cursed himself. Stockholm syndrome for sure. "Fine. Done."

"Good. We can negotiate along the way on everything except me letting you leave."

And turning me over to the feds, unless I escape first. "Fine."

"Good." He turned to leave.

"Wait," Travis called. "I, uh..."

Slowly, Loch turned, a half-smile on his face. "Problem?"

Travis took a breath. He had to get control over this situation. Over himself would be better but he'd take what he could get. "I'm hungry."

Loch sighed. "What do you want?"

"Chinese."

"Fine. I'll order a variety." Then he closed in on Travis, murmuring, "And if you think about screaming when I open the door..."

He only managed to say "I wouldn't..." before the ball gag was stuck into his mouth. It was a small one but dammit to hell. He slammed around as best he could in protest.

"Just until the food is safely inside and the delivery guy's gone. Beyond that? This place is soundproofed."

Travis didn't doubt that. He lay there and seethed, uncomfortable as hell and seriously thinking about ripping the bed apart. But there was something inside of him that told him this was the safest option. If he'd been compromised...

He refused to think about that. He was safe. He just had to live thought this. And he'd been doing that for his entire life.

Finally, Loch came back and put the food down...and placed a butter knife in Travis's bound hand. "Dropping that is giving your safe word."

Fuck. His cock swelled and there was no way to hide it. And before Travis could recover, Loch was between his legs, pulling his jeans off and pulling his shirt up and over his head, where it remained on his bound arms.

Loch leaned in and sucked one of his nipples hard and Travis's entire body jolted at the intimate touch. He was dazed, shocked, because he was the working one in this equation, and as such, he should be the one doing all the work. In fact, in the majority of cases he was expected to be.

But Loch? Was taking his time, like he was continuing his investigation to learn Travis's body...and that thought only made Travis's dick harder. He heard his whimpers through the gag as his body surged helplessly against Loch—a fully clothed Loch, which made the whole thing more of a turn-on somehow.

And when Loch crawled down between his legs, Travis stared at him, their eyes locking as his cock slid inside Loch's hot, wet and too-damned- talented mouth.

Travis wasn't going to make twenty-four hours of this. He had to find a way out. Anyway out.

At any cost.

But first, he was going to come. Hard and fast, an orgasm that shook him to the core. And finally, as he was still feeling the aftershocks, Loch took his ball gag out and freed his arms, taking the knife away. He massaged feeling back into Travis's arms as Travis prayed that Loch would stay and do more.

Because sleeping alone under this new threat...*Fuck.*

But Loch simply pointed to the food and said, "Call if you need anything." And then he left...closing the door behind him. And locking it.

That's when the first quiet sob caught in Travis's throat.

Loch waited in the shadows just outside the closed door, waiting to see if Travis would call for him. But no, Travis was too damned stubborn to do it.

And you're too stubborn to go to him.

Loch shook his head, remained in place and ate some noodles with chopsticks from the carton as he listened to Travis's harsh breathing. It finally settled in, and then Loch heard the television turn on. He took that opportunity to dial Tar from his office as he checked Travis's apartment on his laptop.

"Guess you saw what went down," Tar said, forgoing hello completely.

"The Russian was the real deal. Travis recognized him."

"You'd think the kid would have a better poker face," Tar mused. "You've really gotten under his skin."

Loch ignored that. "Did you neutralize the threat?"

"Of course not," Tar scoffed. "Why would I give him a head's up? I let him search and then I made sure he got out of there without hurting Dodge. But this guy? He's a body-guard—name's Vadim—and he's a wanted man. He'll be back. In fact, he hasn't exactly left. He's sitting on the building."

"Travis isn't going anywhere."

"Good. I'm getting the next safe house ready."

"Give me the word and we move," Loch assured him.

"This could bring the feds out," Tar warned. "You've gone rogue on Park, and word is, he's not happy."

"Let it leak that I lost Travis. That should help."

"Already a step ahead of you," Tar said before cutting the line.

Loch cursed, then carried a chair into the hallway and sat just outside the door where Travis was. He should be spending this time planning, figuring out the safest way to keep the Russians off their tails. Because although his safe house was off the grid, the Russians were good, and Travis held the key to their freedom in his testimony.

There was no way they'd want him alive, and they'd be ruthless enough to make sure it didn't happen, no matter the cost. Tar was monitoring the situation and Loch trusted his friend with his life—had from the time they'd been fifteen. But still, being a caged lion instead of being the one doing the stalking never sat well with him.

Then again, behind the door was a man he'd been subtly stalking, and it was time to get him talking.

Travis figured he'd been left alone for about an hour before Loch came back. Before that, Travis looked through the keyhole and saw Loch waiting on the other side of the door and had no idea why...and he refused to read into it, no matter how badly he wanted to.

Don't trust him. Or anybody.

He'd turned on the TV, and then he'd taken some time to eat, because he'd learned that keeping up his strength was tantamount to a proper escape. Now, he sat on the edge of the bed and assessed Loch coolly.

He took a few steps into the room and leaned against the dresser. Crossed his arms and said, "There's a bounty on your head."

"Who's the highest bidder?"

"Not your concern."

"It's my life."

"Should've thought of that before you got in bed with the Russians."

"I was fucking one of them. I wasn't part of the mob." Travis sighed, guessing Loch was finally ready for him to start talking. "So you're working for the government."

"I work for myself," Loch told him. "And if you don't tell me the truth, you'll spent the rest of your life in a cage."

It was a lie. Travis was pretty sure of that and that made it worse. He tried to breathe, to keep it together and keep calm, because the sound of the box's lid slamming closed echoed inside of his head, until that was all he heard. Loud. Deafeningly so.

"Travis—Travis, dammit, breathe." Loch acted like he could command a panic attack away and that would be a great trick if he could pull it off.

Travis felt the bag at his mouth, opened his eyes as Loch instructed him to breathe into the paper and he did, because his sense of survival was stronger than his urge to not follow an order of Loch's.

After several minutes, his heart stopped beating out of his chest. His skin was sweat-soaked and sticking to the sheets. The headache started behind his eyes and extended to the top of his head, like it wanted to split in two.

"Cage, not box," he murmured as Loch laid a cool washcloth across his fevered forehead. He broke out in goosebumps, alternately sweating and shivering, but Loch seemed to instinctively understand what to do.

No way this guy has panic attacks. Maybe the last lover.

He snorted weakly.

"Glad this is funny to you," Loch said dryly.

"You wouldn't understand." Inside his skull, the cage door was banging like a planned prison break. He could almost hear the click of the key in the lock, the slow creak of the door opening. His handcuffs falling off his wrists turned his attention away from the internal. Loch had gathered him up, mostly carrying him into the shower. He turned the water warm at first, then hotter as Travis's body temperature regulated.

For lack of anything else to hold onto, he wound his arms around Loch shoulders and hung on as the water rushed over him. He closed his eyes, confused as hell about why he was clinging to the man threatening his entire existence.

Survival.

The cage door creaked a little more, but opening or closing? Travis was too turned around to tell.

Loch was soaping him up, even as he remained fully clothed. Travis blinked hard, then looked up and began to unbutton Loch's shirt.

When Travis stared at him, his eyes bluer than they'd been before, pupils blown, he looked angry and exhausted... and somehow, hotter.

"I'm not taking advantage of you like this," Loch told him, even as his cock hardened.

Travis cleared his throat and yanked the wet cloth off Loch shoulders, as if not hearing him.

Or ignoring him.

"Travis," he warned, but Travis was nipping at his jaw, hard bites followed by licks. Loch tried to ignore him, using soap and shampoo as professionally as he could. Which was hard to do with his dick in the way.

Finally, he put Travis under the spray to rinse him. After that, Travis smiled, his eyes glowing in the soft light of the bathroom as he unbuttoned Loch's jeans.

"Travis —"

"Let me." His voice was lower, rougher, his hands insistent and even as Loch prepared for a fight he didn't get anything of the sort. The younger man yanking his jeans down was intent on pleasure, and how had he gone from full on panic attack to wanting to fuck? Loch didn't know, but didn't really care when Travis put their cocks together and began to stroke them.

"Yeah Loch," Travis groaned when Loch pushed his hands away and took over, faster, harder, rougher.

Loch pushed him away, but held onto his biceps. Travis leaned lazily against the wall staring at him with flushed cheeks and swollen lips.

Loch grabbed for a towel and wrapped it around his

waist, leaving Travis to get his own. He waited for Travis to dry himself, staring all the while.

"Tell me about the panic attacks."

Travis shrugged. "You saw it—you tell me."

Loch shook his head. "Is it going to keep happening? Are there meds that you're missing?"

"No meds." He said it loudly. Definitively. Then more quietly. "No more fucking meds."

CHAPTER SIX

BY THE TIME Loch saw the nondescript sedan drive past the house for the third time, he was already on high alert with his go-bags in the kitchen, near the back door. Russians or feds? Didn't matter—either way, he needed to get Travis dressed and out.

He texted Tar with *911*, and the immediate response was a latitude and longitude location as he raced up the stairs to the bedroom. Travis was attached to the bed with one ankle cuff and he was sitting back on his elbow, watching TV. Or pretending to because he didn't seem surprised to see Loch.

And here he'd always prided himself on being quiet. He *was* quiet, dammit, so he tucked that information away as a reminder that Travis was definitely dangerous. With that, Loch prepared to free him.

"Problem?" Travis asked with a forced calm.

"We've got to go," Loch told him firmly. "You need to shut up and listen to stay alive."

Travis nodded. As Loch slipped the ankle cuff off, he was

already dressing. Fast. Then he followed Loch down the stairs and toward the back door. Loch went to grab the bags but Travis did instead, slinging them over his shoulder.

"I'm assuming you need your hands free to shoot at people," Travis explained.

Loch nodded and motioned for him to follow out the back door.

"Shouldn't you set some kind of trap?" Travis asked quietly, still in the doorway.

"What makes you think I haven't?" Loch walked away and Travis followed through the darkened backyard at his heels. The path Loch led him down cut through to the next street, where Tar was waiting with a car. Tar got out, wearing a cap and a hoodie pulled up, and Travis gave him a once-over.

"Get in the back seat and lie down," Loch instructed tersely. Travis handed him the bags and complied.

Loch shoved them into the passenger's seat and went toward Tar. "They'll be in the house by now."

"I'd like to know who they are," Tar said.

"Then you need to hurry before the house kills them."

"Dammit, Loch." Tar took off with a light jog, and Loch got in and took off. Tar had the coordinates to the safe house on paper in the car because he didn't want to risk having them traced. He'd also laid out the best route to take that would avoid cameras—because the feds had access to pretty much any camera they thought could help them find a criminal—and the CIA agent helping that criminal.

After driving for ten minutes, Loch told Travis, "Try to escape and I'll kill you myself."

He got a light snore in response.

When Travis woke, the car had stopped moving and it was dark out. He raised up on his elbow slowly, assured that things were all right because Loch was in the driver's seat on his computer.

"If you're awake, we can go inside," Loch said, without looking back at him.

"Inside?" He realized quickly they were in a garage. "Why didn't you go in already?"

"Someone needed to guard you."

Travis wanted to point out that, rather than sit uncomfortably in the car, Loch could've simply woken him, but Travis didn't say that. Instead, he rolled that point around in his mind as Loch got out of the car and motioned for him to do the same.

The house looked similar to the other one on the inside, just much smaller—only one floor—and he quickly spied a roomful of technology off the kitchen.

He glanced out the window, surprised. The inside of the house didn't match what he saw, and he figured that was the point.

"Windows are bulletproofed and darkened for privacy," Loch told him now. "And yes, this house blends in."

Which meant it must look like shit, just like the rest of the neighborhood. The kind of row house that someone driving by would overlook since it just faded in with the others. There was even a broken down car in the driveway, and Travis figured Loch and his accomplice were smart enough to make sure the registration matched whatever fake identity owned the house.

Travis hadn't been able to see much of the man who'd brought them the car earlier, but under the faint glow of the streetlight, he'd seen the man's eyes—an ice blue that held his for a moment too long.

And you looked away first. But hell, that was more about survival than fear.

"You can use the bathroom and grab something to eat," Loch was saying, and Travis realized the sun was already up.

"Same rules apply," Loch told him.

"All the same?" Travis asked, feeling the heat rise in his cheeks.

"What do you think?"

"I think you just hid me from the feds," Travis said slowly. "So who the fuck are you, really?"

Loch stalked toward him, and Travis noted he was hard through his jeans. He stood close—so damned close—and Travis realized how much pent-up adrenaline was still coursing through him, looking for a release as Loch murmured against his cheek, "I'm either your best friend or worst enemy. That's up to you."

Yeah, that was. Travis smiled, took a step back and stripped his shirt off, leaving it where he tossed it. He took his shoes off and let his jeans drop, all while heading toward the door he assumed was the bedroom like he didn't have a goddamned care in the world.

When he looked over his shoulder, Loch was staring at him, his eyes heated, his expression unreadable.

Loch was annoyed as hell and already tired of running. He called Tar. "We're here. Maybe instead of running next time, we can just blow some shit up?"

"I'm sure the FBI and Jasper would be pleased with that," Tar said calmly.

"Fuck you." Dammit, he needed a drink, badly.

"How's your prisoner doing?" Tar asked

"Fuck off. He alternates between scared shitless and pissed at me," Loch admitted.

"Are you being gentle with him?"

"Are you goddamned joking? I'm not a gentle man. I'm not emotional. I'm a fucking bastard," Loch roared.

"I hope you're not looking for me to disagree," Tar said dryly.

"I'm looking for guidance, dammit. This needs kid gloves."

"By all means, pass him on to me."

"Right," Loch muttered. "You're like the lions who eat their young."

"Those would be sharks. And it's called survival of the fittest," Tar protested. To be fair, Tar's methods usually worked, especially because it was like to like. "You just don't want to admit that you're a big softie."

"Fuck off or I'll have to beat the shit out of you. Again."

Tar snorted. "In your dreams. Never happened."

They'd actually beaten the shit out of each other. Walls had dents in them and both had come out bruised and broken, panting and only slightly less angry than when they'd started. "I know what to do next."

"Want to share your plan?" Tar asked.

"Not especially."

"I think we need to see a counselor about our communication skills," Tar said pleasantly.

Loch wanted to hang up on him, mainly because he had no plan and Tar knew it. Instead, he asked, "I'm assuming we can't stay here more than twenty-four hours?"

"Correct. Your new location is set to go—confirm with me before you leave," Tar told him. "I did call Park to try to calm him down, but he's pissed."

"Learn anything?" When Loch had accepted the job, he hadn't given a shit why the feds wanted Travis. He wanted to do the favor so he didn't owe Parks anymore, but he realized he'd never *not* owe someone.

"I did a little digging. They definitely think Travis has intel on the Russians—especially their human trafficking endeavors."

"No wonder they're so hot to get him back. Are they sure Travis has intel they can use?"

"Well, several of the Russians allegedly involved in the trafficking ring were found dead three weeks ago. Definitely murder—execution-style."

Loch's throat tightened. "Their throats were cut, weren't they." It was more statement than question.

"Yes."

That method of execution was a Snow specialty. Of course, he wasn't the only one who trained assassins to cut throats, but still, having Travis that close to these murders was no coincidence. "Do they suspect that he might be the assassin?"

"I don't think so—not yet, anyway. They believe he

knows general intel on the trafficking ring, and I have a feeling they believe he was helping with recruitment." Tar's voice was tight. Anything to do with hurting children tugged at both of them in a way that was too hard to bear—but they did anyway. "Have you asked him?"

"No. I've explained that I needed intel from him and when I had what I needed, I'd basically hand him a bag with a new life. But he doesn't trust that—or me. Not completely."

"You have to push him, Loch. Under a controlled circumstance. One that has you armed and ready for anything," Tar reminded him.

As if he needed reminding. "He killed bad men, Tar. That's a good sign, isn't it?"

"We don't know who else he killed. We don't know if he blacked out. Maybe it was a test of Snow's—because killing the traffickers throws everyone off track, including us. No one would think he was a completely bad guy for doing that... unless he's doing it for his own gain. Or Snow's." Tar wasn't telling him anything he didn't already know, but dammit, none of this was good. "I'll come there and question him with you."

"We both know that won't work."

"Fine. You're fucking him. Forming an attachment. Making him beholden to you—"

"Beholden?" Loch scoffed.

"I know *you* don't need me, Loch. But do you need me there?" Tar asked bluntly.

"You don't trust me?" Loch asked, even though he knew that wasn't it.

"It's not that and you know it. I'll be close. Wait until you change houses tomorrow night, but once you're there? You can't waste anymore time. Parks isn't going to be put off much longer."

The FBI would expect Travis turned over to them in forty-eight hours, and the Russians had the same amount of time to find and take him out.

Not a lot of choice here. "And we've got a potential explosion on our hands," he murmured. And a potential new lead on the man who still had a hold on them.

"Check in, Loch," was all Tar said before hanging up.

Loch went to find Travis, following the smell of breakfast cooking.

Travis looked over his shoulder. "I made breakfast—I was just going to come and find you. And I don't cook bacon naked for anyone."

Loch bit back a laugh and went to see what Travis made. Since it was the first time Travis had been allowed up, unfettered, he'd made good use in making himself at home. He'd checked through all the cabinets and found the food that Tar managed to keep stocked and fresh.

There were eggs—over easy—and bacon and toast and coffee, and Loch stared at it, trying to remember the last time he'd had food cooked for him at home and then...

He remembered... because it had been over a year ago, and it had been Liam doing the cooking. He almost broke, right there in front of Travis, who was waiting for him to simply sit and eat, which would be the normal human response in this situation.

But there was nothing normal about what was happening here, not to him or to Travis.... now that the ghost of Liam had suddenly loomed up to bite him in the ass.

"Loch, you all right?"

"I'm good. Eat. I'll, ah, be right back." He retreated into the office, pulled out the picture of Liam he kept in his go-bag and stared at it, wondering why the hell he hadn't been able to commit to him, and why the promise of normalcy hadn't ever seemed real.

CHAPTER SEVEN

THEY MOVED OUT AT DARK, driving through the night. Although he slept through most of the ride, Travis woke when the car pulled into another attached garage.

He'd been ruminating about Loch and Liam, pissed at himself for being jealous of a dead man. Pissed at Loch for being so damned good in bed. It was almost enough to make Travis forget the extremely precarious position he was in: running from equally dangerous entities and in bed—literally —with yet another.

Travis heard the creak of the cage door in his mind opening, and he knew it was because of Loch, who willingly and easily opened that cage and let that animal out to play. And Travis happily allowed it, for longer and longer times.

"Are we moving like this every twenty-four hours?" Travis asked now as he trudged behind Loch into the house.

"Better safe than sorry," was all Loch said. "Sit. I've got food."

Travis paused. "So now you're going to trust me?"

"We're in the middle of nowhere. Plus, the place has

silent alarms. You won't get far," Loch told him as he set down bags of take-out that he'd gotten on the road and began to heat them up.

"I wouldn't take you for the McDonald's type."

"There are times I have to lower my standards to survive."

"Yeah, me too," Travis muttered, which caused Loch to choke on the soda he'd been drinking.

"Am I included in that?" he asked when he'd stopped coughing.

"Yes," Travis told him coolly.

"I'm sorry that fucking me is such a burden," he said as he slowly advanced. "I'll try to do better."

The look in his eyes made Travis freeze. Because if Loch got any better?

Travis would shatter.

Immediately, protective barriers of steel snapped into place. He heard the clang in his head, but then Loch stopped, as if he heard it, sensed the wall that came up between them and retreated back to the food. He sat at the table and motioned for Travis to join him.

With a deep breath, Travis did.

They ate in silence for a few minutes until Loch asked casually, "So, how'd you end up grifting?"

Travis eyed him with the same kind of suspicion he'd usually reserved for well meaning teachers and social workers through the years. "How'd you end up kidnapping innocent people?"

Loch stared at him evenly. "I'm not staring at someone innocent."

"I'm not part of the Russian mob. I'm not a fucking

snitch." And then they were back to Loch's original question, dammit.

He'd used *grifter*, not *hooker* though... "Grifting's a life skill I picked up early on."

"Why?"

Warning bells were going off inside the cage, but Travis ignored them. "What's with all the questions? What do you care? You out to reform me before you send me off to die?"

Loch sighed. "Was your childhood that bad?"

"Excellent work, Freud." Confront it—tell the truth. Take away its power. Stop the person trying to gain power. "It was terrible. My parents shouldn't have been. It was poverty and abuse. The usual shit." But it was so much more than that. The image of the box flashed before his eyes but he pushed it away impatiently. Because he would always find a way to stay free.

Something inside the cage stirred. The cage wasn't the box. The cage was big and open, with plenty of breathing room. The feral-ness could breathe in there.

"Did your parents grift?"

Christ, more questions. "They stole the state's money allocated for me, so I guess technically you can say they were thieves. But not very good ones." He took a burger and ate it with all the focus he could, like the conversation hadn't bothered him a damned bit. Whether he was gifting, hooking or kidnapped, he didn't need anyone feeling sorry for him.

Loch was still, just watching him carefully. Travis knew what he saw—a handsome, strong guy with a fucked-up life.

Loch knows you're smart. Never treats you like you're an idiot.

True. Loch negotiated with him as if they were equals.

Which Travis realized they actually were. Because Loch wasn't exactly a criminal, but his moral line was definitely further over the line than most and shifted at will.

"Why Sergei?" Loch asked finally, and Travis supposed there was no harm in telling him, even though it would bring up more questions. Maybe even ones that Loch thought he had the answers to.

"Nothing to do with mob ties," he explained.

"Was it the human trafficking?"

Something clanged hard against the cage, the feral boy throwing his body against it and Travis shook his head. He put the burger down, feeling the anger well up inside of him.

Sergei trafficked children. He didn't say it out loud. Couldn't. And dammit, Loch was looking at him like...

Fuck. "I don't want to discuss this anymore."

"You have to," Loch said. And Loch was angry, but not at Travis. "Tell me what you found out. And why."

Not getting him to open the cage tonight...not that easy... lock it tight.

Travis stared at him, barely able to deal with the clanging inside his head. "I'm not testifying about any of this. The feds know nothing."

"Travis, tell me more about the Russians."

Travis stared at him warily. "Sergei wasn't a very good lay."

"But you didn't let him know that."

Travis scoffed. "Course not."

"Were you his boyfriend?"

"I was getting there — at least I was a regular lover that he didn't pay for."

"He didn't realize he was paying."

Travis leveled his gaze at him. "What your point?"

"What were you grifting? What was your endgame?"

"I was simply Sergei's lover."

Loch slid his palm around Travis's neck and held it there tightly. "If you want my help, you'll stop treating me like the FBI and start confiding in me. The same way you would your best goddamn friend."

Travis snorted. "I'm my own best friend, Loch. I can't see any reason to change that."

"I'll give you two—jail or death. They could be one and the same, depending on how you feel about confined spaces."

There was a shift in Travis, not seismic but rather incremental, a slow slide that settled into the atmosphere and finally settling inside Travis himself. "I'm not going to jail for the Russian mob."

"I've been working the case, I'm familiar with the mob guys you were fucking around with."

"I only fucked Sergei," Travis reiterated. "Do the Russians know about you—what *you* do?"

"You won't be traced here."

"Heard that before," Travis muttered.

"Does this have anything to do with the scars on the insides of your thigh?" Loch demanded and Travis's eyes went cold.

"Fuck you."

"What exactly were you trying to do to the mob?"

"Fucking Sergei."

"If you're going to get through this, then you need to stop

dicking around and save yourself." He grabbed Travis and slammed him against the wall, a hand snaking around his throat. "Tell me your game."

Travis smiled, wasn't scared. Loch's thoughts flicked briefly to the scars and he wondered if Snow was putting Travis up to any of this.

Finally, he said, "Are you involved in the human trafficking organization?" and got the violent reaction he'd been looking for.

Travis jolted like he'd been hit with a taser, an anger burning in his eyes that Loch had seen in Tar's...and in his own.

But he still didn't say a word, so Loch pressed harder. "Tell me, dammit. Because I don't help or protect scum." He shook Travis pointedly.

"I'm not a trafficker, you fucker," he bit out.

"Then what? Because that was Sergei's angle. So don't tell me you were only attracted to fucking him."

"Why would that be so hard to believe?"

"You're not a one-man kind of guy."

"You don't know shit about me," Travis bit out. "And yeah, I knew they were into trafficking. I knew it."

"Did you know that the three main movers ended up dead at the docks in the shipping containers they planned to utilize?"

Travis just stared, chin raised defiantly, not admitting anything. Not with words, anyway.

Loch pushed harder. "Are you a one-man vigilante? Or did Sergei screw you out of a job? A cut?"

"I'd never make a fucking profit off that shit. Never," Travis said firmly.

"Why should I believe you?"

"Because I was trafficked." His words were a weary confession, the look in his eyes haunted.

"So a vigilante." Loch's chest burned, but he wouldn't get dragged in, wouldn't fall into any traps. No guilt.

"Yeah, sure. Better than a trick, right?" His eyes were questioning.

"You tell me," he countered. "Did you start tricking because of the trafficking? Were you forced?"

"I met Sergei purposely. Because I heard about a shipment." By the look in Travis's eyes, he knew far too much about the horrors of human trafficking. Any time Loch caught wind of evidence of it, it chilled him to the bone, and he believed Travis.

"Travis... come on." He moved his hand from Travis's throat to his shoulder. "Come on. Come sit back down."

Travis moved slowly—reluctantly—back to the table, and Loch sat back down across from him.

Travis held onto the chair like he was considering standing. Then he did sit, but he wasn't still. He shifted in his seat, two fingers rubbing against his temple. "I swear, if you tell the feds..."

"I won't," Loch said quietly, and whether Travis believed him, Loch wasn't sure. But he'd meant it.

Travis grabbed for Loch's coffee and drank half the cup. With his hand wrapped around the mug, Loch noticed, maybe for the first time, how big Travis actually was. And how haunted he truly was as his guard came down. "I got a lead on the connection to the Russians from a friend."

"The same friend you stayed with when you left WITSEC?"

Not Dodge, no, but Loch didn't have to know differently, so Travis nodded. "He knows I've got a special interest in those kinds of things."

Loch pegged that as a giant fucking lie, which made him angrier. "So your special interest is grifting rich child traffickers?"

"Of course not." And now Travis had wound himself up in the lie, because it wasn't about the grift. Not monetarily, anyway. It was to stop child trafficking, singlehandedly, as it seemed.

"Then what, Travis? Because I've got reports of several dead men in that same family of mobsters that you were hanging out with—no known assailants. And I happen to know they were involved in the child trafficking," Loch said calmly.

"I don't know anything about that," Travis said with conviction.

"Bullshit. Of course you do. Because you were with Serge the night they were found. But that wasn't enough to give you an alibi—not by my standards. Maybe the feds haven't put together their time of death and the time of the raid—"

"You said you wouldn't turn me in." Travis slammed the table with his fist and the mug, shattering the ceramic and tilting the table violently. He leaned across it, steadying it with his palms. "What the fuck are you after, Loch? Because Travis is a bit sensitive to all this goddamned questioning, but I'm sure as hell not."

Travis is...?

Loch remained still as he watched the man in front of him who suddenly seemed to loom over him. He looked like Travis still...but somehow...things were different.

Something was so different. Recognition became a slow burn that left his senses tingling and the hair on the back of his neck standing up, his entire body on edge as he commanded, "Back up." He left off "Travis" because the man in front of him?

Wasn't Travis.

Whoever it was told him, "Relax. I'm not going to hurt you. Unless you hurt him—got it?"

Loch wasn't sure he bought that reassurance. "I have no plans to hurt Travis. But I don't take well to threats."

"No plans to hurt him?" The man's head tilted. "Does turning him into the feds sound like a good idea to you?"

"That's not the plan—never has been."

"That's how it started."

"If you know that, why haven't I seen you sooner?" Loch held his breath, having taken the stab and the man in front of him rolled his eyes.

"Sorry. Where're my manners? You can call me Creed." Creed crossed his arms. "You think I haven't been there, pushing him to run? You think I didn't get him out from under the marshals? How do you think he escaped?"

"Dodge."

"Dodge helped, sure. Travis and I, we work in conjunction. Our strengths lie in different areas."

Loch tried to latch onto the truth in that statement. He wasn't sure if maybe he'd been drugged, but he felt completely fine. Was this a ploy, meant to get Travis from testifying under some legal insanity plea? To get him to a mental hospital he could no doubt easily escape from? Maybe Travis didn't believe him about not turning him over to the feds after all.

Snow turned Travis. And Loch might've triggered something—someone—he couldn't put back in the cage.

Open the cage. That's what Travis was murmuring in his sleep after falling into a post-sex coma. Loch had assumed it was a metaphor for how aggressive Travis had suddenly been.

But no—*open the cage* meant something else entirely. Travis had been referring to his DID—Dissociative Identity Disorder. And Travis and Creed might technically have been the same person...but the personalities were very different. Creed was harder.

Creed was the hitter.

Go back to the killings. That's what brought Creed out. Travis was just there tonight to... "Open the cage," Loch breathed.

Creed gave a satisfied smile. "I could get out myself, but Travis keeps me in there by being calm. If he's handling shit, I'm cool. When he can't, I'm letting myself out. But I'll tell you this...if you try to pin shit on him? If you go through with turning him in? I'll be forced to kill you, which would be a damned shame."

"Why's that?"

"Because Travis likes you. And so do I. That's a first." Creed uncrossed his arms and placed them on the table again. Loch could get out of his position against the wall easily and flip the table, and he already knew how strong Travis was.

But Creed? Well, that was a different story. Creed no doubt matched him in strength and skill. Street smarts too, probably fought a lot like Tar.

Thankfully, Loch had fought Tar enough times to know

what that kind of brawl was like. "So we've determined we're not going to kill each other."

"For now, no," Creed confirmed. "Wouldn't mind another fight though." And then a slow, lazy smile spread across his face. His eyes went heavy-lidded and Loch knew if he looked, Creed would be hard.

Had Creed been watching? Was that possible? Or had Creed been out before and Loch hadn't noticed?

Had he fucked Creed? "You've been watching?"

"Can't exactly help it."

"And that's all you've done—watch?"

Creed's smile was sly, a bit wicked and it made Loch's stomach tighten. "I like the way you fuck. I've always liked it rough."

Travis's words echoed in Loch's ears. *I like it rough some- times.* "How often?"

"Does it matter?" Creed gave a pretend frown. "Are you going to tell me you only like Travis? Am I ruining your fantasy of saving a poor grifting rent boy?"

With that, Loch turned the table hard, slamming Creed back with the unexpected force and upending him. Loch took advantage, trapping him with the table and Loch's weight against it.

Creed laughed. "Nice one. I guess you like it when we fight too. I was hoping there's going to be more of it."

"What kind of game are you playing?"

"No game, Loch. No game at all. This is my goddamned life—and you've taken it in your hands. I know you like taking Travis with your hands...your tongue. Personally, I like your cock the best. You were particularly creative with the cuffs. I can appreciate that. Turnabout deserves fair play."

"Don't even think about it," Loch snarled, putting more pressure on the table and causing Creed to pale.

"Be careful...the merchandize," he managed to croak out. "Precious...Travis..."

Loch eased up slightly. "Jealous?"

"Baby, you really have no idea who you were fucking, do you? Travis doesn't want to be your ghost lover, baby. I don't give a shit, as long as you keep fucking me."

"You turn him out? Are you his pimp?"

Creed's eyes flashed with anger. "I told you—I don't make him do anything he doesn't want to do. That's his kink, not mine. I like to pick my fucks."

"But you let him do what he wants?"

"He's been through a lot, so yes. I let Travis run wild and free. When he's grifting? It's a true gift. A sight to see. Then again, you'd figure he'd be good at slipping in and out of other personalities, right?"

"I could have you committed."

Creed laughed. "You think that scares me? Look, believe me or don't—it doesn't make a difference to my end game." He rattled his cuffs. "But this? You know how much this shit turns me on. So tell me—do we have the same deal you had with Travis?"

Loch ignored that—and how turned on he was. Thankfully, fear was a good deterrent, because the man in front of him was as deadly as Tar. "Will Travis remember this?"

"Nope. It's like a blackout for him. I'd rather him not see the shit I do. Kid's been through enough."

Kid. Jesus. "I guess you came around in order to take care of him. Nice of you," Loch said.

Creed shook his head. "You don't get it, do you, Loch?

I'm not the alter. Travis is. And I'll kill you if you try to turn him in."

Creed was more worried about Travis than himself. Interesting. "You could try, but you will be disappointed."

"Unless you're immortal, Loch? You have no idea who you're dealing with."

"Yes, I do. But what does Travis protect?"

"Exactly the same thing I've been trying to for years."

Creed's eyes flared and he shoved hard at the table, sending Loch backward. He was on his feet by the time Creed got out from under the trap and tackled him back down to the floor.

"You're not making the best case for freedom," Loch told him.

"I'm never going back there." Creed bared his teeth. "If you try to take me there, I'll die before I go, and I'll take you with me."

It wasn't an empty threat, and Loch was pretty sure he knew where *there* was—a compilation of the Russians, the feds and Snow's camp. It didn't matter because, for Creed, it wasn't an empty threat. Loch put his hands up, the first time he'd fought Tar flashing through his mind. Tar had been feral, covered in what Loch would later discover was his brother's blood, and he'd fought Loch to kill him. Loch, in turn, fought for his life, having no idea who the fuck this guy was and why he'd been targeted.

He'd found out. And nothing had been the same since.

And here we go again.

Penance and absolution always equaled pain. "Creed, listen..."

But Creed had gotten a running start and Loch braced

himself for the impact as Creed's body slammed his. They hit the ground together, but Loch got the roll on him, hooking his leg around Creed's and flipping him. Loch ended up on Creed's back, holding him down roughly.

He twisted Creed's arm behind his back and Creed growled at him, tried to buck him off. Loch held tightly, bringing his knee up to rest between Creed's legs, right at his balls. "I'd hate to hurt them."

"So suck them instead, and then I'll kill you," Creed shot back.

"Ingenious plan, but no, not the dying part. I'll take the sucking under advisement."

"I'm—"

"Not going to Snow. I'm not taking you back there. Even if I knew where the fucker was, I'd never bring anyone back to him."

Creed went still. "Snow's missing?"

"MIA. Underground. Hell, he could be dead. But you're the first survivor we've found in over four years."

———

Loch saw the seconds of struggle and then the immediate confusion before Travis tried to put his mask on, the one he'd tried to wear from the start with Loch. Tried and failed because Loch was squarely on top of him.

It was like losing Liam all over again.

Loch struggled to regain control of his anger as Travis babbled, "I'm sorry. Did...fuck. I didn't. I can't—"

"Control him? I know—Creed told me," Loch told him

flatly. "It's a good act you've got going on." He pushed off Travis, then went to sit back at the table.

After a long moment, Travis rolled to his side and pushed up, hands still chained together at the wrists. He watched as Loch flipped the table back over and poured him a fresh cup of coffee before sitting back down.

"Let's go back to the trafficking," Loch said, trying to keep his voice neutral as he took a seat across from Travis again. "How many shipments were you...involved in?"

"I don't know. I grifted Sergei to get information and then...it was stopped."

"How?"

"I don't know, all right?" he shouted.

"You do know, dammit."

"It was Creed. I know that," Travis whispered his amendment. "But I don't know anything. I'm the way in, okay? I don't...I can't—"

"You and Creed share the same fucking body—if he kills, then you kill too."

Travis shook his head. "I know I can kill, Loch. Trust me."

"So it was you who went after the traffickers—all you and not Creed?" It made sense as to why Creed would suddenly come out to try to shut Travis up and keep Loch out of his business.

Travis sighed as if reading his mind. "Creed tried to stop me—at first. Once he saw how serious I was, he let me do what I needed to."

"So when Creed came out tonight—"

"He doesn't like it when people threaten me."

"He took the blame for what happened."

Travis shrugged. "Does it really matter? It's not like only half of me can go to jail, right?"

Loch shook his head slowly. "I'm not talking about jail, Travis. I'm talking about the dangerous game you started with the Russian Mob. So tell me what your plan was. *Is.* Because I have a feeling you'd still be working on it if you hadn't ended up being arrested."

"Why? So you can keep telling me how dangerous and stupid it was? How it wouldn't matter worth a damn?"

"Travis...it fucking matters, okay."

Travis took another gulp of the coffee, looking like he might be about to throw the damned thing across the room. Or at Loch's head. The silence stretched out for what seemed like forever, but Loch's patience was short. Still, he waited, watched the emotions crossing Travis's face.

Finally, Travis said, "I first heard about a new cattle call on the second night I stayed over with Sergei—they called it a circuit. Seasoning. And I know what that means. A kiddie stroll." He looked disgusted, pushed the coffee away.

"Were you solicited by Sergei? Maybe for your contacts?"

Travis cut him a look so dark it felt like a physical punch. "I was grifting. And I'm good. To this day, Sergei and his people have no idea what I did or who I really was."

Loch believed that. Because the rent boy act? Travis had dropped that the second he knew that pose was over, and he'd slid out of it effortlessly. For maybe one of the first times (when Travis wasn't orgasming), Loch felt like he was seeing the real Travis, the one underneath all the armor. "You need to listen to me carefully. I know you're good at what you do. But what makes you think you're in the clear on that? What makes you think they didn't discover what you did from prison? Because they're after you not to testify...but maybe they know more than you think."

"Shit." Travis slammed the mug hard on the table and stood. "They don't know, okay. I made sure of it—so much sure that they killed three of their own. Guys I framed. And I'm not fucking sorry I did it."

———

After Travis confessed, he'd sagged back into the chair and Loch had stopped questioning him and instead led him by the elbow into the bedroom.

It didn't look much different from the other safe houses they'd been in over the last days, and it was clean, with fresh sheets on the bed. He fell into bed, dressed as he'd been for the ride in sweats and a tee, the chains clanking when he hit the mattress.

In the darkness, Loch stripped on the other side of the bed before sliding under the covers. Travis could barely keep his eyes opened and he wasn't sure how long he slept with Loch's body next to his, but when he woke, Loch was still awake, staring at the ceiling.

And you're still chained.

At least the cage door was quiet. And in the darkness, Travis broke the quiet. "Loch, please...just let me run."

"Travis—"

"It's the best way. We both know it. I can repay you the money you'll lose on me."

Loch turned on his side and propped himself on his elbow. "It's not about that, and you know it. It's not that simple. There will be consequences."

"Right. Consequences. Wouldn't know about those," Travis said flatly.

"I told you I wasn't turning you over to the FBI. You've got to trust me on that."

Trust? A foreign fucking concept to Travis. He accepted help from certain people, like Dodge and Blue. He could even accept that Loch wouldn't tell the FBI about the human trafficking shipment he thwarted or the men he killed, but that was more of an honor among thieves thing.

Trusting his life to Loch? "I can't trust you, Loch."

Loch sighed. "I'm not sure you've got much of a choice. I'm the only thing standing between you and the FBI and you and the Russians."

"We've had this discussion already. Tell me something I don't know."

"You don't know that I saw you look at Liam's picture."

"Is that a crime too?" Loch pushed the covers back and left the bed and the room, leaving Travis alone and cold.

And this is what you're used to.

CHAPTER EIGHT

LOCH DIDN'T CALL Tar until Travis finally fell asleep. Tar picked up on the first ring, like he'd been waiting by the phone. Which, of course, he must've been because when Loch told him, "I need you," it only took a second for Tar to acknowledge, "I'm right outside."

Relief coursed through Loch. "He's split, Tar. I saw it happen."

"I know."

Loch gave a soft snort. "You watched the whole thing."

"I had to. It's a safety issue."

Loch rolled his eyes. "So you saw what I did."

"I had to, Loch. That's why I'm coming in."

"I'm surprised you haven't already."

"I have some restraint." Tar was already letting himself into the house—quietly, at least, with files tucked under one arm. It was only when he came face to face with Loch that he took the phone away from his ear.

This was the first time they'd seen each other since before Liam died, and they just stood there. He wanted to hug his friend but figured that might be overly dramatic at best, so he refrained.

Tar looked guarded. Quiet, and uncharacteristically so. "Hey."

Fuck it. Loch grabbed him in a tight hug and, after a stunned moment, Tar hugged him back. "It's good to see you, Tar. Really good."

Tar gave a small smile. "Same."

Loch's heart tugged at how good Tar looked. He was that all American handsome, blond and blue-eyed, and yeah, now Loch understood why he hadn't seen the resemblance to Liam before this.

Because Tar was far more handsome. Tar and Travis both, and how the hell had Loch ended up in the middle of this bizarre triangle? Because the usual tug to Tar hadn't gone away—instead, it had gotten stronger. It was part of the reason he'd cut Tar off and tried to throw himself into the relationship with Liam. Because Liam had sensed it and had driven a wedge between the men, and Loch had let it happen.

Because he'd never thought Tar returned the feelings. At least, with their threesomes, Tar had been close enough to him to make things okay.

Just invite Tar into it. That's what they always did. Then it would be business as usual.

Except this time, it would be a foursome, and definitely far different than anything they'd ever done. "Need coffee?" Loch asked.

Tar put the files down on the table. "You look like you need it more."

Loch didn't deny it. Instead, he poured large mugs of the

hot liquid and sat across from Tar, much in the way he had with Travis earlier. The table only wobbled a little, and Tar noticed and silently stuffed a pile of napkins under one leg. And then they sat in silence for several minutes, until finally Tar acknowledged the bruise on Loch's cheek. "Things got heated. Creed's got a temper."

Loch shrugged it off. "It could've been worse. Much worse."

"Did Travis stay Travis?"

Loch frowned. "You don't have the bedroom wired?"

Tar smiled. "I'm trying to give you some privacy."

"You're pretending to give me privacy."

"Deniability is a big part of my life."

"Child. You're a fucking child," Loch muttered. "You saw everything."

"Sometimes I walked away to get food. Or shower." Tar smiled, then grew serious. "He's not mentioning Snow at all."

"Neither one of them. I figured getting him to talk about the trafficking was enough. And I checked it out—as I'm sure you did too. The facts match.

"He could've looked them up," Tar offered halfheartedly, because having Travis truly being one of Snow's meant that Snow was still alive and still training... and that he'd been successful.

"This could've just been dumb luck," Loch said. "He might not have created the split. Travis might've already been there."

Tar sighed. "That would make Snow one lucky bastard. So, what's next?"

"I'm leaving that up to you. You've got more perspective on this kind of thing," he said diplomatically.

"This about my time in the nuthouse?" Tar asked.

"Yes." Because Loch was confident Tar could recognize an alternative personality versus a fraud.

"What're we talking about?"

"You've got to see it for yourself."

"You like this guy," Tar said finally. There wasn't any judgment in his tone but his eyes? They looked haunted. More so than usual.

"I...yeah. He's different."

"You fucked both of them."

"I think so. Yes."

Tar nodded then placed a file on the table between them. "This is going to be hard for you to hear."

"Was it hard for you?"

Tar's jaw tightened, and he nodded. "None of this shit ever gets easier. If it does, it's a sign to get out." Tar opened the files and began to page through them, then turned the papers to face Loch and pushed them in front of him.

"You've read it?" Loch asked as he took the file and opened it. Tar nodded and Loch looked at the slim volume of papers in front of him and brought himself up to speed.

"What are the sources on this?"

"Jasper found them, thanks to West. Dark web search," Tar confirmed.

"West, huh?" Loch asked, and Tar nodded without saying anything further. Loch didn't press it because West was always a source of tension between them. Not Liam levels of tension, but still, he didn't like thinking about Tar with anyone, and the irony wasn't lost on him. He forced his focus back into the file. "It makes sense now—the names. Travis is definitely the alter."

"Creed. They named him Creed, not Travis." He said it more to himself than to Tar. According to the papers in front of him, Creed had been abandoned as a baby, kept in an orphanage until he was two and abused by his foster family.

By all accounts, they were a strict, religious family. *Punishment is life* types. And Creed hadn't been a *sit still and be good* kind of kid.

There were several reports of abuse, all ignored and chalked up to risky childhood behavior. A psychologist's report noted the parents were counseled to allow Creed room to mess up and then give lockdown punishments.

Creed had been six.

There were school reports from various teachers that Creed didn't have clean clothes or lunches or snacks or any money for books or pencils. There were signs that someone should've picked up and followed through on. Creed had been abandoned by all the adults in his life.

Loch cleared his throat before he spoke again. "He didn't ask for any of it. Those fuckers took him in, got money, and spent it on themselves." He seethed for the hurt and pain Creed had suffered and vowed to seek revenge against the bastards who simultaneously forced Creed into being a bad kid and then punished him for it.

He wasn't sure he wanted to read on, because he was sure there was worse to come...but Creed had lived it. The very least Loch could do was read about it.

He paged through drawings that Creed had made, ones that punctuated his permanent school file. They showed what was a cartoon drawing of what was most likely him, in a closet, curled up, and the words, *No one can love you because you're bad*, written over and over again.

A powerful statement for a three-and-four-and-five-and six-year-old to repeatedly have drummed into him. Creed had no doubt absorbed this lesson well, and there was a part of him craving the love he'd never received and yet too scared to ask for it. Loch was as sure of that as he was anything because he'd watched Tar live through it...and Loch dealt with it himself.

Loch wanted to burn the fucking folder. Burn it, then go find Creed's parents and burn it all down, and maybe he would. But that wouldn't help Creed—or Travis— to stop thinking of himself...and everyone else...as a commodity. "We can't turn him over to the feds."

"Absolutely not. Jasper already knows he's ours."

He's ours. Christ. "So he's going to make sure Travis disappears? That he's no longer a viable witness?"

"I didn't ask. Deniability."

Many witnesses they happened on in their line of work weren't so much innocent as they were the lesser of two evils. The small fish who'd done terrible things but was willing to bite the hand that fed them in return for freedom—if a life of WITSEC could be called that.

Their new charge wasn't an angel, but the people he'd taken money from weren't either. He hadn't preyed on the weak; he'd taken from those who'd thought themselves too powerful to be conned.

And he'd shown them how wrong they'd been. "Jasper knows...that he killed traffickers?" Lock asked.

"I think he suspects. But it's not entirely clear who killed them, or how." Tar shrugged. "Travis and Creed seem to be covering for each other. And we need to know the truth so we can cover for them."

"You think the triggers made him kill the traffickers? Even after what he told me last night?"

"I don't know."

"Maybe he doesn't have triggers."

"So Snow was able to split him—"

"Maybe he was split before Snow got him," Loch broke in.

"Then he'd have even more time to plant triggers to try to create an assassin," Tar finished.

"What if he created an assassin...just not one who works for him? He's got someone with a conscience and he couldn't beat it out of him. It wouldn't be the first time."

When Tar spoke again, his tone was grim, his expression mirroring his emotions. "His markings..."

"Nothing like yours."

"They wouldn't be," Tar said flatly. "Unless they had him marked for death."

Only Loch knew how close to that promise of Snow's Tar had come. "So he's got the FBI, the Russians, and Snow after him."

"He's ours," Tar said flatly. "No exceptions. No matter what he needs. Because if he's Snow's..." He couldn't finish his reiteration. Loch didn't press him to. He didn't want to know more—his imagination was already leading him down that dark path. "He's got to remember — all of it."

"He's already started to."

Tar stared at him steadily. "Let me bring him to —"

"No."

"Loch, this is complicated. The doctors who took care of me —"

"I'm not against him getting help, Tar, but it's too soon." Loch took a breath and tried again. "He trusts me."

"Point taken. Still, he's got to remain restrained...and I'm not sure what that's going to do for his trust issues."

"All the time?"

"Yes, especially when he starts to remember."

Loch knew that, knew that if the triggers came back full force...then neither Creed nor Travis would have any control over themselves. They'd revert back to being a Snow killing machine. "Is it possible only one of the personalities are?"

Tar pressed his lips together. "You can't take that chance. I need to talk to him. See what—if anything—he remembers. I'll do it here, because I don't want to lose his trust either."

"Won't Jasper have something to say about that?"

"Jasper will understand, as long as we're careful. And I need to do this alone with him. Travis has already seen me talking to you, so that should make him accept me being here. But I need to stress him... and you shouldn't be here for that."

"I'm not leaving."

"You can wait next door." Tar took keys out of his pocket and handed them over. "It's all wired up."

CHAPTER NINE

TRAVIS WOKE a couple of hours later to the angry sound of his handcuffs hitting together and he cursed himself for not running. Granted, then he'd be chased by three separate groups—because Loch was definitely some kind of agent—and Travis wasn't sure he'd be able to get away from all of them.

Apparently, Loch was the best enemy to have at the moment. But this handcuff shit still sucked.

He pushed himself out of the bed and, feeling Loch's eyes on him, turned to find him standing in the doorway.

"I'm going to shower," Travis told him and walked into the bathroom without further comment. And Loch didn't stop him—or offer to take the cuffs off, and hell, they were loose enough for him to be able to wash up easily enough. It was just awkward, which, yeah, it all fucking was.

When he emerged, in a towel, Loch was still there. Travis ignored him, rummaged through his bag and grabbed a pair of jeans. He dropped the towel and slid them on, sans underwear...and noted that Loch watched the entire show.

"My friend is here. His name's Tar," Loch said finally.

"So why are you here staring at me?"

"He's here to talk to you."

Travis rolled his eyes, grabbed a t-shirt, and pulled it over his head. "He a shrink?"

"No," Loch said.

Travis ran his hands through his wet hair. "Is he going to try to get me to admit more shit?"

"It's not about you admitting anything. We're not going to turn you over to the feds. But we do need to get to the bottom of what exactly happened. What you—what Creed—did."

"It's not like I have a choice in any of this, right?" In the back of Travis's mind, the cage door was creaking, like it was swinging back and forth, the door completely open...for whenever he needed to lock himself inside.

He followed Loch into the living room where Tar stood, waiting—a blond, blue-eyed man who looked a lot like...him. Travis felt a flush of familiarity rush over him, which was odd, because...

He blinked. The cage door creaked and Creed was suddenly flying across the room at Tar, handcuffs and all. He took Tar down but, to Tar's credit, he quickly subdued Creed with a surprising strength and sat on his chest, holding Creed's cuffed hands above his head. Creed felt himself get hard and didn't give a shit. Tar?

Just smiled.

"I'm guessing I'm stirring up some memories for you." Tar stood suddenly. "Why don't we sit and talk about it."

Creed immediately missed the body contact. He got up slowly, leaning on one elbow to get himself completely off the floor. "Asshole," he muttered in Tar's direction, then tested the cuffs. Pulling on them would only result in broken bones. "I don't know you."

"Seems like you know something."

Creed looked around for Loch and realized he and Tar were alone. "I'm not talking about the Russians."

"I'm not asking about the Russians," Tar told him, and Creed bared his teeth and growled. Tar reciprocated that gesture, then learned close and said, "We come from the same box, Creed."

Box? Not box. Cage...and yet, Tar's words rang true to him.

Box.

He blinked, and suddenly, Snow's voice echoed inside his head. The boy I built the box for never broke either. Creed stared at Tar, realization crashing down, and his voice sounded hoarse as he managed, "Why should I believe you?"

"Because you saw what was carved inside that box." Tar stared at him. "Over soon."

Creed froze for a second, and then an involuntary shudder ran through him. "You could've seen that anytime."

"Maybe," Tar said, and then he slowly unbuttoned his shirt. Stripped it off and then yanked off the T-shirt he wore underneath off.

And then he turned around.

OVER SOON.

Those words were tattooed in black and gray scale on his back, between Tar's shoulder blades. Creed's mind flashed to the letters carved into that box—all caps, a mantra he'd repeated to himself over and over.

Sometimes, he still did.

He'd hated the boy who never broke. And that boy he'd

hated all these years and the reason Creed had survived was one in the same...all because he'd wanted to make some previous inhabitant of the box proud.

Creed stared down at the table in front of him, his fingers reflexively tracing the words from his memories. Things he tried not to think about ever, things that he'd sworn he'd buried so deeply that they'd never come up again. Not for him or for Travis, but now? He'd stepped right back into that world. "I don't want to talk about this."

"I need to know what you remember, Creed," Tar pressed. "Let's start easy. How did you escape from the box—from Snow?"

"How did I escape?" Creed repeated slowly, frowning. "How did I?"

"You don't remember?" Tar frowned.

"Did you help me?"

"No. You weren't at the compound I freed. I'm assuming you were held in a different place for a while after Loch and I thought Snow's reign of terror had ended. We were focused on finding the survivors, not liberating more guys from being tortured." He sounded troubled.

Creed felt the confusion crowding in. "How many were there with me?"

"I was hoping you could tell me."

Creed snorted. "Travis isn't talking. He's the one who escaped."

"I thought you were the violent one."

"I am." Creed sat back, the restraints heavy on his wrists. "Travis must've fucked his way out, or stolen a key."

"Or you were let out on purpose."

"Why would Snow do that?"

"Because you're a human trigger." Tar looked as troubled as Creed felt.

Tar stared at Creed then, like he was trying to assess the danger by staring into his eyes. Finally, he moved toward Creed, took out the handcuff key and freed him. Creed remained seated even after the chains fell away, only bringing his arms forward to rub his wrists absently.

It was only then he noticed that Loch had come back into the room. The memories from last night flashed hot and he gave Loch a look that let him know that Creed remembered.

"Tar was explaining that we've got a lot in common," Creed told Loch, whose expression tightened.

"He wasn't there, Loch," Tar added.

"That doesn't make me feel better," Loch admitted.

"So what now? Hypnosis? Electrodes?" Creed asked as he looked between the men.

"I'm taking you to the hospital," Tar explained.

"To check me in?"

"To see if you recognize any of Snow's other experiments."

For some reason, having Tar refer to him as an experiment didn't bother him, because Tar was just as much of one.

Creed watched Loch walk over to where Tar had dropped his shirts and picked them up. He paused for a long moment to stare at Tar's back, and Creed knew from his expression it wasn't the first time he'd seen the tattoo.

But Creed knew from experience that each time could be equally as painful as the next.

Seeing the tattoo for the first time in years could break Loch
—if he let it. When Tar turned to him, he stared at Loch
before taking back his shirts.

"Don't," was all Tar told him, then pulled on the T-shirt.
They were both acutely aware of Creed watching them,
assessing their dynamic.

"I'm sorry," Loch said quietly. Because, during his time
with Liam and the time after Liam's death, Loch had
forgotten why he'd started working with Tar in the first place.
All he remembered was the terrible, burnt-out feeling, the
constant suffering pulling him under.

He'd forgotten how much worse Tar had it—and how he
never, ever complained...

*After he and Tar almost killed each other, Loch followed
Tar back to the place he'd claimed he'd escaped from.*

"It's missing," Tar had told him.

"What?"

*"The box." Tar looked troubled. "The box he'd built
for me."*

Years later, they'd find it, or it would find them. It had
been left on Tar's back porch. And Loch knew that if they
searched the prints they'd found inside, the ones that hadn't
matched Tar, they would match Travis and Creed.

Tar had freed all the boys when he'd escaped, and they
hadn't waited around. It took a while but, before and after
they began working for Jasper, they worked on recovering
them.

Tar rescued at least ten of the boys himself while Loch
covered for him and let the CIA take him into custody.
After that, he and Loch worked together. They found
several more, but there were still many they never found.

"*Not yet*," Tar would say, but he had a list, both written and committed to memory, of all the boys he knew who'd been with him during Snow's reign of terror at that compound.

Of the ones recovered, some managed to kill themselves even while in protective custody—they never trusted that they'd ever truly be free, and neither Tar nor Loch could disagree with them. Some still resided at the hospital, brutal killing machines housed for their own safety. Some who were deprogrammed? They were too fragile to live on their own and also remained in the hospital, scared of what their own bodies and minds could do to betray them.

And Tar? He took care of them all. Loch was honored to help him and to call him a friend. Because what Snow did was take vulnerable kids and fuck with their mental health. He created multiple personalities where there might not have been any. He also used children who had shown any kind of psychic ability, feeling that they might be easier to break and remold in the image of the assassin that he claimed the CIA wanted.

God, how could he have been so selfish? He couldn't blame Liam or the alcohol, just his own selfishness. Because he'd done the one thing, the one unspoken thing he'd promised he'd never do—he'd abandoned Tar. Left him alone.

Technically, he hadn't—Tar wasn't trapped or hunted, not the way he'd been. And he had the support of Jasper and plenty of friends in various law enforcement agencies, plus the other men of Snow's who he helped—and who'd helped him.

But Loch had gone off on his own and left Tar alone. He hadn't been watching his best friend's back at all. Hadn't checked in with him, hadn't bothered to make sure that Snow wasn't hanging around.

He'd completely checked out.

"Loch, stop," Tar warned him now. "It's enough. It's not necessary."

"I'm sorry," Loch repeated, his voice nearly breaking as he pulled Tar in for a hug. For a long beat, Tar let him, and then pulled away.

"Like I said, it's not necessary. It never was."

"I didn't want to get involved again."

"I know you're angry you got dragged back in," Tar said. "It's my fault. Again."

"Again? Tar...fuck, no. Stop. That's not true. Never was," Loch told him, but Tar had already walked away, was staring out the window, just the way he'd been that night, with the blood he'd spilled on the floor between them.

"We're all products of the same monster," Loch said finally. "But that doesn't make us monsters ourselves."

"You need to convince yourself of that, Loch. Because you're the only one out of us who doesn't believe that," Tar told him, his voice quiet but firm before he left the room.

Inside Loch's head, Tar's voice sounded like a scream.

CHAPTER TEN

"I HATE it when Daddy and Daddy fight," Creed drawled.

Loch broke from his reverie, having forgotten Creed was there and watching the exchange between him and Tar. "Just a lot of water under the bridge." He didn't want to turn around and deal with Creed being an asshole, but he was on the job.

"Is Tar coming back?" Creed asked finally, after several moments of silence.

"Why? You don't want to talk to me?"

"Personally, I'd rather fuck both of you than spend time talking." Creed said back, his body languid and his expression suggestive. "How'd you two meet, anyway? You kidnap him or vice versa?"

Loch considered that. "We fought...and then we ran. Together."

Creed leaned forward on his elbows. "Tell me about it."

Would it hurt anything? At this point, they had to assume Creed was going to be on their side with a mutual enemy in Snow. If he turned out to be programmed? Well, he had Tar here who'd help him take Creed down. But telling the entire truth wasn't going to happen. "There was a fire in Snow's compound. I don't know who set it, but it was probably Snow trying to destroy evidence of what he'd been doing. Trying to kill the men he'd trapped. We freed all the men who were still alive and then we ran. And we hid. And then..." He closed his eyes for a brief second, glossing over the terrible details from that first night. "After that, we decided to find Snow ourselves."

"What happened?"

"Jasper King and his PsyOps Unit happened. He's the man who was charged with bringing us in and then letting us go back out to hunt Snow."

"How old were you?"

"I was seventeen. Tar was sixteen."

Creed frowned and nodded. "So Snow wasn't successful...in programming you two, I mean."

Loch stared at the door that was closed between them and Tar. "Tar was programmed to kill anyone who got in his way."

Creed barely blinked as he stared at Loch, riveted. "What happened?"

"I got in his way." God, this was so much closer to home than he'd anticipated.

"So there's a way to stop it," Creed murmured, almost to himself.

Loch froze, wondering if Creed knew more about his own programming than he was saying. "There's always a way, Creed. That's why we're here. We're not going to let anything happen to you."

"Or to Travis."

"No, you're both safe with us."

"And if I'm programmed?" Creed asked.

"I never gave up on Tar, or any man we saved. I'm not about to start now."

"But you were going to turn Travis in, right?" Creed challenged.

"At first, I had every intention."

"And now?"

"It's odd discussing you in the third person when you're right in front of me," Loch said dryly. "And I'm not sharing plans with you."

"Why?" He tilted his head. "It's not like I share shit with him. I protect him from bad things, including me."

Was Creed a "bad thing"? *He's a killer...who kills child traffickers.* So in Loch's eyes, Creed wasn't bad. "He doesn't know when you do things. So how does it work—because he seems to know what you need, and you seem to understand his needs equally as well."

"It's complicated, Loch. He leads me. I'm sensitive to his stress levels."

"So you control him but he can't control you."

"We control each other, to a point. If he doesn't need me, I don't come out." Creed smiled. "But if you stay in the picture..."

"Tell me when I've fucked you."

"You tell me."

Loch tried to think when he might've had Creed in bed. Travis did get aggressive at times but he'd still been...Travis.

But so was Creed.

Jesus Christ, he was losing his mind. Maybe it was better

this way. Loch changed the subject. "Do you feel like you might be programmed?"

"Fuck, I don't know. I don't know enough about what actually happened to say yes or no. It's hard to tell if it's programming...or if it's me being protective of Travis."

"So you might've..."

"Hurt you, yes. If you'd been hurting him for sure. And it was confusing, coming into that." Creed shrugged. "I was expecting a fight. And what I got..."

Loch remembered very well what Creed had gotten. He closed his eyes at the memory, thinking about noting the difference in Travis, but how it happened so quickly that he hadn't had time to really process it. Not with an impending orgasm and his cock buried in Travis's ass. "So you stuck around for the sex."

"It was good. I didn't understand why Travis freaked, and then I got it."

"Care to explain?"

Creed shrugged. "Not really."

"We're going to have to discuss the trafficking more."

"I don't think that had anything to do with being programmed. But now I'm..." He shook his head. "Tired. What time is it?"

"Middle of the night." Loch wanted to ask him if Travis was trying to come out, but he didn't. He put the cuffs back on Creed. "Come on—let's get you to bed."

Loch helped him, a hand on his lower back to guide him toward the bed. Suddenly, Creed was turning to him and they were close—too goddamned close—and Creed's mouth was on his. It wasn't the first time he'd kissed Creed, he realized quickly from the weight of the kiss...but it was the first time he knew it for sure.

Creed's tongue slid over his, and Loch's hand slid behind Creed's neck to keep him near as he deepened the contact. The handcuffs between them stopped them from getting too close, but Creed tried anyway, pressing their clothed cocks together. He groaned into Loch's mouth and Loch didn't want to break the contact, wanted Creed to suck his dick and make him come.

Wanted Tar to watch the entire goddamned thing—like the old days, and where the hell had that come from?

Loch pulled away. Creed rested his forehead on his for a long moment and then, for just a second, he swayed before pulling back. And Loch fully expected to see Travis staring back at him.

But no, Creed was still there, watching him thoughtfully before asking, "Disappointed?"

"No," Loch said honestly.

"Fuck." Creed brought a hand up to his head, the cuffs clinking together as he did so. "Head hurts."

"It's been a long night," Loch reassured him. "Everything's okay."

"Is Tar?"

"Are you?"

Creed gave a soft snort. "Almost never."

"So maybe we can change that."

"Stay with me, Loch. Please. And leave me chained, okay? Promise me that." Creed half stumbled into him and Loch caught him, mouths mashed together, hands winding in hair, moans caught in the kisses.

Creed kissed like his life depended on it. So did Loch, to

be fair, so together it was the most purely combustible reaction he'd ever experienced and he was stripping Creed of his sweatpants while he did so. When Creed pulled back, his eyes were glazed, unfocused, like he was waiting for Loch to back away, renege, refuse.

Loch did no such thing, but instead shoved Creed against the wall, lifted his cuffed wrists above his head and kept them there with one hand as he freed his cock and then ground his cock against Creed's. And he continued kissing him during the slow, dirty grind, knowing that Tar was watching this. Wanting him to.

In turn, Creed wrapped a leg around Loch and then managed to climb up his body—Loch helped him by grabbing the back of a thigh to leverage and then kept him trapped, pressed between his body and the wall, his cock sliding against Creed's

"Don't you dare come," Loch growled, biting Creed's bottom lip.

Creed growled back but he didn't protest further, just strained for more — more kissing, more contact, more skin. And Loch gave him that by stripping his shirt and wrapping it around Creed's already bound wrists while he was pressed helpless against the wall and held up by Loch with his legs wrapped around him.

Stripped. Tied.

Helpless. "Going to gag me too?"

"No gag. I like to hear you scream," Loch told him as he caught their cocks in his hand and began to stroke them together.

Creed whimpered softly but trusted Loch, trusted him in a way he'd only ever trusted Travis. He needed Loch inside of him, welcomed it even. "Fuck me, Loch. C'mon."

"Don't want to hurt you," Loch told him. "Don't feel like letting you go to find lube or protection."

"I don't care what the hell you use—I want it—and I'm clean," Creed pressed. Loch frowned, then slicked his hand on their pre-come and spread it on his own cock. "Yeah, that's good—do it, Loch."

"You think you're in charge, don't you?"

"If it'll get me fucked, I'll say anything you need me to," Creed promised. "Please."

"I'm clean too, Creed. Get tested regularly," Loch told him as he slid his cock in between Creed's ass cheeks, teasing him and Creed felt like he could come just from the promise of what was about to happen. But then Loch began to press inside of him, and Creed closed his eyes and arched into the intrusion. A hiss escaped his throat as Loch's thick cockhead breeched him, and he dug his nails into his own palms.

Loch leaned forward and bit his shoulder, hard, and the pain sensations seemed to fire from all Creed's nerve endings. He groaned as he sank down further, forcing Loch deeper, until Loch hit his gland and he almost came apart right then and there.

But he wanted this to last, didn't want Loch to let go of him...didn't want Tar to stop watching this because Creed knew that, somehow, he was. The thought of both men's eyes on him, watching him get fucked, watching him helpless and slack with surrender made his cock throb.

He was unable to brace himself as Loch drove into him in a series of brutal thrusts, his cries growing more desperate with each snap of Loch's hips. The face that he was giving away the only thing he had—his protection—needed to mean something to Loch, and judging by the way the man watched him, almost tenderly, it did.

And then the wild feral part of Creed came lose, blew apart, shattered like he'd never ever be able to put himself back together. The intensity shook every muscle, his body bowed, mouth opened with a silent acknowledgement of just how deeply he felt his orgasm.

And Loch was controlling it, riding him, rutting into him like a charging bull, spearing him and not letting him go. His ears rang, his eyes watered and his mouth stretched into a taut smile in acknowledgement of the kind of pleasure he'd never been allowed to have before he escaped. Even after, the kind he never allowed himself to feel. Travis turned this off, treating his climax like the currency it was. But Creed let it course through his entire body, head to toe, seized in Loch's grip, with everything a haze.

For several long moments he remained in that zone, staring hazily at the opposite wall with Loch's come inside of him. Loch rubbed his back and wrists, pleasure zinging along his skin with every touch of the man's fingertips, like they were laced with some kind of pleasure drug.

No wonder Travis retreated during sex with Loch. The first time, Creed hadn't expected it, had gone from the cage to finding himself knees in the air on his back on the mattress, the dark-haired man above him pounding into him. It'd felt too damned good to even think about protesting, but he knew why Travis had—this was somehow too familiar. Too intense... and far too intimate.

Travis sucked at all of those things. Creed wasn't much

better but he could handle them, didn't need to run and hide. But he'd never blame Travis for his retreats. No, he thanked him every time he woke to find Loch pushing inside of him with fingers or tongue or cock. And in the aftermath, he lay there basking in the warmth of Loch's arms and the bed, his own skin still sex-flushed, and he wished he never had to retreat back into the cage.

But eventually, he'd slept, and Travis's protective instincts had kicked back in. And so Creed waited, heard the familiar buzz in his head, but it wasn't as loud as it usually got. And then...nothing. Just blessed silence in his mind and Loch's calmer breaths against his neck.

Now, Loch lifted his head and reluctantly pulled out of him before lowering Creed to the floor, still holding him as if to make sure he was steady. He let go of Creed's arms, and Creed winced as Loch rubbed some circulation back into them.

And then they were face to face and Creed didn't know what to say, except, "I'm going to shower," and Loch nodded and followed him into the bathroom. Ran the water for him and joined him, although it was more utilitarian than anything with both men washing and drying themselves.

"Hey." Loch's hand went to his shoulder once they re-entered the bedroom. "You okay?"

"I needed that, so yes."

Loch nodded, handed him his sweats and a T-shirt, and Creed slid into them, slicked his damp hair back from his face with his hands. Loch pulled on the cargos he'd had on earlier, same T-shirt, his hair similarly brushed.

And Creed was just about to ask Loch to get into bed with him...until he saw the red dot on Loch's cheek and heard the shot. It missed them by a mile and hit the plaster wall behind them. Before the gunman could steady up and find a better target, Creed slammed Loch to the ground and rolled with him behind the bed, pure instinct and adrenaline taking over, even as he heard the cage door slam.

Creed felt the quick jolt of Travis's panic, the buzz loud inside his skull, but he'd gotten Loch down on the ground and out of harm's way, so the panicked feeling receded as fast as it had come. Loch struggled under him, obviously pissed off until the shots rang out and slammed into the sheetrock above their heads. He heard Tar yelling. Creed and Loch stayed low and followed him out through the door between the kitchen and the garage. Creed got Loch into the front seat and he got into the back just as Tar called, "Hang on," and peeled out of the garage, barely waiting for the door to rise to an appropriate level. "Truck's bulletproof but I don't plan on waiting around to test it out."

Creed watched intensely out the back window. "Can't see shit. No men, no cars, nothing. Why bother pushing us out if there's no one waiting to grab us?"

"That's the million- dollar question," Tar muttered then pressed a button on his phone.

Creed watched the explosion as the house they were just in seemed to just...disintegrate. Without touching the houses next to it. "Cool fucking trick."

Tar gave a tight smile. "Not leaving evidence behind for any of those fuckers."

CHAPTER ELEVEN

"FUCK, THIS IS BAD," Loch muttered two hours into the ride, and Tar wondered if he was in shock. It'd been a while since he'd seen this kind of action, and this Travis/Creed thing already had him well off his game. The whiskey consumption definitely wasn't helping make shit better.... and neither was the sex that Tar had, of course, watched which was why he hadn't noticed the sniper earlier.

Tar glanced at him and then at the side mirrors. "We've got what's important."

"I still maintain that shit with the house was impressive." Creed's cuffs clinked as he continued to make himself comfortable in the backseat. Early into the trip, he'd stretched out on a commandeered pillow and now appeared to be in it for the long haul. "So...Russians or Feds?"

Loch and Tar glanced at each other. "You tell us," Tar said.

Creed considered the situation "Whoever it was didn't want us dead. They were meant to drive us out so we could be taken. I guess they didn't count on the truck. Which is odd...if it's supposed to be one of Snow's."

"We never said anything about Snow," Tar pointed out.

"You didn't have to." Creed still looked relatively unconcerned. "Any trackers that might've been letting them find us were destroyed...unless we're implanted. Shit, did Snow do that?"

Loch and Tar both raised their brows. "We're not chipped. Think you might be?"

"If I was, wouldn't he have come after me long before this?" Creed was silent for a long moment, then told them, "That wasn't Xander."

Tar cursed under his breath. "What do you know about Xander?"

"What do *you* know about Xander?" Creed shot back.

Tar jerked the truck off the road, hard enough to make Creed slam off the seat. Before he could rally, Tar was out of the truck and around to the back seat, yanking Creed out onto the grass on the side of the road. He shoved Creed to the ground and sat on him, pinning him.

Creed smiled up at him. "Taking your turn? Because I'm sure you watched Loch fuck me last night."

Tar put both hands around Creed's throat, cutting off his air for several minutes until Creed began to turn an unnatural shade of purple. Then he eased off, demanding, "Who's fucking with us?"

"Jealous. I like that." Tar rolled his eyes and repeated the choking. Finally, Creed bit out, "You tell me, dammit. I ran. I'm out."

"No one's ever really out," Tar muttered as he got off him

with a single, vicious shove. "And you know more than you're saying. Either you or Travis—you're holding back."

Creed propped on his elbows. "I knew Xander. He trained at the camp I was in. Bastard used to use the weakest guys for target practice—live prey—with Snow's permission." He grimaced at the memory. "If Xander wanted us dead, we'd be dead. If he was driving us out, he would've had a team waiting to scoop us up."

Tar had to agree. "So who is it?"

"Someone unstable. Or someone who really didn't want us dead." Creed shrugged. "Good job saving us though."

"Fuck off, Creed." He marched back around to the driver's side, impressed that Loch hadn't moved from his seat, but merely rolled down the window to watch the action.

"Guess we weren't followed, or the sniper could've easily taken out you two assholes," was all he said after Creed got back in and Tar pulled back onto the road. "What now?"

"We wait until the smoke clears and then we go to the hospital," Tar said.

"Where are we going now?" Creed asked.

"Someplace safe," was all he'd say.

Three hours later, Loch's eyes narrowed as they pulled up the long, hidden drive to the cabin, like some long-forgotten sixth sense whispering to him. When Tar pulled into the garage, Loch remained stock-still until Tar touched his shoulder, and then he jumped.

"C'mon. Been a long ride. A long day."

Loch nodded woodenly and followed Tar into the cabin. Creed was behind him, nearly tripped over him as Loch stopped dead in his tracks and looked around for a long moment before muttering something under his breath and breaking off toward one of the bedrooms.

Maybe that same sixth sense called to Creed as well because he finally asked, "How close are we to Snow's old place?" His voice was near to a whisper, like if he said it any louder, Snow himself would come walking in.

"Close enough," Tar muttered.

"That's not an answer."

"We're safe here. Trust me." As soon as he spoke, Creed grabbed him and Tar fought the urge to slam him against the wall or the floor. Instead, he growled, "You're taking your goddamned life in your hands, Creed. Hands off."

Creed stared at him and then did so. "Loch's got whiskey with him in his bag."

"Big fucking surprise."

"He's drinking to kill memories."

"Never works. He'd have to kill himself first."

"Maybe that's what he's trying to do."

"You've known him for less than a week and now you're an expert on all things Loch."

"Doesn't take a genius to see what's happening between you two," Creed told him. "He doesn't look good."

"Because he's not good at all," Tar muttered. "Get some sleep. Let me worry about it."

"Too late," Creed said irritably. "And I fucking hate this weather."

Tar wanted to agree with him, but this cabin brought back too many good memories for him to buy into that completely.

Nothing much had changed—Jasper's cabin was a luxury log cabin with amenities courtesy of a CIA spy, including bulletproof glass, generators, a kick-ass security system and networked computers. Plus enough weapons to keep them safe during any kind of apocalypse. Plus food.

But that damned fireplace...

He shook his head but couldn't repress the memories of the young boys who shivered in front of it all those years ago.

They stripped as soon as they got into the house. They'd been driving like mad against the wind and weather and they'd jacked the heat up but their clothes were still damp and reeked of smoke. Jasper's house had a washer and dryer, so they'd stuffed their clothes, and then they'd gotten into the giant shower together. Tar had been so used to being naked and hosed down, he hadn't given it a second thought, and Loch looked too shell-shocked not to follow suit.

Now, wrapped in towels, Tar started a fire while Loch gulped down some whiskey he'd found in the kitchen. He shared it with Tar, who couldn't get past the taste of the stuff and went for soda instead. He didn't want to ever be fuzzy-headed again in his goddamned life.

"Fire's going," he called back to Loch, who'd been staring at the pictures that lined the walls. Later they'd learn it was Jasper's old Delta Force team, with most of the men wearing camo paint on their faces to render them unrecognizable. Later, they'd also learn that most of them had been killed in a raid after being betrayed by one of their own and that Jasper was one of the two survivors. The other man would never walk again, and Jasper still visited him almost daily.

"Think we're okay here?" Loch asked as he came toward the fire. Tar grabbed blankets and put them on the floor and they wrapped up in them, their backs against the couch.

"No one's getting through tonight. We barely did," Tar

said firmly, wanting nothing more than to believe it. But he kept a rifle next to him—he'd found more of them plus ammo in one of the bedrooms. If anyone came in? He'd defend them. He was never going back to that place.

But where the hell are you going?

Loch had been thinking about the same things. "What are we going to do now? Where the hell do we go?"

"Let's just get through tonight, okay? There's cash here— we can take that to get us started."

Loch nodded. "We can pay it back when we get some of our own."

Some of our own...so Loch was planning on staying together. That comforted Tar a great deal. He'd fully expected to be put out on his own. Not that he couldn't do it, but hell, teamwork would pay off in this instance—he was sure of it.

Fuck. He shook off that memory because there were too many before it that threatened to overwhelm him. They were closer that night than they'd ever been, but in order for Loch to even remember that, he'd have to go back to the beginning...and that was a place he used the goddamned whiskey to help him avoid.

Tonight promised to be no different.

CHAPTER TWELVE

LOCH GRABBED the bottle and took a long swig—and then another and then yet another, until the bottle was nearly empty. He sat on the floor, his back against the bed, the bottle between his legs and he watched the world spin around him, out of control...just like him.

And he didn't give a shit. Wished he had another goddamned bottle.

Instead, he reached for his phone and dialed Tar, not giving a shit that the man was probably less than forty paces from him. "You know what your problem is?" he asked without preamble.

"I guess you're going to tell me," Tar said agreeably.

"You're a self-righteous asshole."

"I'm a lot of things, but self-righteous? That's the best you can do?"

"No problems fitting in. No addictions. You can handle anything, right, Tar? Takes a lickin' and keeps on tickin'."

"If you say so."

"You're just going to agree with me?"

"I could take you to a meeting instead," Tar suggested.

"Aren't you the perfect one? Swooping in to rescue me."

"I told you, I'd be there every time."

"Right. Mr. Perfect." Loch took a last swig of the bottle and threw it off to the side, more pissed than he was when he'd started. "If you were here—"

"What would you do, Loch, if I was in the room with you right now? Take all your anger out on me. I'd let you, you know." Tar's voice was smooth and hot and it ran through Loch's blood like lava, warming him. Filling him. "Just say the word and I'll be there."

Loch's mouth opened but nothing came out. He squeezed his fists together, hard, because that was exactly what he wanted. Exactly. Tar. Travis. Creed. All of them. "I need more whiskey," he said instead, before he hung up.

Fuck. What had he done?

You've been sitting here drinking since you walked into this fucking cabin, with all its memories. He thought about getting up, walking out and finding Tar and asking him what the fuck was wrong between them...

But you know what it is. You caused it.

And then Tar was there, in the doorway, holding a bottle of whiskey in a bag, letting it dangle from his pinkie. "You ask, and I'm bound to answer."

"What? Like a genie?"

"Rub me and find out." Tar held the bag close to Loch and then pulled it back once Loch reached for it. "Reflexes are a little off tonight."

"Don't, Tar."

"Don't what? Give you whiskey? Comply with your

wishes?" Tar asked, finally dropping the bag with the bottle into Loch's lap. "Go ahead, babe. Drink up."

"So fucking perfect," Loch muttered. "Must be wonderful."

"Yes, I'm perfect. Yes, it's difficult. But I'd be happy to show you the way."

"You can leave."

"Leave? No, I'm just getting started." Tar knelt down, straddling Loch's legs, and Loch's sensors went off.

Too close. Too close. Tooclosetooclosetooclose...

"Loch—can't you even look at me?" Tar asked softly. He used his finger to lift Loch's chin, forcing their gazes to meet. "I hate to see you torturing yourself like this."

"You don't understand. Just because you don't have demons..."

Tar laughed. "I don't have demons? Loch, my demons have demons, okay?"

"Maybe you need this whiskey more than I do."

"That's not what I need."

"Then what?" Loch asked, started to feel too sober and too drunk for this conversation all at once.

Tar took his finger away and brushed Loch's cheek with his knuckles. "I've been trying to tell you for a long time. I'm too much of a coward, so this is as much my fault as it is yours. But don't think I'm not tortured. Don't ever think that."

"I don't want you to be tortured. Let me help you fix it."

Tar smiled sadly. "You do...every time you're around me."

Loch dropped the bottle and grabbed for Tar, causing him to land halfway in his lap. He put his mouth on Tar's and began to kiss him like his life depended on it, even as the world swirled around him. God, it felt so familiar and so fucking perfect with Tar pressing him and Loch holding him in place.

"Want to fuck you, Tar. Lay you down and spread your legs and bury my cock inside of you until you goddamned scream," he murmured after he pulled back and Tar choked out a groan. "Yeah, you'd be begging for it."

"Yeah, I would," Tar managed. "And fuck it all, I want to strip for you right now, let you do anything you want to me. But you won't goddamned remember—and I need you to."

Slowly, reluctantly, he pulled away from Loch and handed him back the full bottle of whiskey. "Here's your company for tonight. Tomorrow, I need you functioning."

Loch watched him walk away, watched the set of his friend's shoulders as they disappeared. He'd left the door open, and Loch could see straight through to the main room where there was a roaring fire in the fireplace, throwing light into the darkness...the memories flooded him and he wanted to drown them with whiskey. But tonight, the whiskey only succeeded in making them more vivid...more real...

The night was already on fire. It glowed over the landscape, more beautiful than frightening, a wildfire so out of control it promised to engulf everything in its path.

It would be too easy to liken it to a phoenix rising from the ashes, but that was exactly what was happening. Because Loch had just come to the mansion straight from his boarding school, had barely made it home because of the traffic after the school had been forcefully evacuated. Otherwise, Christmas break meant nothing to him. This mansion that would go up in flames before the night was over? Again, nothing, except pain and misery and bad memories that would stick with him for eternity, it seemed.

This house, his uncle and his own goddamned brother were oppressive, and if that had been all he'd ever known, that would've been horrific enough. But after his parents had been killed, he'd already had ten amazing years with them, only to be shipped off to his uncle's house, a mysterious, cold, terrifying man who'd almost immediately shipped Loch off to military boarding school... and kept Loch's brother all to himself.

The fire was definitely happening on the property—the smell flooded his senses and he tamped down a mild feeling of panic as he went upstairs to get a better view. It was there that he first encountered the wild man—he had blood on his hands and his bare chest, a wild look in his eyes. Loch's brother was dead on the floor.

"You're next," the wild man told him evenly.

Loch put his hands up. "Look, if you were caught in the fire and need help..."

"I didn't come here for help." Wild man's voice was a rasp, underused and damaged from screaming and the smoke. It hadn't fully recovered, even to this day. But he'd paused and looked over Loch curiously. "Who are you?"

"I'm Loch. I'm...that's my brother," he said stupidly. "I hated him. What did he do to you?"

The wild man paused, as if considering how to answer that. "It's more what he didn't do. Which was everything."

Loch nodded. There were times he'd heard screaming in the night and when he'd asked his brother about it, he'd been told that there were wolves and other creatures on the property. But looking at the man in front of him... "Where's your family? Did you come in here looking for help from the fire?"

The wild man shook his head almost sadly. "You really don't know fucking anything, do you?"

"I was at school. I've always been at school. I don't come home, but the fire..." He realized he wasn't scared of the man with the knife. He expected violence when he came home. "Where's my uncle?"

The wild man laughed. "I'm looking for him next."

Loch's next words came out in a rush. "I hate it here. I've always hated it here." And then he rushed at the wild man because there was no one else to take out his sudden rage on.

But that wild man had been safe. He'd taken it—and given as good as he'd gotten—and he'd never used the knife, just his fists. They'd taken their fear and frustration out on each other for several long moments, until the wild man ended up on top of him, his forearm pressed against Loch's throat.

"My name's Tar. I think I'll let you live, so you can see what your family's been doing while you've been at school. And I think you're going to wish you died tonight. Hell, I already do."

It was midnight, pitch black outside because Tar had cut those lights and the alarm systems, but the main house had a hidden generator. The ceiling light cast eerie shadows against the corners of the room, on Tar's bare back that was scarred and bloodied, and on the body on the floor as well, throat cleanly slit.

Loch was covered in blood, some of it his and Tar's from their knock-down, drag-out fight and some, his brother's.

Now, the truth was laid out there, much like his brother's body.

"Ready?" Tar asked, and then they were downstairs, with Tar lighting the mansion—with his brother's body in it—on *fire.* They sat for several minutes and watched the place whoosh up in fast flames. Then, in Loch's uncle's car, they drove the two miles into the secluded property, where a whole insular world welcomed him.

He'd gotten sick two feet into the camp when he'd seen the first body. He stared into the smoky haze and saw cages. Chains.

"I let them go before I went to the main house," Tar told him. "If we call the police, they'll take us."

"Who are they?" Loch asked. "What the fuck is this place?"

"No time to explain now. We need to get the hell out of here."

"Where's my uncle?"

"Snow's gone," Tar said flatly.

At that point, Loch didn't know the true danger he was facing, but Tar had. And all Loch could think about at that point was freedom.

They were long gone in a stolen car by the time the police and fire caught up to Snow's compound that was being eaten alive by the fire.

They hadn't counted on the CIA looking for them, had no idea Snow had once been a CIA agent. Loch was wanted. Tar? No one knew he existed. Still, it took a while for Jasper and his agents to catch up with them, but eventually, they had.

It took even longer for Jasper to believe them, but ultimately, and especially because he knew who and what Snow was by that point, he did. They were eventually deemed too dangerous to not work for the CIA, and since they'd bonded so strongly, Jasper kept them together. And then he'd honed them both into weapons. Weapons against Snow.

But on that day, all they knew was that Snow had escaped, and so had they. Thanks to Snow's emergency kit, they had IDs and money and weapons. They'd left Snow's car behind when they stole another one and got as far from the house as they could.

They holed up in a house an hour outside the fire zone that was full of Christmas lights, drank all the booze, and showered the smoke smell away from their skins. They attended to each other's wounds.

"This is the best night of my life."

"Yeah, mine too," Tar sighed. "How fucking pathetic are we?"

"We're free. And it's Christmas."

There was a fire in the fireplace. The old cabin that meant freedom, for both of them. Drunk. Naked. Waiting for their clothes to dry. Falling asleep like puppies, sprawled together in front of the fire, neither admitting to the other that they remembered everything that happened that night in front of the fire... and it not mattering, because their friendship had been forged that night, created in the flames and rising from the ashes.

They'd risen together. They'd fight together.

But when Loch woke in front of his own fire...he was very much alone.

Fuck, *that night....*

Naked. A tangle of limbs. His and Tar's, the sudden urgency between them undeniable, born of a shared pain, adrenaline and youth. They were free, and nothing else mattered.

He'd been whiskey warm. Loose. Free.

Tar's mouth was on his, his hands everywhere, and Loch's dick was buried inside of him, Tar's strong legs wrapping around his body, pulling him in deeper. Raking his nails down Loch's back.

The full bottle rolled away from him on the wood floor. He watched it, mesmerized as the movie played in his mind.

That night...a fire, a snowstorm. And an empty whiskey bottle and his dick buried inside of Tar as Tar chanted his name like a prayer and clung to him. He was suddenly completely fucking sober and more contrite and confused than he'd ever been.

That night, everything had finally been right. But the memories had been blunted by alcohol.

He'd been numbing himself ever since.

CHAPTER THIRTEEN

TAR AVOIDED both Loch and Creed for the next couple of hours. He stayed on the couch by the fire, Loch stayed in his room with his fucking whiskey, and sometime during the night, he'd closed the goddamned door between them.

Hell, you had to be the bigger person and walk away from the kiss. From everything.

One of these days, he wasn't going to have that kind of control left in him.

Creed had curled up in one of the spare bedrooms and Tar kept an eye on him with the help of Jasper's monitors, dozed on and off, stroking the fire, his only company the raging storm outside...and the one in his own head as he revisited that goddamned kiss over and over again.

Creed stirred first...but once his eyes opened, Tar could tell he was watching Travis. There was something about the way he moved—with no less confidence than Creed, but less of a bull in a china shop and more like...a thief.

"You don't have to stay in there, Travis. Come on out and

grab something to eat," he called, his voice low so as not to wake Loch.

He wondered if Travis was worried since Loch hadn't stayed with him.

"Who's there?" Travis called.

"It's Tar—we met for half a second today before Creed decided to hijack the meeting. I'd really like to take some time to talk with you," Tar said, keeping his voice neutral.

Finally, Travis appeared in the doorway of the bedroom. He hadn't come out in over twenty-four hours, and he looked confused and more than slightly defiant. He had a blanket wrapped around him and the cuffs around his wrists? Gone. "What time is it?"

"Just after one in the morning."

"Where are we?"

"We had to move last night. Do you remember the sniper? You saved Loch's life."

Travis nodded slowly. He looked groggy, like the transitions were harder on him than they were for Creed. Tar wasn't a doctor, but he'd been prepared to bet his life that Creed had DID from the second he'd seen the first transformation on camera. Travis and Creed were different people in the same body, but there were slight physical changes between them. Creed was battle weary and Travis was younger, but nowhere near innocent.

"Where's Loch?"

"Sleeping off the whiskey." Tar had stopped covering for his friend a long time ago. He didn't say it with any bitterness, but with the recognition of someone who understood addiction and that tiptoeing around it didn't do any good.

"Shit," Travis bit out. "Has he always..."

"Yes. It's worse at times. After..." After Liam, that fucker. But he wouldn't say the goddamned thing out loud, so he left his sentence to dangle. "Why don't you come on out here." Tar motioned to the other couch and Travis walked over slowly, like he was waiting for Creed to come bursting out. Truthfully, that's what Tar was figuring would happen and he was surprised when it didn't.

Instead, Travis settled into the couch, still wrapped in a blanket. "Creed talked to you?"

"Yes."

"Was he angry?"

"At first. And then I explained to him that we had a common enemy."

Travis frowned. "I'm guessing you're not talking about Sergei or the FBI."

"I'm not, but I don't much like them either, so I guess we've got a lot more in common than I realized."

That got Travis to smile a little. "Can I grab some coffee?" he asked and Tar nodded. "Want some?"

"Sure, I'll take a cup. Milk and sugar."

Travis dropped the towel and went into the kitchen. He glanced over his shoulder before he poured. "Loch likes it black."

"I never understood the point of that. At least make it enjoyable."

Travis handed a mug to Tar and sat back down. "You and Creed talked about Snow."

"About the box," he said carefully, wondering if Travis would make the connection to the other boy in the box who wouldn't break.

Travis just sighed. "He spent a lot of time in there. He liked it better than being outside."

"What about you?"

"I hated it in there," Travis confessed. "Creed preferred it to dealing with Snow."

"You've been with Creed a long time."

Travis gave a small smile. "I like the way you say that. Like it's normal. Like Creed and I are friends and it's perfectly reasonable to have two distinct personalities in the same person."

"You bodyguard each other. I'm not sure who wouldn't want a built-in protector."

"You've seen it go badly with DID?"

"Very," Tar agreed and knew he needed to change the subject. "You need to tell me about the trafficking."

Travis sighed. "I already told Loch about it. It's complicated."

"Because you're not sure which one of you is doing the killing?"

"Did Loch tell you that?"

"Yes."

Travis nodded. "I told him already—I killed those three men, not Creed. After I did it, I don't remember anything about the actual killing, but I knew that I wanted to do it. I knew from the first moment I heard about it. That's why I seduced Sergei and pretended to be his lover. I wasn't playing rent-boy with him, although he did buy me shit. And, in the aftermath of the killings, I guess Creed moved fast to get me out of there and save me."

Tar considered that. On the surface, Creed was definitely the hitter, the assassin. But with Travis, most people wouldn't see it coming...and maybe that's what Snow had been counting on. "Did you feel in control when you killed those men?"

"Are you asking if I think Snow's controlling me and forcing me to kill? The answer's no. Like I told Loch, trafficking isn't something I take lightly. Because I was a victim—or Creed was. Either way, it's not something I want to see continued. Why would Snow let me kill bad men when they bring him what he needs to continue his experiments?"

"That's what I'm trying to figure out," Tar muttered. "I can't tell if you're bullshitting me, Travis."

Travis stared down at his coffee cup for a long moment. When he looked back up, Tar was staring at Creed. The eyes were darker, the planes of his face somehow sharper. And Creed's energy was unmistakable. It made sense—Creed liked sparring with Tar. He'd been hard during their fight yesterday.

And so were you. "So Travis can't handle curse words?"

"Fuck you, Tar. You don't get to treat him like that."

"He's not such a fragile flower when he's killing people."

Creed shrugged. "I don't know anything about that."

Tar leaned back. They'd circle back to the killing topic later—he'd make sure of it. But for now... "So what do you want to talk about?"

"Tell me more about Snow," Creed demanded.

"You first."

Creed gave a short laugh. "Bastard was a sadist."

Tar couldn't argue. He'd put a lot of it behind him, but he would bear the scars—physical and mental—forever. You couldn't go through the length and breadth of torture he'd endured without a couple of issues, and he could still break into a cold sweat just thinking on it too much. "Is that all you've got?"

"How does Loch feel about Snow?"

"You can ask Loch yourself. You spend enough time with him. At least Travis does."

"Jealous?"

Tar didn't want to admit that he was and he hated Creed right about now. "Loch's a big boy—he can fuck anyone he wants."

"What about his precious Liam?" Creed asked. "Feels like there's no love lost between you two."

Tar's gut clenched at the mention of that fucker...and what the hell did Creed know about Liam? "What makes you say that?"

Creed smiled. "Just a hunch."

Fuck, maybe this had been a mistake. Maybe Jasper was right—taking Creed directly to the institute might've been the correct course of action, instead of leaving him and Loch to deal with this shit. He didn't need anyone else inside his psyche.

But he brought you back with Loch.

And Loch was breaking the fuck down. Tar kept reliving that damned kiss over and over in his mind.

"Loch and Liam were together for a long time, right?" Creed pushed.

"A year," Tar confirmed. And during the time Loch and Liam had been exclusive, Loch and Tar continued working together. But picking up and fucking men together—his and Loch's mainstay—had come to a dead stop the second that prick Liam entered Loch's life.

And Liam *had* been a fucking prick. It didn't have

anything to do with the fact that Tar was jealous as fuck. He could admit that straight out, if only to himself, but still, there was *something* off about Liam. The fact that he'd gotten himself blown up by a car bomb after Loch had broken things off with him made him some kind of saint in Loch's eyes.

It was like Liam had been programmed to know exactly what Loch thought he needed and Tar was immediately suspicious. But Loch threw himself into the relationship hard and fast. *Pussy-whipped*, Tar had told him. Toward the end of that relationship, Loch and Tar could barely be in the same room, and for Loch's sake, Tar gave him a wide berth. Because hell, he wanted his friend happy.

"Who told you about Liam?" Tar asked Creed now.

"Loch did. He told Travis. Called Travis that the first night we were all together." Creed smiled a goddamned knowing smile that Tar wanted to smack off his face. "He stopped using Liam's name after he and I fucked."

Creed knew more than he was saying, but Tar refused to push it. He didn't give a shit who knew he hated Liam...but why was Creed so interested? That's something Tar needed to know about. "Creed, I'm not here for games."

"Right. You're an open book. So what—tit for tat?"

"Fine," Tar bit out.

Creed frowned. "What's the worst thing Snow did to you?"

Tar felt his face go hot with anger, at Snow, and at his own helplessness. "The sex."

"Why?"

"Because it was a power play." Because it was humiliating and painful and so fucking public.

Creed was studying him carefully. "Yeah." His voice was

hoarse and it seemed that he regretted asking the question because of the memories it stirred. "Liam was an asshole. Your instincts were right on." He offered that like an olive branch, his voice contrite...his eyes haunted.

"You don't know shit about my instincts." He stood, moving closer to Creed, who didn't appear threatened...even though he damned well should. "You knew Liam?"

Creed sat forward but didn't attempt to get up when he demanded, "What does it matter? What the fuck does any of this matter? I've been away from Snow and the damned camps for years now. I haven't crossed paths with him. If I'm under his influence, I haven't seen any goddamned evidence of it. I'm just all fucked up, probably beyond repair and you and Loch were the ones who yanked me into this shit. So again, what the fuck does it matter?"

Tar shoved his shoulders back against the couch cushions and held him there, his voice low and controlled. "It matters because you were probably the last person to see Snow before he went dark."

"Not me. *Liam.*" Creed's eyes were navy with anger but he didn't fight Tar's hold. "He would've been the last one to see Snow."

"How would you know that?"

Creed sighed impatiently. "Do we really have to play this game? Liam was Snow's."

Tar went cold inside. It must've shown on his face because Creed tilted his head and narrowed his eyes as he studied him. Tar attempted to yank his expression back into submission before this whole thing was shot to shit. He moved away from Creed. "No way. Liam didn't have the marks."

"So?" Creed shrugged. "He stopped doing that. Said y'all were getting too good at identifying his men."

Fuck. Fuck. "For someone who didn't remember..."

"Whoever said I didn't remember? I remember every fucking minute I spent with that sadist. I've just said that I don't like remembering."

Tar had told Loch the same thing, many times. "And Travis?"

"He wasn't around much during that time. I took the brunt of it." Creed took a gulp of his coffee. "Things changed when Snow brought Liam in. I don't know where the guy came from, but it was like the second coming of Christ."

This made so much sense. Tar's head began to spin and he glanced toward the closed bedroom door Loch was safely behind.

"You don't want Loch to know this, I'm guessing," Creed said.

"I want to know more about Liam." Needed to. Because what if Liam wasn't really dead after all?

Creed nodded. His tongue traced the corner of his lips as he gazed up at Tar before starting. "I don't like..."

"Going there." Tar moved and sat down next to him. "There's no choice."

"You think Liam shot at us?"

"I don't know shit at this point."

Creed absorbed that while outside the wind howled, slamming at the windows like it wanted in. The wolf was most definitely at the door. Tar had never realized what an apt description that was.

Finally, after what seemed like an eternity, Creed's hands fisted on his thighs and he said, "Liam was a soldier. One of the torturers. I don't think he was ever...one of us. It didn't seem that way. There was always a pretty clear divide between the real guards and the ones like us who cooperated and got a few special treats, you know?"

Tar definitely did. Those men had been deemed traitors by the rest of the prisoners, although Tar could understand their push to become what they saw regularly. But Snow tended to punish those men the worst, not making the small rewards worth it. "Keep going."

Creed closed his eyes like he was seeing it play out in front of him. "Snow would...let him use us. Whenever he wanted, however he wanted. He had free reign with us. It was really fucking bad to be chosen as one of his experiments."

"Were you?"

A shudder went through him before he opened his eyes. "Yeah. Too often. Fucking bastard. If he's not dead? I'll kill him myself."

"Join the club."

Creed glanced at him. "I saw you and Loch kissing."

Tar tried to dismiss it quickly so Creed couldn't continue exploiting his weakness for Loch. "It only happens when he's drunk."

"Liquid courage."

Tar needed to change the subject. Badly. "If you can escape your bonds..."

"We're too dangerous to stay," Creed finished, holding up his unfettered wrists. "But here I am, right? Don't tell me you're scared of the big, bad man with two identities."

"People with DID aren't always dangerous—most of the

time their alters are younger kids who protect their adult. People who have it induced by a psychopath can be."

"Sounds like you know something about it. Been doing some reading, have we?"

Tar snorted. "I don't have to read—I lived it."

Creed obviously hadn't expected to hear that, and the wiseass immediately left his expression, replaced by intense interest. "You're not pulling some kind of mindfuck on me, are you?"

"Trust me—I've had enough of that to last a lifetime." Tar's own personalities had melded, but he still vividly remembered the blackouts. The loss of control.

"I want to know more," Creed told him.

Tar wanted a lot of things, but revisiting that? Not one of them. Not when the horrible thought had already bloomed in his mind. He wanted to bury it deep down where he didn't have to confront it or deal with it, and he'd never wanted to be so wrong in his goddamned life. But he'd learned a long time ago that when there was nothing to be done about a situation in the immediate, worrying about it didn't do a damned bit of good.

He'd just remain vigilant and pray that he was wrong.

———

Creed sighed loudly when Tar found stronger cuffs and chained his wrists—again. This time to the goddamned bed he'd claimed earlier.

"I thought we got past this. I thought we bonded," he told Tar in a fake, mournful tone.

Tar snorted. "This is safer—for all of us. Last thing I need is Travis getting spooked and running off into the storm."

"Travis seems to be doing just fine," Creed sniffed, then rattled one of the cuffs. "Is this because of the time I spent with Liam? Because I thought people went with the honesty is the best policy rule."

Tar rolled his eyes but his response was serious. "It's because of everything."

Creed nodded, like he accepted that. But Tar had to know these wouldn't hold him for shit, so why bother with the show?

He guessed everyone had their own lies they needed to tell themselves to keep the peace. He knew his, but learning about Tar and Loch's was a far more interesting challenge. "I'm not even sleepy, so what am I supposed to do here like this? I can't even jerk off to amuse myself."

"Tell me about Snow."

"Is that an order?"

"A request," Tar countered.

"Is this like before—you show me yours and I'll show you mine?"

"Yeah, something like that."

"So show me." He glanced at Tar's crotch and then dragged his eyes back to the man's handsome face.

"Calm your dick down. Question for question is what I'm agreeing to."

"Fine. But I'm betting Loch would agree to dick for dick," Creed murmured. "You can go first, as long as we're in the land of no fun. And no dicks."

Tar sighed, like Creed was impossible. And how was that new information to him? Creed prided himself on showing that outright. "How long were you with Snow and when did you first go in?"

"Seriously? You're already trying to get two for the price of one." Creed crooked a finger at him, already annoyed at his bound wrists. "Fine. But this better be worth my while. Travis and I were with Snow for almost six years. If you ask ages, I'm not really sure. Maybe nine or ten when it started." Creed leaned forward on his elbows. "How long for you?"

"Eight years, and I was eight years old," Tar admitted. "How did you get from pre-Snow to post—the whole lead up?"

Instead of reminding Tar that he wasn't sticking to the spirit of question for question at all, he decided to answer in a more roundabout way. "I started to help Travis before he got to Snow's."

"So life pre-Snow wasn't a walk in the park."

"Right."

"Foster?"

"Does it matter? They were abusers either way. Wouldn't it be worse if they were my real parents?" Creed demanded. "Whatever—whoever they were—Travis thinks they sold me to Snow because of him. He feels guilty about that, but I was always too hard to handle. Travis actually helped smooth the edges. I think the only reason they kept me around so long was because of him."

"He played the role of the good kid."

Creed turned to him unexpectedly angry. "Travis was no fucking wimp. You need to understand that, if nothing else. Travis has his own way of dealing. If anything, he should blame me. Because he doesn't remember what an asshole I am. But I remember all of it, dammit. And all he's done is protect me." He was suddenly furious.

"Sounds like you protect him too, Creed. Remember that."

Creed turned to him, his expression half smile, half snarl. "You should remember that too, Tar."

CHAPTER FOURTEEN

THIS WAS ALL TOO GODDAMNED personal, and Tar didn't know what he'd been thinking. He should've grabbed Travis and shoved him directly into the hospital, put Loch right into rehab. Then he wouldn't be dealing with any of this.

Instead, he was sitting next to a trained assassin—his split personality tucked away for the moment.

"You seem agitated, Tar. I'm all tied up with no weapons, remember?" Creed rattled his chained wrists for emphasis.

"You are a fucking weapon. Just remember, so am I."

Creed's eyes glinted. "Keep talking like that. You're making me hot."

"The Russian didn't do that for you?"

"So completely boring—after the first two times, I stopped popping up. Travis dealt with him way better than I did. Now Loch? He was fine, but he hasn't touched me since you came into the picture. Why is that?"

Creed knew that Tar had watched everything...or else he was just poking around and hoping to get lucky. By the time he'd thought of his answer, he glanced over to see Creed turned on his side, eyes closed, breathing calmly.

For now.

Should've known better.

Because the soft mattress lured him into a dangerous sleep. Normally, in a situation like this, he and Loch would be taking turns sleeping, but no such luck, and Tar wasn't a goddamned machine. The quiet and stress won out... as did the view of the fire, even from across the room...

When he woke, he was in the box. The lid wasn't locked. It rarely was anymore. He'd become too stubborn to climb out of it, always doing the opposite of what his torturer wanted.

With his arms bent at the elbows and stretched over his head, his fingertips reflexively traced the carvings in the wood. His elbows hit the top of the box whenever he did that, and he could easily lift the lid and get out of there, but his act of defiance was staying in the box and refusing to break.

There was no way off the actual island for him—and no, it was a wooded expanse of area around Snow's mansion—but it was surrounded by guards and alarms and escape meant more beatings. No, it was far easier to stay in the box and refuse to do anything Snow wanted.

He'd become a pro at knowing when and where he'd be checked on, knew to exercise when no one was watching. When the time did come for escape, he was gone.

But then he smelled the smoke. At first he ignored it, thinking it was one of the fires the guards used to keep warm at night. But the smoke grew heavier, until it became oppressive and it was hard to breathe. For once, the screams he heard were not from torture, but for survival.

He climbed out and saw the slaughter, walked through it

because no one was interested in touching him. No, even in the heat of this mess, they were still afraid of him.

He took off towards the main house at a dead run. He knew just where they'd be.

He woke with a gasp in the dark room. The fire in the main room had burned out and he was cold and having trouble breathing.

It took him several seconds to realize that was because Creed's forearm was pressed against his throat. He'd fallen asleep on the bed next to Creed, and Creed had waited and watched until he'd taken his opportunity.

Tar's arms were stretched above his head, handcuffed and held down by Creed's free hand. Creed was straddling him, looking too damned pleased with himself.

He was already hard, so he stared into Creed's navy eyes and murmured, "Do your worst, Creed."

"Suppose I don't want to give you my worst?" Creed asked, his voice rough with need.

Tar swallowed hard. "I'm your captive audience. What do you want to prove here?"

"You're not scared of me? Worried that I'm split? Terrified that I'm programmed and going to turn on you?"

"You don't think I worry about myself every fucking hour of every goddamned day?" Tar snarled. "You couldn't get me any other way but this? Now you've got me. So come on, tough guy—do your worst."

Creed bared his teeth and whipped Tar's belt out of his jeans. He used it to wind it through the cuffs and secure them to the headboard before viciously bringing his mouth down on Tar's for a kiss that was like trying to ride goddamned lightning. Everything sparked, everything hurt...and Tar didn't want it to ever fucking end. He wanted to explode, wanted Creed to take him, to hurt him, to make every goddamned thought in his head go away... wanted to be wrung out in every way possible. And Creed? He could do it. Loch could too. And that thought made Tar shudder.

"You're thinking about both of us, aren't you?" Creed asked, breaking the kiss. "Dirty boy."

"Not your fucking boy," he bit out.

"Right now you are." Creed used his teeth on one of his nipples and immediately soothed it with his tongue.

Tar strained to keep his mouth shut, because dammit, he hadn't wanted anything like this. Until he realized he did. And the moment he surrendered, the moans built up in his throat. Creed heard the sounds and gave a soft chuckle.

"C'mon, Tar—moan for me. Need to hear it." He bit and sucked and licked at Tar's jaw as his fingers continued to explore his ass. "Tight. Been a while for you?" Creed asked as he stroked Tar's ass. When Tar didn't say anything, he bent down. "I'm going to make you answer. Trust that."

Tar took a deep breath in, the loss of control devastating and exhilarating all at once. Could he try to get out of this? Yes.

Would he?

No. Maybe it was penance, maybe it was because he was pissed as fuck at Loch, but either way, he'd spread his legs for Creed and let him inside. All the way.

He lifted his chin, a show of submission and Creed seemed fascinated by it. He moved to rub his stubble against Tar's cheek and Tar breathed in his scent as he licked.

Haven't—" he muttered as Creed's fingers continued to

rub against the tight ring of muscle, a blunt finger pressing more insistently but not breaching. "It's been a long time."

"I'll go slow for you, baby."

Fuck. How was Creed so in control and why was he so out of it? "I'm not fucking glass. I don't break."

"No, you don't. And I don't want you to. I just want you to enjoy this." Creed's finger moved to rub the sensitive strip of flesh behind his balls and Tar couldn't help the moan that escaped his throat.

"Good boy," Creed told him and Tar didn't bother to correct him, because his dick was a total traitor that didn't mind the endearment.

Creed brushed a kiss over his racing pulse, skimmed his mouth along Tar's jaw, and felt his dick throb against Creed's even as his breathing quickened.

No way was Creed being...tender. Because it'd taken Tar years to learn to be softer, but to accept tender?

Never.

But Creed seemed to be pushing the envelope.

"You checking to see if I'm programmed?" he asked.

Creed smiled. Dipped his head back down and bit Tar above his collarbone. "I'm just testing the floor, seeing if it's really lava. Testing the perimeters."

"Looking for my weaknesses."

"You won't do the same to me?"

"Of course I will."

"Good. Then just lie back and accept your fate. And I guess you can be as loud as you want." He jerked his head toward the next room, where Loch was in his whiskey-coma.

"Is that what you want—me to be loud? Is that what turns you on?" Tar asked, and Creed smiled that goddamned, enigmatic, wicked smile and Tar bucked his hips up in response. "Do it."

"Likes it hard and fast? Or maybe slow and sweet and you're trying to throw me off track so you don't feel."

"Fucking fucker," he bit out.

"If Loch wasn't drunk, would you be sharing?"

A second image of the leather daddies...and that night... flashed through his mind, and so he lied. "We never shared me. It would be you being shared. How do you feel about that?"

Creed frowned. "I'm not sure. But I obviously have time to think about it."

"What are you waiting for?" Tar asked irritably. His cock was already hard and the fuck or fight instinct was kicking in hard.

"Are you sure you were never shared?" Creed asked suddenly.

"Go wake up your fuck partner next door and ask him. Or, you know, you could just fuck me."

"Your avoidance of certain topics is so interesting."

Tar didn't think so, felt completely exposed because yes, Loch would often make him the center of their threesomes, especially in the months before he'd met Liam. Tar always wondered if Loch had gotten scared of the intensity of those sessions...because they'd come so close. Especially that last time.

Creed's hand pressed his throat. "I'm the one in the goddamned bed with you tonight."

"Didn't take you for the jealous type," Tar smirked, but stopped when Creed's free hand dragged the length of his shaft.

"Yeah who's holding you in his hand? Who woke you up from your nightmare?" Creed asked as Tar's breath hitched, and he moved his hand off his cock and between his ass cheeks. "Whose name are you going to call tonight?"

"Fuck you," he managed.

Creed sucked hard on his finger, which he pressed inside of Tar. It burned...until a knuckle brushed his prostate and Tar saw stars. And he did it again and again, and then he pressed against Tar's throat at the same time and asked, "Whose name, Tar?"

"Yours," Tar heard himself say. "Only yours."

Creed grabbed his hair and held him fast, brought his mouth down roughly on Tar's, dragged his tongue along the seam of Tar's lips. Finally, after a couple of tugs on his hair, Tar relented, opened his mouth. Steeled himself against feeling any goddamned thing and fuck—it didn't work, because the second Creed's tongue took possession of his mouth there were feelings flooding through him.

Because Creed took his mouth the way he'd no doubt planned on taking Tar's ass—leaving him breathless, wrung out, turned on, needy and achy all at once.

And Creed knew, goddamn him and his psychological games. Because his kisses weren't subtle or shy—they were intimate...and they made Tar feel desperate.

Tar felt thoroughly taken—stripped—just from that kiss. He wasn't sure how he'd handle what would come next.

Creed sucked his neck, marking him, right out in the open, where Loch would see it. It was a warning, a dare...a taunt, all wrapped up in one. He could almost hear Creed telling Loch, "*I took what's yours. Now it's your move.*"

Creed would take what he wanted, what he needed. He'd

be selfish about it and, in the process, Tar had no doubt that he'd get off. "You don't have to fucking seduce me. I'm letting you fuck me."

Creed shook his head slowly. "I don't want you to let me. I want you pleading for it. Needing it like you need air."

"Why's that so important to you?"

"I don't know—it just is." Creed's voice was urgent and suddenly, Tar wanted him, maybe as much as he wanted Loch. Because, next to Loch, Creed was the only one he'd been this vulnerable to who knew exactly what he'd been through.

They were so similar and yet so different. "Then go ahead—keep seducing me. Make love to me. Make me beg."

Creed smiled. "Been waiting to bend you over and fuck you. Hear you yell my name. Jerked off thinking about you. And you and Loch. About both of us fucking you. But I want my turn with just you first." His hands left trails of fire behind wherever he touched. "You like that, baby?"

"Yes," Tar managed.

"Good. I want you to. No more hell tonight."

Tar smiled. "Yeah, works for me."

Tar lost himself in Creed's searing touches and he relented fully, let his body enjoy everything Creed gave it. Creed was hell bent on exploring, like he was cataloging every scar he came across, and laving them with extra attention, as if he was trying to change their energy—and fuck it all, maybe he could.

He worshipped Tar's cock, sucking, kissing along the prominent vein that ran along its underside.

Tar blushed when Creed spread his legs. He stared up at

the ceiling until he felt Creed's tongue, wet and hot against his hole.

He didn't recognize the sounds that tore from his throat as Creed ate his ass, not stopping when Tar begged him to... probably because he was moving his hips in time with Creed's tongue, his cock dripping pre-come.

His cock needed something—friction, a touch. Anything.

"Creed, I want..." Creed's fingers joined his mouth, and he was sucking, kissing, brushing Tar's prostate. Overstimulating him. And finally, Creed's hand moved up to tug his cock roughly and the combination of his hand and his tongue made Tar rise off the bed with each stroke.

A shot of fear went through him that threatened everything—he was so vulnerable and needy, and he stilled, trying to keep the memories at bay, but Creed was too talented—and too insistent.

Creed was pulling all of his strings. "Come on, Tar. Give it up for me," he demanded before spearing his tongue back inside of him and giving a few fast, hard strokes on his dick... and suddenly, Tar couldn't think of a single goddamned reason strong enough not to.

He stared into Creed's eyes and he followed his directions.

Tar's voice held a level of desperation that Creed recognized...recognized, and pushed him anyway, pushed them both in a direction there was no coming back from. But the faint tremor of fear he'd felt run through Tar wasn't what he was after. Not at all. He'd sought to reassure Tar by reaching up and stroking his cock, letting Tar come in hot ropey spurts all over his hand, belly and chest.

Now, Creed worked his way up, licking the come from his skin. Grabbing Tar's hair and making him lick his own come from Creed's fingers. Fed him his own come and then kissed him, and Tar did it, blushing and growling.

The fact that Tar could still blush after all he'd been through—Creed swore his heart opened for the man underneath him. Protective urges kicked into place as he covered Tar's body with his and rubbed his shaft along the seam of his ass, riding him like that and Tar spread his legs willingly.

"Ready, baby?"

"Please." Tar tugged at his bonds. "Take me."

And Creed did, pushed past the first ring of resistance and Tar shouted—a mix of a laugh and a groan—and then he stared up at Creed and stilled, as if trying to keep memories from flooding in again.

"Hey," Creed said roughly. "It's me—Creed. Not going to hurt you. I'm going to make you feel better than you've ever felt. So stop thinking and start feeling."

With that, he started to move, his palm sliding up to remain on Tar's throat... a warning, a promise, a goddamned turn on nonetheless.

There was no easing him into it. No chance for him to back out of it. Not that Tar would—he was the boy who never broke.

Then why are you trying to do it yourself?

"Creed—oh God, please," Tar moaned, shoving Creed back into the present and the man underneath him.

The heat and pressure on his cock was indescribable. Tar's ass latched onto him, engulfed in all his heat and friction and suddenly, inexplicably, Tar was in total control of this fuck.

He was rocking against him, his mouth tugged in a satisfied smile. His eyes locked on Creed's—Creed grabbed Tar's hips and held them still so he could fuck Tar as hard as he wanted, keeping his legs spread and him helpless from stopping the hard thrusts and the constant throb of Creed's cock against his gland.

Tar was groaning, arching his back and Creed would make him come again, didn't care if it might be painful. He wanted to push Tar past the point of reason and he thrust violently against him, holding him close, leaving no space between their bodies. And Tar's body clawed at Creed's for more—begged for harder, deeper, faster. The friction was delicious, and Creed leveraged his body weight to make Tar scream.

It was a brutal, snarling race to the finish and Creed felt the violent shudder that went through Tar when he realized his body was on the brink of another orgasm—his muscles tensed, and Creed felt out of control for the first time in a long time. He lost it, his hands on Tar rough enough to leave marks as his hips snapped. His vision went hazy and his dick began the warning throb. His balls drew up and he was coming and so was Tar, his ass contracting, milking Creed and drawing out his orgasm further.

In the aftermath, Tar's breath sawed in and out of him as Creed kissed the sweat from his neck, wiped his hair off his forehead. Held him, cradled him, released his hands and massaged his arms.

"Sleep if you want. I've got you," Creed whispered. Tar folded against him and closed his eyes. It wasn't for very long but this extended trust had done something to Creed, strengthened a resolve he didn't even know he had.

If you were honest with yourself, you knew it was there from the first.

And when Tar stirred in his arms, he looked flushed. Refreshed. Not scared or wary...for several moments at least, and then something changed in Tar's expression, and no, Creed didn't like that at all.

He stroked the side of Tar's face. "I didn't...fuck, Tar. I didn't mean to hurt you or scare you. Please..."

Tar grabbed his wrist. "Stop, Creed. I could've gotten away if I'd tried. I wanted it too, although maybe without the nightmare."

"I wanted you to wake up happy."

"Next time, avoid the press-on-the-throat, blocking-the-windpipe thing and it'll be more of a success," Tar advised.

"You didn't seem to mind it when you were coming."

Tar sighed and stared up at the ceiling. "Are you okay?"

"Do you think I'm too dangerous"

Tar dragged his gaze downward to meet his. "I'm just as goddamned dangerous."

"Okay. Good to know. But I do have questions," Creed admitted.

"About how I didn't mind things when I was coming?"

"No, about what happens after this. Before we go to the hospital—and I will go, Tar, okay? I'm not thrilled about it, but I'll go...I want to know more."

"About the hospital?"

"About you."

Tar shifted to his side, the blanket just above his hip and Creed stared longingly at the dip of muscle that ran along

Tar's side. He ran a finger along that dip, unable to help himself. He'd never been a good fan of self-control.

Tar watched him interestedly. It was easy to see his cock harden under the sheet. "I thought you said you wanted to talk?"

"I like making you scream too," Creed said absently.

"And here I thought it was my turn now."

Creed suddenly leaned in and kissed him, needing to feel Tar's mouth again, needing that connection. Wanting that closeness. They'd get Loch in on this—he was sure of it, but Tar was hurting. And Creed didn't like seeing anyone hurting...least of all, someone who'd been helping him. "Is Loch going to be okay?"

"Yes, he will be. He's been before. He'll be again."

"Good." Dammit, he was suddenly needy as fuck, wanted to ask if he could stay with Tar and Loch after all was said and done. If he was a good boy and did everything they said. Instead, he asked, "How many personalities did you have?"

"Two, just like you."

"From Snow?"

"I don't think so. I think...I'm a lot like you. I think my DID already came through and that's why Snow targeted me."

"No real memories?"

"I didn't have them. The other guy did."

Creed didn't bother to ask Tar for the other guy's name. It didn't matter. "Did the doctor make you merge? That hospital you're taking me to?"

"That hospital didn't exist then. Not until after I merged. And no, the doctor didn't make me. I wanted to merge, because one of my personalities was a killer, and I couldn't control him. Snow could, though. So first, I was deprogrammed...and then I wanted that. Then I wanted that killer melded in with me, because then I couldn't switch off. I'd feel it. I'd know." Tar was gritting his teeth, fisting his hands at the memory.

"Did it hurt?"

"Still does," Tar said honestly. "But it's better this way. For me. I was...uncontrollable."

"Did you hurt anyone?"

"Yes." But he didn't get into it then—because talking about Loch and his brother and that night? Torture, in so many different ways.

Creed didn't push. Maybe he wasn't really ready to know either.

CHAPTER FIFTEEN

TAR FELT THE FAMILIAR, predictable anger pulse through him. It was irrational but, after all these years, controllable. It was easy for him to recognize the red hot flash of fury for what it was... and that it wasn't something he had to act on. It was like having an uneasy truce with the Incredible Hulk inside of him. And he kept that Hulk on a very short leash.

Of course, Creed zeroed in on it immediately. "What's wrong?"

"Like I said...it still hurts." He didn't want to scare Creed, but he didn't want to lie to him either. Unification wasn't a perfect science—the devil inside of him would never be completely eradicated. Tony had been honest with him from the start and Tar was lucky, in the sense that the CIA had access to many things to help him that the general public didn't. Some of that was because of the major risks involved with what Tar went through in order to merge his secondary personality, and because the government had a very definite interest in keeping his inner assassin at bay.

Creed frowned. "Did you go to the doctor willingly?"

Tar flashed to Jasper hog-tying him down and dragging him down the hall to the (then) horrified doctor. Today, Dr. LaSalle didn't blink. Back then? Tar almost broke both of them. "Very willingly."

He was grateful Loch wasn't present to hear the lie because hell, Tar barely got the words out with a straight face. Even Creed looked doubtful but tactfully ignored it. "Am I going to have to merge because of the traffickers?"

"Did they deserve to die?"

Creed didn't hesitate to say, "Yes."

Tar shrugged. "Not so worried about them. But I don't know how you or Travis felt. Whether it was planned or out of control. Do you remember killing them?"

Creed sighed. "I remember coming to and finding the men dead. Usually, that's my thing—the muscle, you know? But this? It was well thought-out. He wasn't freaking out or out of control. I think he was saving me from having to do it. He planned it—it was neat. Cleaned up. Thought through. That's how he didn't get caught."

Tar nodded.

"So what do you think? Snow or not?" Creed pressed. "Or is Travis showing serial killer qualities?"

"Been watching Netflix a little too much?" Tar asked, then got serious. "If you thought you had a monster inside of you that was controlled by Snow, would you be content to live with it?"

"No."

"Good." Tar trailed his knuckles across Creed's cheek and Creed flushed. Tar was pretty much convinced that both Creed and Travis had a conscience, which was a good sign. It was hard for Snow to do much with boys who had consciences, but that provided an irresistible challenge for him. "More questions?"

"A couple."

"Go ahead."

"Your name," he started.

"Snow named me."

"And you didn't want to change it?"

"Why? So I could forget?" Tar let out a harsh laugh. "Why didn't you change yours?"

"My parents—whoever they were—named me. And same reason." Creed looked abashed, like he'd admitted a weakness.

"Hey, you took control of your identity. I felt like changing it would mean I was trying to escape me. Like I was ashamed of myself and things I'd done. And I've done a lot of things but I'm not ashamed because I fucking won. I'm still here."

"Survived the box." Creed paused, then put his hand on Tar's back and ran his fingertips along the tattoo. "Over soon. But sometimes, it feels like it might never be."

As he spoke, Creed's hand strayed to Tar's throat again and pressed hard and suddenly Tar was tired, so fucking tired of all of it—of fighting to stay alive, of looking over his shoulder, of searching for an elusive madman. So he didn't fight Creed's hold, didn't say anything else, just closed his eyes and waited for the inevitable.

Because he was also tired of trusting. Because he'd obviously been wrong. "Gonna kill me? Just get it over with."

"Jesus," Creed whispered, warm breath on Tar's cheek. "Tar, come on. I wouldn't...I didn't..." A sigh, and then his weight rolled away. "Don't give up, Tar. Don't give up on me." He sounded vulnerable as hell, probably more than he'd ever felt in his entire life, if Tar had to guess. "I just...fuck... doing that earlier was hot."

"So that's your way of seducing me?" Tar asked, finally opening his eyes.

"Kind of. Is that wrong?"

Tar rolled his eyes. "It's my turn, isn't it?"

"I thought it was still my turn," Creed corrected.

"Why's that?"

"Because I'm not done with you yet." He leaned down and crushed his mouth down on Tar's, his palm once again on his throat and Tar didn't fight it because yeah, it was hot as fuck. Even so, Tar tried to wrestle his way on top of Creed, and the combination of slow dance and wrestle continued until both men were panting with need.

Creed won when he circled Tar's cock with a rough palm and Tar wasn't complaining about losing as he hissed in a breath. Creed smirked down at him. "Gonna resist?"

"If I do?"

"Only makes things hotter."

"Take him, Creed. Go ahead. Don't stop on my account." Loch's voice was heavy with lust.

Loch.

"Yeah, you like to watch, Loch?" Creed asked as he stroked Tar's cock roughly. "What do you want me to do to him?"

So much...

So much that Loch was sure he couldn't explain it with all the time in the world on his hands. Directing the two naked men in front of him would be the best way, and maybe the only way right now he'd allow himself to be involved.

He'd been standing in the doorway, watching Creed kiss Tar, watching Tar respond. Based on the fact they'd been already naked in bed, he knew it wasn't the first time they'd slept together. And he was pretty pissed—at himself for being too drunk to know what was happening last night...

Mainly because he'd wanted to watch. But now he had his chance. "I guess I missed the earlier show, so you'll have to make it up to me."

Creed smiled and Tar frowned, but he didn't protest.

"Tar, move between Creed's legs and start sucking his cock. Now. Stay on your knees with your legs apart too. " Loch held his breath as he watched Tar, after a brief hesitation, settle himself on his knees. He leaned forward and nuzzled Creed's cock and Loch wondered if he'd get through this without coming in his pants. "Creed, hand in his hair. Take control of him. Tar, spread your legs so I can get a good view."

Both men did as he asked, and Creed began to guide Tar's head so he bobbed up and down, swallowing Creed's cock. And Creed couldn't take his eyes off Tar.

Loch watched the two men, mesmerized by them. "Is he good, Creed?"

"Fuck yeah," Creed breathed. "So hot and wet."

"Did he tell you about the last time we picked up guys together?" Loch asked Creed, who glanced at him in surprise. "About him on his knees, sucking two leather daddies off while they called him their boy?"

Creed looked back at Tar and groaned.

"It was so hot. One of them held his nipple the entire time. Controlled him with it."

As if on cue, Creed reached over and grabbed Tar's nipple. Loch watched Tar's body buck in response, heard the hum of pleasure he made around Creed's dick that made Creed hiss and rock his hips up.

"Fuck his face harder." Loch fought the urge to free his own dick and start stroking, tried not to think about how good it would feel to shoot his load over both men, mark them with his come.

For now, he contented himself with watching Tar's talented mouth push Creed over the edge as Creed cried out Tar's name while he came.

The night Tar had been fucked by the leather daddies? He'd called out Loch's name.

Tar watched Creed's face as he swallowed the man's come, then continued to worship his dick until Creed tugged him up. He climbed up Creed's body and Creed leaned in and kissed him, an unexpected kiss that was hard and fast and really fucking good. Creed's tongue danced over his, licked the roof of his mouth and his hand remained stroking Tar's dick the entire time. Tar's hips were moving to his rhythm and he felt helpless. Exposed, to both men.

Which, he supposed, was the entire fucking point. Both of them, wanting him. Vying to give him pleasure, each in their own way.

But Creed looked protective as fuck, like he was going to

make sure Loch didn't hurt either one of them, and Tar realized he was in the middle of a pissing contest.

This was exactly the way he and Loch used to play—except that the man between them, the one they'd pick up together, was their center of attention and Loch and Tar didn't play with each other. They took turns. But Loch directing Creed to fuck him? Was pretty close to what happened the last time he and Loch had picked up a guy together. And Tar wasn't sure what the hell to do with it.

Enjoy the fuck out of it.

The threesome Loch referred to was the last one they'd had—because right after that, Loch had gotten serious with Liam. At the time, they'd only been dating—fucking, really—and it hadn't been serious.

Suddenly, after Tar and the leather daddies, Loch was moving in with Liam, leaving Tar spinning.

But as painful as it had been to think on that night, it was also the focus of a hell of a lot of fantasies for Tar—the two leather daddies had nearly brought him and Loch together and they'd definitely brought Tar to his knees.

It'd been Loch's turn to pick up the guy they'd ultimately share. They'd been at a leather bar because the city they'd been in at the time didn't have a ton of options, and hell, neither of them minded leather.

So Tar was sober—by choice—and Loch had a few drinks. At that time, he'd been able to control the drinking far better and the promise of sex had both men amped up.

When they were together, they were safe. Bottom line.

But at some point, Loch had hatched a plan and changed up the way they'd usually done things. "Let's head out."

"You didn't find anyone?"

"I did. They're meeting us back at the hotel."

"They? Feeling ambitious?"

"Very.

Tar had been curious but the anticipation was a big part of the thrill, so he hadn't asked any of the questions. Instead, he'd pretended to wait patiently in the bedroom portion of suite of their hotel, his heart jumping out of his goddamned chest when he heard the knock on the door.

He was lying on the bed, the TV blaring, when Loch walked in...with the two leather daddies right behind him, and all three of them had a locked and loaded focus directed at him. It'd been suddenly hard to swallow—or hide how aroused he was.

Of course, they all noticed. One of the leather daddies moved closer and said, "We heard you're in need of a spanking."

Tar glanced between him and Loch, who agreed, "He definitely needs some discipline."

Tar had been too stunned at the turn of events to argue and by the time everything had sunk in, one of the men had clamped his thumb and forefinger around Tar's left nipple and had Tar kneeling on the floor between them.

A lot of it was a blur—an intense, overwhelmingly sexually charged blur that found Tar coming more times than he'd thought humanly possible.

And Loch directed the entire show, although the men had been very creative in their own right. And Loch had watched, fascinated...until both men decided that they wanted to fuck Tar, at the same time. Tar hadn't done that ever—and hadn't since, mainly because of the memories of what happened. Because, after he'd agreed to let it happen, and he'd been strad-

dling leather daddy one's lap and impaled on his cock while leather daddy two worked his way inside, Loch came over and kissed the shit out of him, taking away all the pain and stress, soothing him. Making him enjoy all of it.

Tar had cried out Loch's name when he came, sure that a wall had finally come down between him and Loch.

It was up, taller and wider than ever, hours later.

But now, with Creed, Loch was back to solidly directing. It was the oddest feeling, knowing that Creed was playing with him to Loch's specifications. That Loch was watching him, studying him, making sure Creed gave Tar all the pleasure. Like a do-over for the night that, at the time, Tar was sure broke them forever.

They knew each other's deepest darkest fantasies, watched them play out in front of each other—with the threesomes. Now, Loch was going to tell Creed and with him, make those come true.

"Put him on his back, Creed. Hold his legs tight while you rim him," Loch instructed now. "Make him helpless. He loves that."

"Loch, shut the fuck up."

Creed laughed. "I'd rather he didn't. God, this is going to be fun."

"You do love it," Creed told him with a smirk.

Tar grunted as Creed grabbed his legs roughly and spread them. Tar whimpered, then did so again when Creed blew on his hole. He teased it with his tongue and then speared inside, burying his face. Tar's cries only made him harder. His cock jutted upward, dripping, finding no relief and Creed licked harder, more intensely, getting deeper inside the man's walls and driving him crazy.

"He loves this and he hates it at the same time," Loch murmured. "He's blushing like crazy. Always does. And Tar? No coming yet."

Fuck. Tar kept his eyes closed and whimpered.

Tar understood why Creed had overwhelmed him. It wasn't just about physical strength. No, it was the palpable energy and drive that radiated off the man in waves. It pulsed through him and into Tar and Tar wanted more.

"Don't fucking baby me," he warned Creed. "Don't you dare."

Creed smiled, almost reassuringly. "Not in my plans, baby. After all, you and I? We're from the same box."

Creed's fingers took him, his cock jutting out, hard again. "Hurry, Creed—please."

"Oh no, he's not rushing you, is he Creed?" Loch asked. "He needs some discipline." Tar's body drew up tight at his words. "Put him on all fours, Creed."

Creed bit his inner thigh to make him open his eyes, then helped him turn over. "Good boy," he murmured and rubbed Tar's lower back, like he knew what Loch was going to ask him to do—and how would he know that?

"Spank him, Creed. Don't let him come though—not yet."

Creed's hand trailed down his ass and Tar fought to remain silent. But the first slap surprised him, even though he knew it was going to happen, and he let out a keening cry that had Creed smacking his ass over and over, hitting the perfect spot on each cheek to keep him guessing. "Stay still, baby. Just like that," Creed crooned as he paused to let Tar catch his breath. He screwed his eyes shut against the tears that threatened, because that pain/pleasure line had been breeched and he was in the zone. Half floating.

A few more hard smacks left his ass burning and then Creed was mounting him, burying his cock so deeply inside that Tar's body bowed tightly in a desperate attempt not to shoot. The room smelled like sex and fire as Creed bit the back of his neck as he came hard inside of him. Finally, Loch ordered, "Come now, Tar. Right fucking now," and he did, his body bucking, hands clawing the sheets, his dick taking over every possible brain cell.

He didn't know how he ended up on his side on the bed with Creed pressed close, pushing hair out of his eyes, and murmuring to him. He was all wrung out but his dick still twitched because he wanted more. He wanted Loch too. Imagined what it would be like to have him in the bed.

Creed wanted both men too. Tar could see it as he kept looking between them. As hot as their scene had been, with Loch involved...forget it.

"Loch, come join us," Creed said finally.

Loch shook his head. "This one isn't about me."

Creed snorted. "Of course it is."

"I don't deserve him." Loch ran a hand through his dark hair, his countenance completely serious.

Tar frowned and Creed looked pensively between the two men. "Then I'll take care of him for you...until you're ready. Until you do deserve him."

CHAPTER SIXTEEN

"STORM'S SUPPOSED to taper off tomorrow," was the first thing Loch said to him.

Tar? Just snorted and sat across from him. There were circles under his eyes, a high sex flush still on his cheeks and his hair was damp from a recent shower. "Really? That's what you're going to start with?"

Loch shook his head and bit back a smirk. "I'm not going to drink anymore."

"Ah, Loch, let's stick to promises you can keep. Hour by hour. No shame in it."

For the first months after escaping Snow, Loch recalled that Tar couldn't sleep for more than an hour at a time, not without a nightmare. He wasn't trying to be a dick about this. "I'm tired of apologizing to you. But I'm not sorry about last night, or the kiss before that. And I'm not sorry I finally fucking remembered what happened that first night here, with us, in front of the fireplace."

Tar's eyes were clear and bright, and a small smile played

on his lips. "About fucking time, Loch. Did you enjoy directing the show last night?"

"What do you think?"

Tar shook his head. "You stayed out of reach, as usual."

"Because I don't deserve you. Not yet."

"Sounds like avoidance to me."

"No, it's not." Loch studied him. "It was hard not to jump in bed last night and take my turn."

"Then I'll make sure I keep trying to seduce you," Tar promised.

"You never give up on me."

"Never will."

"Last night? Hot as fuck."

Tar flushed more deeply. "You know the right buttons to push."

"You and Creed?"

"Yes." He narrowed his eyes at Loch when he looked away. "You can't be jealous."

"Why can't I be?"

Tar muttered, "Gotta be kidding me." Then, louder, "You and Creed fucked like right in front of me."

"Because you watched on camera."

"You guys were loud as fuck. And the door was open. You would've watched last night if you hadn't been passed out. Oh wait, you did get to watch after all."

Loch stared at him with a pit in his stomach. "Don't be mad at me, Tar. Please. I'm trying."

"I know. But I also don't bullshit you." Tar took a long drink of orange juice. "Are you screwing him because you're trying to replace Liam?"

"No."

"You said he was the love of your life."

Loch shook his head. "Not even close." He saw the softness return to Tar's expression. "I won't hurt you again."

"I'm already at risk, Loch," Tar told him. "Have been since the day Snow grabbed me. So really, you can't bring me any danger that I haven't already brought on myself."

"I know," Loch told him softly. He also knew that Tar would never put him in harm's way, not without warning. "Tar, I can deal with this."

Tar chuffed a soft breath. "Right, tough guy."

Not so tough. He always thought it after Tar said that... and he'd never had to say it out loud. Because Tar knew him better than anyone. "What happened last night?"

"Yeah?"

"I want it to happen again. With all of us. And alone, with you."

Tar's smile was lopsided. "It will, Loch. If I can only promise you one thing, it's that."

Creed stayed in the shower for a while, not wanting to walk out of the room and deal with the two men talking in the kitchen. He'd woken to an empty bed, the memories of what happened last night burned into his brain forever.

It's not like you like to snuggle, you asshole.

Finally—and only because he didn't want to kill the hot water totally—he emerged, dressed, and tried the casual thing, walking into the kitchen and nodding at both men. Like no big deal.

Except he was about as casual as a bull in a china shop.

Always had been. "So, I guess we're still stuck here," was his opening line.

Tar barked a laugh and then muttered, "More weather bullshit," and Loch just shook his head.

Creed ignored him and poured a cup of coffee. "Are you two friends again? Because I can't keep up." He couldn't keep the irritability out of his voice and it had nothing to do with lack of caffeine. He didn't know where he stood or what the fuck he was supposed to with a morning after. Up until now, Travis dealt with it...at least Creed assumed he did, since he was never there for it.

Most of the time, he pieced shit together from things other people said, like Dodge, for instance. Because Dodge didn't know anything about Creed and neither did any of his associates, and Creed had to get good about being dropped into things and avoiding conversations he knew nothing about.

But here, he had no real escape, and no way to claim memory loss...at least not about last night. He was stuck here, with Loch and Tar and their issues.

Finally, he turned to Loch and motioned to Tar. "You should be with him. And you should leave me the fuck out of it. Both of you."

With that he walked away, shoving the coffee aside. But there wasn't really anyplace to go, so he found the furthest room away from them, the loft that took up half the space of the lower floor. It was all windows and overlooked what was no doubt gorgeous scenery in the Spring. Now, it was complete whiteout conditions, so he sat on the floor, his back to the couch and stared out as his head began to hurt.

What did you think? That you'd be a happy threesome?

Because that had never happened for Loch and Tar. No, they used a third person to keep distance between them, and so far, their plan was working perfectly.

Except for the person caught in the middle.

He rubbed a hand along his chest which had started to hurt as well, and his throat tightened. He was sweating, too, and fuck, he felt awful. And it hadn't happened to him in a long time.

He heard Travis buzzing in his brain but Travis wasn't trying to come out...and still, the pain in his skull was like a chainsaw, attempting to break out.

"Creed, hey...talk to us." Tar's voice floated by him, but Creed couldn't answer—he was too busy trying to breathe. He felt Tar and Loch's hands on him, and he wasn't threatened but he was sinking deeper inside of himself.

Drowning. He reached his hands out and felt nothing.

"What's happening to him?" Loch asked while they tried to help Creed as he thrashed around the floor.

He'd been the one to find him first, quickly calling for Tar when he found Creed having trouble breathing, but it didn't seem to be a purely physical problem.

"It's a panic attack," Tar said as he wiped Creed's head with a warm washcloth. "He's burning up."

"Seems more like a nightmare."

"It is." Tar looked as concerned as Loch felt, especially because Creed had begun to thrash between them. All they could do was talk to him, touch him, assure him that he was okay.

And finally, after what seemed like forever, Creed stopped struggling, and even though he was still panting, he was pulling in easier breaths. His expression relaxed slightly.

When he opened his eyes, it took him a few moments to register where he was, and he looked between Loch and Tar with slight suspicion before realizing what had happened. He closed his eyes and murmured, "Fuck. *Fuck.*"

Tar looked over at Loch and smiled, relief evident in his face, and Loch's gut tightened at how handsome Tar was. He reached out and put a hand on his friend's cheek and Tar frowned, but didn't pull away.

"I'm sorry," was all Loch said, to both men. He took his hand away and Creed opened his eyes.

"Yeah, me too." Creed groaned and went to sit up. Tar helped him so his back was against the couch.

"Does that happen a lot?" Tar asked him.

"Not really, no. But it's not the first time." Creed sighed. "It always sucks."

"Thinking about Snow?" Loch asked hesitantly.

"Wasn't about Snow." Creed took a long slug out of the water bottle Tar handed him. "Before that. With...those people."

Loch assumed he was talking about his parents—or the foster family. Jasper hadn't been able to verify exactly which one they were, but Loch suspected they were the latter. That Creed had been trafficked to them, and that they'd been paid by Snow to turn him over. "Do you remember...anything?"

"Some. None of it good."

"Yeah, same here." Tar sat shoulder to shoulder with Creed. "I guess we never talked about how we got to Snow."

"Does it really matter?" Creed asked. "I mean, if life was good before it for any of the guys there, I'd be shocked."

"Mine was," Loch heard himself say. "Until my parents died."

Creed would assume that Loch somehow ended up at Snow's camps after that—and he had, but definitely not in the way Creed thought. But Loch wouldn't clarify it. Admitting the reality to Creed now, no matter how shitty it was, would be the stupidest thing ever because it could trigger Creed, worse than he already was.

Even with the small admission, Creed's eyes looked haunted. "Yeah, that's worse. At least I went from shitty to shitty. If things had been good beforehand, I'm not sure I could've survived."

Tar remained silent, his stare that of the thousand-yard variety, and Loch reached over and touched his arm. "You all right?"

"I don't like talking about this shit—at all." His voice was tight. He wasn't in panic attack mode. No, Tar didn't do that —he just got angry. Creed put a hand on Tar's thigh and Tar seemed to relax a little. "The people who sold me...I can't remember who they are or anything else; I just remember darkness."

"But it's not dark here," Loch reminded him, and Tar frowned, then looked at him. "Safe, remember?"

"Are we, Loch? Are we really?" Tar asked.

CHAPTER SEVENTEEN

TAR MIGHT BE safe with Loch and vice versa, but Creed knew he couldn't promise the same thing to either man, no matter how strongly he felt it to be true.

"What if..." He paused and then confessed his worries in a rush. "What if I lose control? You've put your trust in me. What if I fuck that up?"

Tar put his hand on the back of Creed's neck and pulled Creed in. "Stop, Creed. We all fuck up. We chose this risk. I'm not implying you're not safe...but we all come from the same place. I think safe is a relative fucking term, and that it's a choice. When I said that to Loch, I was really wondering if we're safe for you. Because I don't want to hurt you—and neither does he."

Loch nodded in assent.

Creed knew that. "So you do guys sleep with the men you rescue?"

"We've never done this," Loch admitted. "And we've only been with each other once. Here."

"Here?" Creed asked.

"This is where we came...just after we escaped." Loch shook his head as if to try to clear the memories.

Creed looked around as if he could feel the ghosts of who those two men used to be. So much history between them and all of it seemed to be playing out in front of him.

To know they'd never taken on anyone else like him, to know he was the first? "Why? Why me?"

"At first, I didn't know. And then, it just felt right," Loch admitted. "Tar seemed protective of you from the start, even before he knew."

No wonder Travis let his guard down and why he hadn't fought Creed emerging at all. Now he sat between the two men, realizing that for all his talk, he was nervous as hell. He never did the sweet talk seduction shit. He was in it for the hard fuck and not the emotion...and yet, what he felt for these two men? Maybe it was because they were kindred spirits or had a common enemy.

But he couldn't deny the pull, his want and his need to discover the obvious and unexplored attraction these men had for each other.

He needed to be a part of it. So he leaned his head on Tar's shoulder. Loch had a hand on his thigh. "I don't know where I fit in. Travis fits with Dodge. He's fine moving along, pretending, with everyone. But I don't think he's lonely."

"Are you lonely?" Tar asked.

"Not...here." Creed closed his eyes and where the hell had this emotion come from? Maybe Travis would come out and save him...but even the low buzz in his head had stopped.

Loch's hand moved to the back of his neck, massaging. Comforting. "Good."

Creed glanced between them. "Am I in the way?"

"I don't think either of us feels that way," Loch assured him.

Creed knew they loved each other, knew that he might possibly be a third of convenience only.

For the moment, he was okay with that. Because at least for once, he'd be left with good memories. Like Tar said, safety was a relative term for assassins with multiple personalities anyway. A part of him felt the urge to barge in, strip, and exorcise all their ghosts. And that feral, caged part of him urged him to push hard and do that, even though he had no real idea of why.

And here he sat, in the middle this time. He turned his head to the left and kissed Loch, surprising him for half a second before his mouth opened to allow Creed to slide his tongue in and lick the roof of his mouth.

And then he turned his head to Tar and kissed him, groaning into his mouth as Loch cupped his crotch through his pants.

"God, you two look hot together," Loch told them as he moved to nuzzle Creed's neck, licking and nipping the sensitive flesh. Creed pulled his mouth off Tar's—because this was happening. Loch was actually joining in, and Tar smiled like he knew what Creed was thinking.

Tar grabbed pillows off the couch behind them and laid them on the floor, tugged Creed down onto his back. Loch ended up straddling his calves in order to take off Creed's pants and then Tar helped him take his shirt off before leaning in to kiss him again.

All of this felt safe... and yet he was unsteady as fuck. His world spun even as he gave in to the insistence of Tar's kiss. He put his hands on both sides of Tar's face and held him there as Tar's tongue slid over his. The heat between them surged as Tar deepened the kiss and Creed's hands fisted as Loch's hand ran up his inner thigh. Then his breath hitched as Tar's mouth pressed lightly against his neck, that spot right behind his ear that made him goddamned nuts.

Tar moved behind him then, spreading his legs and tugging Creed back against his chest. Loch moved in between Creed's legs and spread his thighs, forcing his calves over Loch's shoulder.

Loch looked between Creed and Tar and smirked, like all of this pleased him greatly. As he licked the precome off the head of his cock, Creed almost jolted with pleasure, but Tar had him, was playing with Creed's nipples, tweaking them, tugging them taut as Loch licked and nipped along Creed's hip before moving back to lick his cock.

"Fuck," Creed bit out as they worked in perfect unison, all for his pleasure.

Were they trying to break him? To get more out of him? Was this a way to make him want to stay with them?

Did it matter? Because Creed was ready to hand himself over for more, willingly and gladly. He watched Loch tease his cock, his groans giving way to flat-out begging—to come, to be fucked, for this to never goddamned end. Tar chuckled in his ear as Loch's head moved down, his tongue licking a strip over his hole.

Creed arched up, his back pressing Tar's chest. Tar's hand wandered across his belly and wrapped around his cock, stroking in unison to Loch's tongue, which was now spearing inside of him, fucking him, taking him, and he closed his eyes, lost...and found.

Loch pressed a pad of his finger against Creed's hole now,

then began licking and laving again as he pushed one finger, then two inside.

Tar snapped the cap off the lube that suddenly appeared.

"You carrying that around, hoping to get...lucky," Creed managed and Tar laughed, and laughed more as Creed cried out when Loch's fingers found their mark.

"Think you're lucky, baby?" Tar asked and Creed could only nod.

Loch sat up. "I've got to fuck him now." He took the lube. "Condoms?" he asked and Creed shook his head no. "I'm clean, Creed."

"So am I. We'll compare tests later," Creed told him impatiently. "Right now, hurry up and fuck me."

Loch spread the lube on his cock, then took his lubed fingers and pressed them back inside of him, opening him. Preparing him. Tar moved away so Creed was lying flat on his back, save for the pillows under his head and then Loch was on top of him, his cock at Creed's entrance.

He put his mouth on Creed's, and there was a desperation in their kiss, especially after Loch push inside of him. Creed wrapped his legs around Loch and arched up, demanding to be taken, to be filled immediately. And Loch obliged him, sliding up to his balls and, without pausing, snapping his hips, forcing Creed into his rhythm. Creed's arms went to Loch's back, and he raked his nails down his spine, which made Loch pound into him even harder. He caught sight of Tar watching him, knowing he was in line to take his turn—and fuck, the thought of having both men spilling inside of him was enough to make his balls tighten. He shot between their bellies as Loch cried out his name and came, his dick pulsing inside of Creed. His body shook from the intensity of his climax, his muscles tensing for several long seconds as his orgasm slowly receded.

He rested, his forehead pressed to Creed's chest for several moments. Tar leaned over him, brushed hair from Creed's eyes. "How're you feeling, baby?"

"Fuck me, Tar. C'mon," he said, his brain fuzzy and floaty. He wanted the pleasure to continue.

"Let's give him what he needs," Loch murmured, then eased up and out of Creed.

In seconds, Tar was between his legs, holding Creed's hips so he could drive himself inside, his cock sliding in with the help of Loch's come. Then he leaned forward and dragged Creed's arms upwards, holding them, then winding his fingers in Creed's. "Still so fucking tight, Creed. Like a glove. No idea how good this feels."

Tar pounded into him, holding Creed's body immobile, forcing him to take the pleasure, their hands fisted together. Loch moved between both their legs, his fingers pressing in around Tar's cock as they both took him. The storm slammed the windows like it wanted in—but Creed had wants too. He understood its unrelenting fury because all of that lived inside of him too, a swirling, unrelenting cacophony calmed by Tar's climax as he throbbed and shot inside of him, and Creed cried out both men's names as all the puzzle pieces finally clicked together.

CHAPTER EIGHTEEN

TAR LOOKED at the weather report and realized there was no more putting off getting in touch with Jasper. He opened his laptop, went into Jasper's office and locked the door behind him. The place was soundproofed but he still refused to give Jasper any intel on Liam.

It wasn't even that he didn't trust Creed or Travis. No, as much as it pained him, if Liam had programmed Loch, Tar could be putting all of them in more danger than they already were.

You'll get them to the hospital and then you'll figure it out.

He shifted, his ass still sore, a bittersweet reminder that getting exactly what he wanted might have an expiration date. But not if he could help it. He knew how to fight like hell.

Jasper had no doubt tracked them here, so there was no reason to lie. And Jasper, being Jasper, didn't force him to.

"How're you doing, kiddo?" Jasper asked, and Tar wanted to roll his eyes at Jasper's daddy-ing, especially since the guy was only ten years older than he was, but hell, it still made him feel protected.

"Not bad."

"And how is he?"

"Which one?"

"Loch." Jasper leaned back and Tar gave a wistful smile that he knew Jasper recognized all too well. "That good, huh?"

Tar shrugged. "It's not easy. Lot of memories coming back into play, and none of them are all that great."

Jasper understood, which was why he chose to monitor this situation closely. "Maybe you should all come in."

"It's not time yet. I think...I think Creed remembers more than he realizes. Travis too. And they both trust us."

"That's good, Tar. Really good. The clean-up crew didn't see anything," Jasper confirmed. "But a sniper shooting at you is never a good thing."

"Creed doesn't think it's Xander, and I'm inclined to agree. Then again, I can't make heads or tails of Snow's plans these days." He watched as Tony LaSalle walked in and sat next to Jasper at the monitor. "Hey, Tony."

"You're not okay," was all Tony said.

"I've been better," Tar admitted. "Loch's drinking again. A lot."

LaSalle nodded. "He's going to have to dry up in-patient."

"They'll bring Creed in to visit soon and then we'll surprise Loch—it's the only way," Jasper said. Tar felt a kick of relief that he wouldn't necessarily be the bad guy. Loch knew his credit cards were monitored and trips to the liquor store wouldn't go unnoticed.

There was definitely value in the ambush.

The storm had been over for two days, and they couldn't put the trip to the hospital off for much longer. No matter how badly Loch wanted to.

Jasper's cabin had, once again, become his safe space. It had brought him closer to Tar again, and it brought them both closer to Creed. The thought of giving that all up...

You know you need help to kick the drinking.

It'd been so much worse since Liam's death. He's always had trouble with drinking. When his parents were first killed and he'd been sent to Snow's, alcohol had been the only way to numb himself, the only thing that made it better. Hunting Snow had been enough to make him kick the habit, and he had, for a long damned time. Until Liam. The urges had started when they'd been dating, but they'd increased tenfold after his death. Whiskey was the only way to stop the buzzing in his brain, the thoughts of Snow and the many, many ways he'd failed Tar.

"Loch, you hungry?" Tar was asking. "We'll stop in half an hour for lunch and then drive the rest of the way through."

"Yeah, works for me." He glanced over his shoulder to Creed, who was quietly staring out the window. "Creed? What's up?"

Creed's nerves were palpable. "What's going to happen to me? I mean, I get that this hospital shit needs to happen, but fuck...when do I get to just be?"

"Ah, Creed," Tar murmured, before he pulled the car over and turned to face Creed. Loch did too. "Travis is coming out less and less. Does that bother you?"

Creed shrugged. "I'm not sure. What does it mean?"

"'That you're comfortable," Loch said quietly. "Once you get to the hospital, or under situations of stress, you might need Travis, and he might need you."

"Are they going to make me try to merge us?"

"I think Dr. LaSalle will listen to what you've got to say. And what we've observed so far," Tar assured him. "We're not into forcing people to do anything. You've got to believe us."

"I do believe you." Creed glanced between both of them. "It's everyone else that freaks me out, okay? And supposed Travis comes out?"

"It's okay if he does," Loch assured him. "I know about slipping into different identities when the situation warrants it. I also know it's hard for men like us to shake off those identities internally. Because you can get used to being numb. Depersonalized. It makes it easy to do the job, but it's not an easy way to live."

"You think I can control my identity?"

"Can't you, to a point?" Loch asked.

Creed stared at him. "It's not the same."

"I never said it was. But you seem to be able to physically protect yourself just fine. What does Travis protect? Exactly the same thing I've been trying to for years." Loch paused "I'm trying to say that I understand. And that it's okay."

"Thanks for your permission," Creed snarled.

"It's not about permissions. It's about us," Tar reminded him.

Creed blinked at him. "What? Not ready to give up a fucking nutcase?"

"No, I'm not," Tar said.

"I'm not ready to give you up either," Loch agreed.

"Package deal," Creed muttered.

"I think we can handle it."

"It's a novelty. You'll get sick of it, trust me." Creed shook his head. "It's exhausting."

Tar shook his head. "Then let us give you a comfortable place to lay your damned head."

"It's that simple?" Creed asked.

Loch smiled. "I don't know. It's worth trying, no?"

Creed drew a stuttered breath, rubbed his head. This was a lot of stress for him, all of it a trigger for Travis to come to the surface, and Loch watched with baited breath to see if Creed would let Travis come to his rescue.

Creed shook his head, hard. "Not happening. Have to prove it."

"The anger you have inside of you? That's all right," Tar told him gently.

Creed frowned. "It is?"

"It is," Loch said firmly. "You can be angry. You can be sad. So can Travis—if he's what you need."

Creed wondered if he'd ever really know exactly what he needed. Then again, maybe no one else knew what they needed either.

CHAPTER NINETEEN

HOURS LATER, Tar's truck was ushered into what seemed like a private estate behind imposing wrought iron gates and Creed stared up at the house as if it might swallow him whole and never spit him back out, like that "Hotel California" song Dodge loved so much.

"I'm not sure I want to know anyone who lives like that," he told them.

Tar snorted. "Don't let it fool you, okay? Trust me—you'll be fine in there."

"Dr. LaSalle and Jasper will both see you in there, okay? And then we'll come back and go visit the hospital with you."

"You think I'm okay to meet with the doctor here, not the hospital?" Creed couldn't keep the surprise out of his own voice.

"Definitely," Tar told him firmly. "We'll come back to get you when Jasper calls for us."

"How long will that be?" Creed asked, suddenly wishing he hadn't agreed to meet Jasper without these men with him.

"Not too long, Creed," Loch told him, his tone encouraging. "You need to get answers from Jasper—and Tony too. This is the best way. And don't hold anything back...about us."

"About us or..." Creed let that hang in the air because he hadn't planned on bringing up the fact that he'd fucked Tar and then had a threesome with him and Loch.

"Jasper won't care that we've slept together," Tar assured him. "But if it makes you uncomfortable, you don't have to tell him."

Creed put his hand on the door handle, but paused before he got out. "Before I go, will you guys promise me something?"

"What is it?" Tar asked.

"Go somewhere and fuck each other's brains out."

Tar blinked. "Is that an order?"

"Yeah, if you need it to be. Because it's the only way that you're going to know—if I'm going to know—if what happened between us was a substitute for you wanting to be with each other," Creed told them honestly. "So you two need to fuck for your own sakes, and for mine, and whatever way it ends up, I hope you'll both still be there for me."

Loch frowned. "Of course we will."

"Definitely," Tar added.

"Good. Go. Have fun. Try not to forget about me too much. And you could always tape it for me." He smiled as the front door opened and a tall man nodded in their direction. He looked imposing, all wide-shouldered with a shock of blond hair and dark eyes that seemed to center on him, even behind the tinted glass. "Shit."

"Yeah, that's pretty much how we felt the first time we met him too," Loch reassured him. "But he's cool."

Creed figured that if they were going to throw him to the lions, they would've done so earlier, like the first time he attacked Loch. And Tar. So yeah, he got out of the truck and went toward Jasper, who extended a hand to shake.

Creed did, and fuck, the man's grip was crushing.

"Good to finally meet you. I'm Jasper."

"I'm Creed." He liked that Jasper hadn't just assumed which personality he was meeting.

"Will I meet Travis today?" Jasper asked as they walked inside the wide doorway that accommodated them side by side.

"I'm not sure. It depends."

"On?"

"If Travis feels like I'm going to get too angry. He's used to me getting in trouble and tries to save me."

"And the reverse holds true as well, I'm guessing." Jasper closed the doors behind them and motioned for Creed to follow him.

And yeah, the inside of this place wasn't what he'd expected. It was expensive, yes, but it was more like part command center, part bachelor pad. Giant bachelor pad, with big leather couches and TVs everywhere. It was warm and comfortable and the tension immediately began to uncoil.

He sank into one of the couches across from Jasper. "Tony LaSalle will talk with you when we're done. But I figure that you've got questions. I'll answer what I can—what's not classified. Unless, of course, it's something you already know."

"I guess I need you to tell me why Snow had the agency's backing."

"Seems hard to believe, I know." Jasper frowned, and then began telling a story that he had to have told hundreds of times. "His full name is Jabez Snow. Son of Marin Snow. Jabez was supposedly an unwilling victim of a cult his father ran. Marin Snow joined the cult, True Believers, when Jabez was just three years old, and soon rose up the ranks. He was, by all accounts—including Jabez's—a brutal leader. And Jabez escaped when he was fifteen during an FBI raid and helped take his father down."

"Shit." Creed leaned forward.

"Yeah, don't feel too bad for him. So he's taken into the FBI and supposedly deprogrammed, although the profilers at the BAU were fascinated to discover that he'd somehow managed to not be indoctrinated into the cult. What they hadn't realized was how well his father's lessons had been burned into Jabez...he just bent and twisted them to his own uses. Then the FBI handed him over to the CIA—or the CIA stole him, depending on which agency you talk to. What the agencies both agree on is that Jabez Snow was a homegrown criminal mastermind who was also aided and abetted by the CIA for years, unwittingly, via a special program to create assassins. The original mission was to build a better soldier. The government needed all the help they could get against the US's enemies, foreign and domestic."

"And no one was watching him?"

"They were, but everyone saw what he wanted them to see. He's brilliant—and if he'd used his mind for good, I can't imagine what resources he'd have created. Initially he culled the men and women who weren't up for the special forces jobs. He gave the agency a blueprint for what traits made a good agent, and there were a lot of surprises in the pool he chose. Some men and women who wouldn't have been deemed fit for the field ended up being the best operatives we'd ever had. It was a whole new way of looking into the mind of an agent. Then it got more specialized. What would, or could, break an agent? Could we train that perceived weakness out of them? Could their minds learn ways around the pain of torture?" Jasper sighed. "And then we realized that Snow believed he had the power to create "super agents"—a whole group of assassins, and had a special way to weed out the unstable ones."

"So he really had a background in mind control," Creed mused. "And you guys were only too happy to capitalize on that."

"Snow wanted to be one of the good guys and for a while, he was," Jasper said wearily, without a hint of defensiveness.

Creed shook his head. "There was never anything good about him."

Jasper nodded, his expression tight. "I agree with you. He's a psychopath, and while a great many agents share that quality, most of them aren't depraved. Jabez Snow is, in every sense of the word."

"So why the obsession with breaking men's minds—forcing a man to split?"

"He splits the men in order to create a front man. That front man protects the killer. Passes lie detectors. He's a built-in alibi—he's a whole other person."

Creed shook his head. "I never..."

"Never killed?"

"Not for *him*," Creed emphasized, refusing to say Snow's name.

"Tell me about it."

"And have it turned against me?"

"Were they innocent?"

Creed scoffed. "Of course not. They were trafficking."

"And you killed them?"

"Travis did. Apparently he killed three men and got their cargo back to Child Protective Services, since they were mostly kids from within the US. Travis had a case number and used a burner phone."

Jasper nodded. "The CIA already has this background information."

"So you're fact-checking me."

"Part of my job." Jasper gave a tight smile. "It was the Russians."

"Yes." Creed clenched his fists. "I'd do it again."

"You...or Travis?" Jasper countered.

"Travis," he admitted. "But I don't think he did anything wrong. So what, that means the next step for me is allowing myself to get locked up in a nuthouse until I remember if Snow broke me and programmed Travis to be a killing machine?"

"You need to be examined, yes." Jasper leaned forward, his voice not unsympathetic. "Once you're deemed fit, then staying at the facility or not is your choice. You don't seem like the kind of a man who would want to hurt innocent people at the mercy of Snow."

"I want all traces of that bastard gone from me," Creed growled. "Can you do that?"

"We can try."

"What if I don't want to lose Travis? I mean, he's not killing random people."

"You and Travis can't just—"

"Kill human traffickers? Why not?" Creed demanded.

"Because I don't want you going to jail."

"Jail? For killing scumbags that the CIA can't catch on their own?" Creed snorted.

"How about capturing the traffickers and then let us arrest them?"

"Because it's easier to kill them where they stand. They deserve it."

Jasper sighed, but he didn't look upset. "I can't decide if Tar and Loch have corrupted you or if you're perfect for them."

Jasper's words gave Creed more than a small burst of happiness, although he tried to hide it. "Why don't you head through there?" He pointed across the hall. "There's a woman named Lucy and she's making lunch for you. And she's an amazing cook."

"And then what?"

"Then you can talk to Dr. LaSalle. Unless you need to know anything more from me?"

"If I pass the mental health shit, can I work to find Snow —like Loch and Tar?"

"I've got my opinion, but Tony's will count for an equal amount, so let's cross that bridge when we come to it. Any other questions?"

Creed stood, immediately creating a plan to escape from wherever they'd shove him if he didn't pass Tony's test. "What did you learn by talking to me?"

Jasper sat back, looking completely relaxed. "I already knew what I needed to the second Loch and Tar refused to turn you into me immediately. Enjoy your lunch."

CHAPTER TWENTY

JASPER WATCHED CREED WALK AWAY, and dammit, he was Loch and Tar all over again. Having them all at his house during the storm reminded him of the first time Loch and Tar had broken in there. He'd known they were there the entire time, and they'd had no idea, and still didn't, that he'd been wired for picture and sound even back then, and that he'd been watching them from his office in the CIA. He had no idea who they were at first...and he'd been unable to find Snow for years before that...until those two young men broke into his house and mentioned Snow's name. After that, the reports of a massive fire came in, his agents discovered it was indeed Jabez's mystery hideout, and Jasper put two and two together.

His throat still tightened when he thought about their first kiss. He'd turned off the cameras after that. They'd been so goddamned young and scared and just searching for comfort, but there was no doubt that something happened that night between them that bonded them forever. And as much as he'd hated the thought that they'd go to jail, he'd had no choice but to drag them in and figure out what the hell had happened.

But they hadn't been captured right after they stayed in his house. No, they'd had the sense to escape, and Jasper had to hunt for them for two years after that while they searched for Snow...and for men just like them.

Loch was first brought into PsyOps, to question his possible involvement in his uncle's teachings. Tar had been dragged in as well, since they'd been caught together blowing up a wall they believed led to one of Snow's underground facilities. When dead bodies and equipment that looked like an anarchist's torture essentials were found, the then-sixteen-and seventeen-year-olds were dragged in, taken to separate interrogation rooms and questioned for days.

By the time Jasper had gotten to see them, neither had broken. There was active resistance, sarcasm, and only admissions of innocence that they didn't work for Snow.

Tar had no ID. When Jasper ran his fingerprints, he'd discovered that Tar didn't actually exist. And that's when things really started to get interesting.

Nine years later, *interesting* was one term Jasper could think to use for the two of them. *Assholes* was another.

Good men was a phrase he often used too, but never out loud to them. Those assholes didn't need praise. They thrived on opposition, and Jasper made sure to present that to them in the form of criminals on a regular basis.

"No lunch for you?" Tony asked as he walked into the room. "I just met Creed. He's thrilled with Lucy right now."

"I figured I needed to feed him before he talked to you."

"Do you think he's satisfied with what you told him?"

Tony asked, balancing on the arm of the couch where Jasper sat.

"I told him the truth. Not sure that's always satisfying." He leaned his head against Tony.

"Headache again?"

"Just tired," he lied.

"Lying to your doctor again?" Tony murmured. "I'll get you something for it, and then I'll talk with Creed...if you think he's up for it."

"More than. Thanks."

Tony ruffled a hand through his hair before he left in search of Jasper's pain meds for the headaches that were more and more frequent. But he turned before he walked out the door. "We'll catch him, Jasper. We'll catch him...and then someone else will emerge. Just remember how much good you've done already."

"We've done," Jasper corrected him, enjoying Tony's soft smile before he left to go dissect Creed.

Creed didn't mind the doctor. Tony LaSalle looked strong enough to handle whatever Creed threw at him—literally— and Travis didn't feel the need to come out and play while Tony questioned him about his time with Snow.

And Creed promised Loch and Tar that he wouldn't be throwing anything at the doctor. As much as he wanted them to stay, he knew it was better that they weren't here. It was part of the process.

He also tried hard not to think about Loch and Tar—and what they might be doing at the moment. He wanted them to do as he asked, but he couldn't deny he worried about the outcome. Which was ridiculous.

"Want to tell me what's suddenly got you so pensive?" Tony asked now.

"Shit, sorry." He'd already been feeling slightly drowsy, thanks to the lunch Lucy had provided and his trip down memory lane, and he'd let his guard way down...with all of them. "It's ah...Loch and Tar."

Tony nodded, like he'd somehow known. "Does thinking about them upset you?"

"Do I seem upset?"

"I'm the one asking the questions, remember?" His tone was still light, but he definitely meant it. "But yes, you seem uncomfortable. Like you're trying to convince yourself of something."

"Are you psychic too?"

"I wish." Tony leaned forward. "Do Loch and Tar make you uncomfortable?"

"No," he said honestly. "Kind of the opposite."

Tony nodded, like he understood. "Care to elaborate?"

"Not really."

"Fair enough—but we'll get back to that at some point."

"Today?"

"I think I'll let it go for today."

"Are you going to hypnotize me?" he asked suddenly.

"Do you want me to?"

"Not today."

Tony laughed. "Not today, then. And no, I'd rather not work that way, if at all possible. Are you up for a few more questions—about Travis?"

"I'll answer what I can."

"At times, you make it sound like you have no control at all over Travis, and others like you've got more than a semblance of control. Can you explain that?"

"It's not so much control over Travis. He comes out when I'm stressed about certain things. He comes out to protect me. If I'm handling things, he stays put."

"So you couldn't handle the human trafficking aspect of your youth?"

"What the fuck is it with all of you and the trafficking?" Creed muttered. "Got a fucking hard-on for that shit."

"Definitely, we do," Tony said, making a note on the pad in front of him. "Apparently, so do you. A hot spot, as we say."

"Who's the *we*? You got multiples, Doc?"

"My brother did."

Creed sat back. "That's how you got pulled into this?"

"I volunteered, actually, once I found out what Snow was trying to do...what he had done." Tony played with the pen, letting it roll through his fingers. "My brother killed himself when I was sixteen."

"And that's why you went to med school and became a psychiatrist?"

"Yes. He went through hell. If I can help just one person not go through that same hell..."

"You helped Tar," Creed interjected.

"I did. Unfortunately, I couldn't help much with the 'go through hell' part." Tony smiled ruefully.

"Sounds like you did, though—to hear him tell it, at least." Creed leaned forward. "Tar said I didn't have to—what's it called?"

"Integrate. And no, you don't have to."

"I feel like there's a 'but' in there."

Tony sighed. "Tar's integrated personality was a stone-cold killer. It was either integrate or live in the hospital. And even though he agreed to integrate, there was always a chance it wouldn't take."

"And there are men who didn't make that choice—and they're in that hospital I'm going to visit."

"Yes. Some of them refused, and some of their integrations weren't successful. And some were."

"And where are they?"

"In the facility."

"Why?"

"They feel safer there. They don't trust themselves," Tony explained.

As much as Creed hated to admit it, he could understand that. "I guess everyone who was tortured by Snow's still a victim."

"I don't see you as victims, Creed, and I don't think you see yourself that way—you're survivors. I have my share of guilt for not seeing what Snow was doing earlier...and I know Jasper feels the same."

"Jasper gave the program the green light?"

"No. Snow actually outranked him—he had other men with him to oversee the project. But Jasper knew Snow—met him during training, and he always said that he never truly trusted him."

"He told me that. About what a rough time of it Snow had."

"Did it make you feel sorry for him?"

"No, but it made me see what shaped him. Or hell,

maybe he was born the way he was—either way, it didn't sound like he had a shot."

"It's not your job to have sympathy for a monster. Listen, Jabez Snow is an evil man. He's a psychopath. He wasn't ruined or twisted by his father and the cult—he was mad he didn't have enough power to overthrow him, so he did the next best thing. He had us dismantle them, which in and of itself wasn't a bad thing. But then he used the agency in order to push his own agenda. He's not a victim, Creed. He orchestrated every single thing that happened."

"But if Jasper said anything at the time..."

"Snow was fifteen when he was brought here for his own protection. He became something of the wunderkind around this place. A lot of the adults took him under their wing, like he was the son they never had."

"Or the son they wished they never had," Creed muttered.

Tony smiled. "I like your sense of humor. It's what will pull you through."

"I hope so."

"Are you going to be all right going to the hospital?" Tony asked.

"Probably not."

"I'll be close by. And I'm assuming you want Loch and Tar to be with you?"

"Definitely."

"You've gotten close with them."

Creed narrowed his eyes, not sure how to answer that, but Tony held up a hand and continued. "I'm not trying to trick you, Creed. I know you slept with both men. They disclosed that information."

"Do they always do that?" Creed asked before he could help himself.

"No, they don't," Tony said quietly. "This is the first time either of them have. I found that...significant."

"In a good way?"

"I hope so." Tony held his hand out to shake, and Creed took it. "You'll get through this, Creed, one way or another. I promise you that."

Creed didn't doubt he'd get through it...it was the "one way or another" part that worried him the most.

CHAPTER TWENTY-ONE

TAR DROVE AWAY from Jasper and watched the gates close behind them. "He'll be okay."

"Which one of us are you trying to convince?" Loch asked him, and his friend smiled.

"Where to?"

"I know where I want to be now. In bed with you. Inside of you," Loch told him outright, and Tar blushed. "It's time. Unless..."

"Unless what?"

"We could wait...until after."

"Is that what you want? Because I don't want to wait another ten goddamned years," Tar growled.

Loch grinned. "Me neither."

So, like errant teens—or a couple having an affair on their lunch break—they headed to the hotel they often frequented and checked in for a week. If all went well, Tar would stay here in between trips to the nearby facility, where both Loch and Creed would stay for an as-yet-to-be- determined time.

Creed would be with Tony and Jasper for several hours.

This would be the best opportunity to do as Creed had requested of them.

"You think Creed was serious about wanting us to tape this?" Tar asked with a frown.

"How about we tell him we'll give him a live demo—something to look forward to."

"Something for all of us to look forward to." Tar had nervous energy to burn—Loch could tell by the restless way he moved.

Loch came up from behind him, wound an arm around his chest, and nuzzled his neck. "Do I need to get you naked?"

"That would help. And fuck, let's not make this so precious." Tar turned on him, fisted Loch's hair in his hands, and kissed him, hard.

Loch responded immediately, and any remaining nerves on both their ends dissipated as their tongues danced, and they kissed until they were both panting, dry humping.

Finally, Loch pulled back and began to strip Tar. He slid his jacket off and then his T-shirt. Finally, he took the jeans down, and Tar, having already taken his boots off, shook out of them and stood in front of Loch, waiting.

As many times as he'd seen Tar naked—which happened more often than not, based on proximity, first when they were on the run together and after, when they hunted down Snow together—he never grew tired of the sight. Because he hadn't taken the opportunity, before now, to trace every dip and furrow, every muscle and scar, to spend so much time between Tar's legs that he couldn't look at Loch afterwards without blushing.

He would. But first things first. "Need to hear you say it,

Tar. Tell me what you want." Because he knew—but to hear Tar say it directly to him...

"I want you to fuck me, Loch. You—inside of me. Not by proxy."

"I still don't think I deserve it. You."

"And I'm telling you that you do."

Loch ran his thumb along Tar's bottom lip, until Tar bit at it. "Brat."

Tar smiled...and it reached his eyes.

"No matter what else happens today, you know I've always loved you."

"No matter what happens," Tar promised.

With that, Loch leaned in and lowered his mouth to Tar's again, pressing Tar's naked body to his fully clothed one, Loch's hands roaming his warm skin. Tar was trying to tug off Loch's clothes, trying to take charge.

At some point, Loch would let him, but tonight? Now? Loch was taking his turn. Again. Because after turning their first night together over and over in his mind, Loch needed to be inside of him.

But first...he dropped to his knees in front of Tar's cock, swiped his thumb to catch the pre-come and tasted it as he stared up at Tar.

"Gonna torture me, Loch?"

"Definitely," he murmured, leaned in, flicking his tongue over the ridge, one hand cupping his balls and with the other, a finger pressing against his hole but not intruding. Not yet. Instead, he moved to stroke the sensitive patch of flesh behind his balls, and a moan escaped Tar's throat, held strangled. His hand dragged through Loch's hair. Dammit, Loch wanted more time, wanted to spend hours between his legs.

But beggars couldn't be choosers. And he'd hold on to this to get him through the toughest part of rehab.

"Coming home to you, Tar," he murmured before sucking down the length of Tar's shaft again. He pulled up, a slow stroke that had Tar begging impatiently, and as much as he wanted to taste Tar, to have him come down his throat, he wanted Tar to come all over him. To brand him, claim him. And he wanted to do the same.

He stood and led Tar to the bed. "On your back," he told Tar, who did as he said. He watched Loch strip quickly, grab lube and then mount him.

Loch grabbed Tar's wrists and brought his hands over his head, pinning his arms to the bed. Wanted to tie him, but he also wanted Tar's hands on him because a wild Tar was a beautiful thing to witness. He'd watched other men take off Tar's restraints for just that pleasure.

There's plenty of time to do everything you want to do with him...

Tar's body was hot against his...his breathing was fast, and Loch loved being the one doing that to him...because he'd been as jealous of Creed touching him as he'd been turned on. Jealous, because he wanted to touch and taste. "God, want to hear all those sounds just for me."

"Surrounded by jealous possessive types," Tar murmured. "Creed said the same thing."

"You trying to rile me up?"

"Little bit, yes."

It'd been so long since he'd been this close to Tar's bare skin and fuck, now this was his—not just under his control, but under him. Skin to skin, one on one.

He pressed his lips to Tar's shoulder, then licked, tasting

him. "Gonna eat you up, Tar. Gonna taste you everywhere. But first? I'm going to take you hard." Tar grunted in response. Loch knew what he needed. What he craved. "I'm going to make you lose your goddamned mind, and then? I'm going to come inside of you. Claim you."

"Like we did to Creed?"

"Like we did to Creed." Loch let go of his arms and flipped the cap on the lube, using a generous amount on his fingers before they circled Tar's hole. Tar opened his legs for him, inviting his touches, moving to Tar's rhythm. Rising off the bed and crying out when Loch's knuckle caressed his gland.

Loch heard himself growl with impatience. "You're going to feel me for a week, baby."

"Yes—want that."

"After this is all over, we'll invite Creed in. All of us."

"Yes," Tar agreed.

Loch coated his cock with lube and threw one of Tar's legs over his shoulder as he raised on his knees and pushed inside, watching his dick disappear inside of Tar. "So fucking hot."

Tar arched up into the invasion. "C'mon, Loch—take me," he insisted, and Loch did, grabbed Tar's hips and slid in until he was balls-deep inside of him. And then he fucked him with a ruthless rhythm. It was all Tar could do to hold onto him for the goddamned ride and Loch loved watching him try as much as the pure molten desire in his eyes.

Everything he did was for Tar's pleasure as much as his.

And when Tar's body drew up tight, he snarled Loch's name as he came all over his stomach and chest. Once that happened, Loch knew there was no going back to life without

Tar ever again. He leaned in and kissed him, a brutally rough, perfect kiss, like he was branding himself on Tar's lips.

Waves of desire washed through him as he came inside of Tar, and he knew he'd never need whiskey again.

Tar hated keeping things from his best friend, and it had been easy to forget all about Liam. Easier especially because he'd let the orgasms take away the majority of his brain cells.

He didn't want to lose Loch…not when he'd finally gotten him back.

"I have to talk to Dr. LaSalle—about the drinking," Loch told him, and the guilt hung on Tar more heavily. "He's going to want me in-patient. That's what he told me last time."

"Is that a bad thing?" Tar asked carefully.

"You won't be there."

Tar grinned like a goddamned teenager. "I'll visit. And I'll be waiting when you get out." And if only that's all there was, how fucking simple would all of this be?

"Did you already talk to Jasper about my drinking?" Loch asked finally.

"He asked, I answered. I don't make excuses for you on that front."

"I know." Loch didn't seem upset.

In fact, Tar hadn't seen any real cracks in his countenance. But when rehab—and Loch's withdrawal—started, things would be different. They always were. And even now, Tar didn't bother pretending that Loch didn't have whiskey with him, that he wouldn't take a drink when Tar wasn't looking. "It's going to be okay, Loch. You've had a rough year."

Loch frowned, ran an elegant hand through his dark hair. The guy was so fucking handsome, he took Tar's breath away at the most unexpected times. "It's guilt, Tar. That's all it is. I was trying to have something...different with Liam. Something normal, and it never worked the way it should have. If I'd just listened..."

"You seemed...to really be into him." This was like walking on eggshells, if eggshells were really IEDs and could blow you into a million pieces and fuck, Tar wondered if he could just talk Loch into fucking him again and end this conversation. "I don't fault you for missing him."

"When I first slept with Travis...I called him Liam," Loch admitted, and Tar side-eyed him.

"I'm hoping that doesn't happen here."

Loch snorted. "I told him I was going to call him that."

"Because you missed him that much?"

"Because I was trying not to think about you." Loch brushed his knuckles over Tar's cheek. "Don't give up on me, okay?"

Tar had to clear his throat before he answered, and when he did, he heard the raw promise in his own voice. "Couldn't if I wanted to."

CHAPTER TWENTY-TWO

THE HOSPITAL WASN'T AT ALL what Creed expected. Which he supposed was the point. It looked like a villa that belonged in Italy or the south of France.

He'd been to both with Travis in the lead, but he'd come out to sightsee. Travis was good like that, but he wanted no part of this shit, which could pose a problem when it came to identifications.

"You okay?" Loch asked before they walked inside.

Creed looked at him. "There's no more choice not to be."

"There's always a choice."

"Then I guess I've made mine." Creed stepped in through the door Tar held open. The carpet was an expensive area rug on a dark hardwood floor. An impeccable, elegant desk was helmed by an equally elegant woman, hair in a neat bun, stylish clothes and subtle makeup.

"Hello, Kassia," Tar greeted her. "You remember Loch, and this is Creed."

She nodded in his direction. "Visiting?"

"Yes."

She gave them each passes that clipped on. "This tells the men and women that you're safe. Friends. Vetted." She looked pointedly at Creed. "Don't fuck this up."

Creed frowned. "You're one of us."

She confirmed by holding up her exposed wrists and showing matching crescent cuts to his. "Don't fuck this up," she repeated.

He nodded because all that wanted to come out was, "I'll think about it," and that wouldn't go over very well. And when they were far enough away, Loch answered his unspoken question.

"There weren't many women. Snow used a select few... for breeding purposes." Loch looked like he hated saying the words as much as Creed hated hearing them. Without comment, he followed Tar, with Loch by his side, up the wide staircase one flight. "This is the unlocked wing."

Creed still tensed as they walked through. He glanced into some opened doors to see the non-institutional looking bedrooms. A larger room opened up in the middle of the hall with windows all around that let sunlight stream in. There were couches and TVs and books and everything Creed would've wanted during the days he was chained up.

Two men lay on opposite couches—one engrossed in his book and the other, his iPad. They barely looked up, and Creed hated that. Were they so used to being looked at, like animals in a cage?

They're in here voluntarily. A cage of their own making. Were they locking the world out...or themselves in?

"Recognize either man?" Tar asked.

Creed shook his head tightly and then turned and left.

"They're not social, but they'd make conversation if you spoke to them," Tar offered.

"Is that supposed to be comforting?" His voice sounded tight as his body felt, like the fight-or-flight response was kicking in big time. "I want to see the locked ward."

"We don't call it—"

Creed cut him off. "But that's what it is."

Tar glanced at Loch then motioned for them to follow him into an elevator that needed a code to take them upstairs. "You won't be in the room with any of them. There are two way mirrors—if they agree."

"Do they usually?" Creed asked.

Loch wasn't offering anything, and Creed couldn't tell if he was angry or upset or both. Creed was definitely both, more so when they hit the floor lined with the mirrors. Tar walked ahead, hitting a switch along each one.

"If they want to be seen, they hit the switch on the other side," Loch explained.

"Do they always have that choice?"

"Not from the doctors, but from everyone else," Loch said.

A few windows flickered, but the majority of them remained dark. "Can they see me?"

"If you want them to, sure," Tar said.

Creed took a deep breath. "Let them." And after Tar turned the two-way mirrors on, Creed walked up to the closest one. A man with a shaved head, tattoos on his skull, and a shirtless chest glared at him while otherwise standing still as a statue.

"That's Otto," Tar told him. "He's not allowed out if he asks."

Creed didn't want to sell him out by saying he could see why. "I've never seen him before."

"He used to look different," Tar offered, then flipped through an album nestled inside a door pocket. He handed it over, opened to a picture, at the same time Otto's body hit the glass.

Creed stared at him, Otto's face pressed in a snarl, blood on his forehead, and then tore his gaze away to stare at the photo...and even though he didn't need to, he was already saying, "I know him," before glancing down.

"Does he do this a lot?" Creed asked.

"Never. He's got a history of random violence, which was why he checked himself in here willingly. And he always volunteers to be seen."

Like he's been looking for someone.

"Shit," Tar muttered. Otto continued slamming the glass with his large hands, palms smacking the mirror, head pounding, a wild look in his eyes. Suddenly, the room began to fog up.

"What the hell's that?"

"Gas," Loch said. "It's too dangerous to go in there to calm him down until he's out."

"He was always like that." Creed didn't know why he was whispering. He'd never been scared of Otto, had even fought him in the pit a couple of times, which were fights sanctioned by Snow. Hand to hand, they'd been pretty evenly matched. Whether or not Travis knew him was another story, and one he probably needed to know. "I want to talk to him."

"No," both men said loudly, but Creed was already

pressing the button. "Otto, calm the fuck down, or they won't let me come in and talk to you. And I will come in—alone."

Whether it was Creed's words or the gas, he didn't know, but Otto stopped hitting the glass and instead walked back to sit on his bed.

"Listen, Tony's going to have to assess him. We need to leave for a few minutes and let everything calm down." Tar was tugging him away from the glass, and Creed caught a glimpse of Otto falling to the floor before the two-way mirror was switched off.

"I want to talk to him," Creed insisted, even as he let himself be led into a quiet room down the hall. There was a couch and a chair, and Loch shut the door behind them.

Tar sat next to him and Loch across from them in the chair, even as Creed tried to sort out everything he was thinking.

"Can you tell us how you know Otto?" Tar asked finally because he couldn't seem to make his thoughts do anything but dance around in his brain, too fast for him to grasp and hold any of them.

"He was one of Snow's guards. I used to fight him—like the fights that Snow orchestrated," he added, and Tar nodded, and judging by his expression, he recalled those fights as vividly as Creed did. Fucking bloodsport for Snow.

"Do you remember escaping? Did he help you? Did you fight him to escape?" Loch pressed, and there was a strange energy in the air that Creed couldn't quite label.

He closed his eyes and shook his head against the low level buzz that started reviving inside his brain. "Fuck, no...I don't know. All of the escape was Travis's doing." He opened his eyes. "If Otto was one of Snow's...why would he lock himself in here? Did he escape too?"

"That's what we need to find out," Tar told him. "Up until now, we thought he was another victim. That's what he told us when we rescued him."

Creed frowned. "When you rescued him? When was that?"

"Maybe four years ago," Tar said. "He originally escaped from Snow's compound during the fire, when we escaped." He pointed between himself and Loch, who nodded. "Remember, we lost track of everyone after that. It was only after we met with Jasper and Tony that we were able to go out and try to collect those who escaped, for lack of a better word."

"That doesn't make any sense." Creed was speaking more to himself than to them, his mind working fast to detangle the threads. "Four years ago..."

"What is it, Creed?" Tar cupped his chin and forced Creed to look at him. "Tell me what's bothering you about this."

"I knew Otto. You knew Otto. That meant he not only escaped the fire..."

"He followed Snow," Tar finished. "Is he the only one you recognize?"

"So far, yes." Creed stared at Tar and told him the thing he suspected Tar—and Loch—wanted to hear. "None of the other guys I was locked up with are here. What does that mean?"

"Nothing good," Loch murmured, coming to sit next to him. He put a hand protectively on Creed's shoulder, partially to try to calm him down. Tar moved his hand from Creed's face, and Creed immediately missed the contact.

"I need you to tell me what this means." Creed fisted his hands on his thighs.

Tar sighed. "It means that either all of you escaped and those men are in the wind, like you were—or fuck, if you were the only one who escaped..."

"That Snow could still have a compound out there," Loch finished.

"And Otto?" Creed asked, but Tar and Loch wouldn't have that answer. Creed might have it—or Travis—but fuck, Creed wanted his memories. All of them. For the first time, having Travis tuck parts of his life away bothered him instead of comforting him. "So you really didn't know...about Otto?"

"If we had, we would've put him in a different place. Questioned him differently." Loch shook his head. "So he went from being tortured to doing the torture."

"Looks that way," Tar said, then turned toward Creed. "You want to go in there and get some intel? Or are you worried he'll trigger you?"

"Aren't you worried?" Creed asked.

"Yes. But we're putting off the inevitable otherwise," Tar admitted.

"And if it does, you'll leave me here?"

"You've already seen him. If you trigger, it will be..."

"Something he says," Creed answer flatly.

"And we'll hear it. Figure out how to reverse it," Loch promised. "Snow built in an off switch to the triggers. Otherwise, the men would just kill and kill indiscriminately. He couldn't have that—he'd burn through them faster than he could create them."

Creed took a deep breath. "And if I make it through this part, you'll make me remember everything else?"

"We can talk to Tony," Tar started. "And we can talk to Travis and try to piece your memories together that way too."

"Whatever it takes," Creed told them. "When can I talk to Otto?"

"He's going to try to mindfuck you," Tar warned.

"Of course he is. You think I don't know how to mindfuck anymore?" Creed narrowed his eyes, and Tar gave him a small smile.

"I know you remember how to. I just wish there was another way."

"If I'm going to help you guys find Snow, then this is the only way." Creed sounded more confident than he felt, but fuck it—it wasn't like he didn't have backup here. For the first time, he wasn't alone... and he didn't just mean having Travis to help him out of a tough spot. No, he had the men in front of him, and Tony and Jasper too.

He just hoped that it would all be enough.

CHAPTER TWENTY-THREE

AN HOUR LATER, Creed heard the quiet snick as the door locked behind him. The room was pleasant and cool, and Otto was restrained by chains that allowed him to stand and lie down on the comfortable-looking bed he sat on. He was staring straight ahead at the wall that had some kind of mural drawn on it, but he didn't necessarily look high or spacey—Tony assured him that the effects of the gas didn't last long, and that Otto woke up calm, so they hadn't needed to sedate him.

If things get out of hand, they'll gas both of us and get me out.

It sounded less and less reassuring every time he said it to himself.

"Otto, it's Creed." He spoke quietly, like Otto was an animal who could spook easily. Hell, it was the way most people talked to him, and usually it worked.

Otto turned to stare at him and blinked. "Yeah, I saw you. I don't slam my head against the glass for just anyone."

"I guess I should be flattered."

Otto dismissed that notion immediately. "I was hoping it was Travis. Where is he?"

"He's in...in here." Creed pointed to his head.

Otto rolled his eyes. "Yeah, tell me something I don't know. Can't you bring him out?"

"It doesn't work like that."

"You were always a pain in the fucking ass." Otto leaned back on his elbows, the chains clanking. "Are you slumming? Or checking yourself in? Or did they tell you that you could come look around without letting you know they could always lock you in here without your permission?"

He's just baiting you. And doing a damned good job. "How well did you know Travis?"

"Well enough." Otto's gaze was suggestive. "Your personalities are the perfect mix of fuck and fight."

Creed hated that his body had been close to this man—that Otto had been inside of him. That Travis had to accept it willingly. "That was a long time ago."

"Seems like it just happened yesterday." Otto frowned, like he was trying to remember something. Creed didn't ask if the men and women here were drugged regularly or if there were any other procedures done to keep them calm—to keep them from remembering. "Snow loved Travis. But because of you..."

"Snow wanted men who were split."

"He did, but he couldn't control you. Not the way he wanted to."

"So why not kill me if I was that much trouble? Why expend so much energy on someone who wasn't conforming?"

"Because the ones who conformed weren't the right type

of personality for Snow to work with. And he was perfectly willing to train Travis to kill. And Travis was good at it. Very in control."

Creed kept his expression neutral, not wanting to reveal to Otto—or to Loch and Tar, who were watching—that he felt betrayed by Travis...for the first time ever.

No, Travis protected you. He hasn't been on random killing sprees. He wouldn't do that...

"You zone out like that a lot?" Otto made the 'crazy' motion with his finger near the side of his forehead. "Because if that happens too much, they'll drug you, first chance they get."

Creed heard the cage door creaking, the subtle buzz that happened when Travis went into protection mode. But this would be the worst time for Travis to come out. "Is that what they do to you?"

"I'm calm."

"Really?" Creed asked as sarcastically as possible.

"Never fucking liked you, Creed."

"Yeah, you've mentioned that. But yet, here we are."

Otto tugged at the restraints. "You locking yourself in here? Because I could always use a good fight. And if Travis comes back out..."

Creed shrugged and ignored the need to punch Otto in the fucking face. "I've been out for eight years. I have no idea what my triggers are."

"Isn't that a bitch." Otto stared at him, eyes glazed but still unsettled. "I never got an alter. I'm just a bastard all the time."

"Yeah, well, so am I. We both learned from the best." Creed stared around the room. Otto had taken to drawing all over the main walls in black sharpie marker. It looked like a giant map, half mural and hand figures.

"Recognize it?" Otto asked finally.

"No."

"Look all the way to the right—bottom corner. The path starts before that," Otto instructed.

Creed spotted the path and followed it, first with his eyes only and then found himself touching each individual step, a feeling of dread growing fierce in his chest.

He half kicked the garbage can blocking the picture out of the way to see the final piece of the path and where it led. But he knew before he saw and touched it, and the thick bile rose in his throat.

He stumbled, almost falling, and then Otto was there, chains clinking, reminding Creed of another time and place...

"How'd you get in good with the boss?" Otto murmured as his hands were on Creed's body, steadying him. Holding him in place.

Creed blinked, and his vision started to clear, but the buzz was loud and threatened to drown everything out. *Dammit, not now, Travis.* "Loch and Tar aren't my bosses."

"Oh, you don't know shit, do you, Creed?" Otto sneered. "You don't even know that Loch is Snow's nephew? His right-hand man? You think you can trust him? Haven't you figured out by now that you can't trust anyone?"

At Otto's words, Creed felt the invisible noose around his neck tighten, and the blackness closed in before he could stop it.

"What the fuck did you do to him?" Tar had Otto by the neck while Loch and Tony were on the floor helping Creed.

"Nothing. Remember?" Otto rattled the restraints. "I just showed him his past and he flipped out."

"You were holding onto him," Tar snarled.

"Because he looked like he was going to faint." Otto's voice was hoarse, and it took everything Tar had not to kill him on the spot. The only reason he didn't was because this man was suddenly of great value in the war against Snow.

"What was he looking at and where?" Loch demanded as Tony broke a capsule under Creed's nose to revive him.

"Right corner—right near where he is now," Otto managed. Tar held onto him while both men turned their attention to the spot Otto spoke of, a part of a drawing Tar himself had seen hundreds of times.

When Otto began drawing a map of Snow's compound on his wall, Tony had kept them updated on his progress. The mural had been finished for quite a while, and Tar had recognized it immediately—especially the spot in the corner, which had been his home for eight long years.

So why would that have affected Creed so deeply?

"Which compound is this?" Tar asked Otto now.

"I don't know what you're talking about."

Tar slammed Otto to the floor, the chains rattling, and Otto tried to fight back. But Tar was quicker. Stronger. Had far more goddamned anger, which was probably what Otto had been counting on. He forced himself to breathe through the familiar pain because it would be all too easy to invite the animal that was still inside of him out to play. "Tell me about the second compound. The one where you met Creed."

Otto smiled. "Can't believe there's something the great Loch and Tar didn't know about."

Tar's hand formed a fist, and he began punching Otto's face until Loch pulled him off.

Tar almost fought him—almost. But Loch was murmuring to him, telling him, "It's okay" and "We'll figure it out, but we need Otto alive."

"He doesn't have to be in one piece," Tar said finally.

"Come on, let's get out of here." Loch led him out of the room and down the hall. Medical staff was with Otto, and Tony had taken Creed by stretcher into the medical facilities.

They went up to the third floor and waited outside the locked doors, while Tony was with Creed. There was nothing to be gained by interrupting him.

"Think he's okay?" Tar asked finally.

"He's strong," Loch reminded him. "Like you."

"Like you," Tar answered, the dialogue familiar, spoken almost every time they brought someone new here. But Creed? He was obviously different. "How's your hand?"

Tar glanced down at the swollen and cut knuckles. "Works just fine."

Loch snorted and took Tar's hand in his, brushed a fingertip over his skin. "We should find a first aid kit."

"We should do a lot of things," Tar grumbled. They were both putting off talking about the day's events—and the magnitude of what had been uncovered. How far behind Snow they actually were...and had always been. Tar felt the defeat deep in his goddamned soul. Had they made any progress? Had Snow been laughing at them the entire time?

"We helped everyone in this place," Loch reminded him. "And we took Otto off the streets."

"To what end? He looked like he was waiting for the right person to show up." And that person happened to be Creed. Or Travis, from the sound of it.

"If Travis was trained by Snow, he had ample opportunity to kill both of us." Loch continued to hold his hand, which by now had started to ache.

"He lived in a fucking dirt hole, six feet down with a chain around his neck. A choke chain. And that was actually when he was being good," Tar said quietly.

"Are you thinking about him...or you?" Loch asked, right before the screaming started from behind the door. Travis, screaming like his life depended on it...and it probably did.

Tar tiredly leaned his head back against the wall as the yelling promised to burn itself into his brain. "Is there really any difference?"

CHAPTER TWENTY-FOUR

IN HIS HAZE, Creed was traveling—back to Snow's, with the threat of the box looming over him and Travis buzzing in his brain, keeping him calm.

Travis had always been the cooperative one...but that didn't mean he was at all innocent. In fact, he could be more deceptive than Creed. But on that day, Creed didn't know that, and neither did Snow.

What the latter did know was that he had a ten-year-old boy who was defiant and angry, who took the skull-splitting music and the sensory deprivation of the cave, the beatings and the torture, and still never broke.

In fact, Creed had spit at Snow in the moments before he heard the cage door close.... except he realized he wasn't in the dark box buried in the cool, damp ground. He was still standing across from Snow, but when he opened his mouth to speak, he wasn't the one talking. He reached out but ended up grabbing the cold metal bars to a cage instead, an open air cage. That voice speaking to Snow called to him too, somehow soothingly so, telling him, "Lock yourself inside until it's safe. I've got this. I've got you."

Was this another one of Snow's tricks? It didn't feel like that. It felt...safe. And just like that, the boy who'd never known a friend had one. "I'm Travis, not Creed," said friend was telling Snow, and Creed stared out of Travis's eyes and into Snow's.

"Really?" Snow frowned. "It's nice to meet you, Travis. I hope you can talk some sense into Creed. Because things always go so much better if you simply follow the rules."

"That doesn't sound complicated at all," Travis said, and Creed swore Travis said to him, "Let me handle Snow. I'll do what he wants. You look for escape opportunities. After you rest."

After you rest...

But I *am* you.

Christ, Creed was losing his fucking mind. But even as he struggled to listen to Travis and Snow, he felt himself get heavy. And the cage had plenty of room to lie down comfortably and just sleep.

And so he did. For how long, he wasn't sure, but when he woke, Travis was obediently going through one of Snow's mental ability conditioning tests. Creed had always fought those tooth and nail but Travis was flying through it, and Snow? Was actually smiling.

Back to sleep, Creed.

Whether Travis was on his side or not, Creed wasn't sure at the time. Later on, there would be no such doubt. And it went on like that, a comfortably numb space...until the terror began anew.

It hit him like the slap of a whip, the cold terror, stark and bleak, shaking him roughly from a sound sleep. It took him several minutes to realize he was the one screaming.

No, not him. Travis. Travis was...shattering. Broken glass sparkled into the air in a million pieces, sharp shards piercing inward until Creed growled, and the cage door slammed open.

The pain throbbed inside his skull, threatening to explode, and pain lashed at his back, but the latter was the familiar pain.

He heard Snow's voice clearly now as he was being whipped, and he shut his mouth.

The screaming stopped. Travis calmed and seemed to disappear. Dissipate.

And Snow? Noticed immediately. "Welcome back, Creed." And indeed, Snow did welcome him back until the blood ran warm down the back of his naked thighs.

"Creed...where are you?" Loch's voice, yanking him out of the blood and the box and the torturous rage. He opened his eyes to meet Loch's worried ones and opened his mouth to speak, but only a croak came out of his oddly sore throat.

"It's not good." Tony was never one to sugarcoat anything, and judging by the look on his face, *not good* was a major understatement.

"Figured that from the screaming," Tar said bleakly, even as Tony studied his bleeding hand. It was almost an hour from when they'd first heard the screams, and they'd finally slowed to sobbing whispers.

"Let's get this fixed up now then get some ice on it," Tony told him, and Tar followed him over to one of the tables and sat on it. Loch remained in the corner, staring at the door Creed was behind.

"Otto either saw me, or Snow told him about me," Loch said finally, and Tar's chest tightened because he knew exactly *how* Otto knew—goddamned Liam. He glanced up at Tony, who, to his credit, kept his focus only on Tar's hand.

Tony and Jasper both were going to talk with Loch about Liam today. Probably would have already, if Creed hadn't recognized Otto.

"Is he going to be okay, Tony?" Tar asked.

"It's too soon to know that." Tony finished up the stitches and gave Tar a disposable icepack and some Advil. "You can see him for a little while, if you think that might help."

Tar didn't know if that would help or hurt. The fact that Creed—Travis—knew who Loch was...

"Major damage," Loch murmured. "Should've told him."

"No," Tar said, his voice raised. "You couldn't be sure of what he'd do. He's in the right place to learn this. If he wasn't here..."

Fuck, he didn't want to think about that. Because Loch still had his own shit to deal with, and he didn't even know it.

Loch went in first. Tony had told them one at a time, and Travis seemed to lose it again the second he noticed Loch. He'd been screaming for the last ten minutes, and nothing Loch did or said had been able to bring him back out of it.

"He's got to do it himself," Tony told him. "Travis is screaming. And if Creed's trying to come back out, Travis is blocking him."

If Creed was trying. "This is because of me."

"Loch, he had to know eventually."

"And it was always going to breed distrust. If I'd told him from the first, maybe we could've gotten past it." Loch hung his head.

"He's reliving what happened to him when he first met Snow."

"How do you know?"

"He was muttering about it earlier," Tony confirmed. "He was so young when it happened."

"He's still young." Loch watched Travis's face contort in pain, real or imagined. At least the screaming had subsided... probably because Travis closed his eyes and refused to look at either of them.

He'd endured years of torture already...and had so many more to go. And he was going to have to relive them all.

"He'll come out the other side," he murmured.

"Are you convincing him or you?" Tony asked, although not unkindly.

"Whichever one of us will believe it," Loch admitted.

"Come on—we'll let Tar sit with him while you and I talk."

"The big bad addiction talk?"

"That, and a few other things."

Tar slept maybe a total of six hours over the next forty-eight, and only because Jasper and Tony practically sat on him to do so. But even in sleep, he couldn't contain his worry for Loch and what he was about to endure, nor could he escape the nightmare that was unfolding before Creed. And his own nightmares joined in, making a shitty time even worse. So he spent his time lurking outside of doors, waiting for Tony to tell him he could go in and see one of the two men.

They were on separate floors, so tonight, Tar sat outside of the locked ward which housed Loch's room somewhere behind it, trying to will him to be okay...all the while knowing that Tony wouldn't break the rules by letting him see Loch just yet. Because rehab meant at least two weeks of isolation from outside forces.

He was just heading down the hall to the stairs that would lead him down to Creed's floor to try and worm his way inside because there wasn't any rehab rule happening there—just Jasper and Tony keeping him away—when Tony came out of the locked ward's door.

"Everything okay?" Tony asked him. "Because you look like shit."

"Thanks, Tony. You know how to lift me up when I'm down." Tar rolled his eyes. "You don't look so hot yourself."

Don't ask about Loch.... Don't ask about Loch... Don't....
"So, how's Loch?"

Tony sighed. "Forty seconds—a new record."

"C'mon, Tony. Please?"

"Things aren't going...great," Tony admitted.

"Shit." Tar leaned against the wall and let himself slide down to the ground.

Tony followed suit so the two of them were sitting on the floor together. "His withdrawal has been difficult."

"The meds usually help."

"This time, they're not." Tony looked troubled, and the man was usually pretty unflappable, at least where Loch and Tar were concerned.

"How bad is it? Can I see him?"

"Listen, if I thought it would help, I'd break the rules. But I think it might make things worse—for both of you."

Yeah, that didn't sound good at all. His gut clenched, and his nerves jangled. "He knows...about Liam?"

"We told him before the withdrawals started, yes. Of course, he was upset—more so because he thinks you sensed it and if he'd just listened to you..."

Tony was interrupted by someone slamming hard on the other side of the doors he'd just emerged from. Someone was pounding with their fists, making the heavy door shake, like someone was trying to break out.

And then Tar heard the yelling. "That's Loch."

"It's a new development. He's been doing that all day. He's now the only patient on the floor...with several guards on him."

"And he still manages to do that?" Tar shook his head. "Maybe he's having a bad reaction to the medication this time?"

"I thought of that too. He hasn't taken any for twenty-four hours, and things are just getting worse."

"I can't do this, Tony. I'm fucking helpless here." Tar's throat was tight with anger and fear. "You've got to let me do something."

Tony nodded. "Let's go see how Creed—or Travis—is doing."

Tar felt some relief flood his body. Just then, the slamming on the doors stopped, and fuck, he hoped Loch was going to be able to get through his withdrawals sooner than later. But really, at this point, he and Loch would probably fight, and it wouldn't do either of them any good.

CHAPTER TWENTY-FIVE

TWENTY MINUTES LATER, Tony got Tar the clearance he needed to go into Creed's room.

Creed—*no*, still Travis—was lying on his side on the hospital bed staring into space.

Did it matter that it wasn't Creed? Yes, Tar had to admit that it did. He liked Travis, knew Travis would possibly always be a part of Creed...but ultimately, Creed was the person he and Loch were involved with. Travis was simply another part of Creed, and because of that, Tar would treat Travis gently. Because Travis ultimately had Creed's back.

Whether or not he was a Snow-level assassin remained to be seen.

"He had a bad nightmare about fifteen minutes ago," one of the nurses told them, keeping her voice low. "He came out of it on his own, so we didn't give him anything, as per your instructions."

Tony nodded and motioned for Tar to follow him over.

"Hey, Travis?" Tony leaned down, seemed to be trying to get Travis to meet his gaze. Tar saw a flicker of eye movement, a bit of acknowledgement from Travis and pushed forward. "Tar's here. He wanted to see you. I think it'll be good for you, okay?"

No answer. No nod of the head, but still, Tony moved out of the way, and Tar pulled up a seat close to Travis.

He's unpredictable. Don't get to close to him. Be on alert. All Tony's warnings in the elevator up here went out the window, and all Tar wanted to do now was climb into bed and reassure Travis that Creed was going to be all right, that he should let Creed out.

But hell, none of them could promise that Creed would be all right—not at all. Otto knew more than he was saying, and even though Creed's body had been scanned, who knew what other kind of technology Snow had bought from friends in other countries?

"Hey, Travis—it's Tar." This time, Travis did make eye contact, almost immediately, and Tar felt like Travis had locked onto his soul. "Are you feeling any better?"

Travis shook his head no. And then he brought his hand up to touch the side of his face, and he frowned.

"Does your head hurt?"

Travis shook his head no again and then looked at his hand before bringing it back up to the side of his head. He did that several times, and finally, Tar understood—had first-hand experience with what Travis had been dreaming about.

"There's no gun, Travis. You were dreaming about something that happened to you when you were with Snow. It's not real...not this time." Because it *had* been real, a real game with a real gun.

Travis nodded then seemed to finally notice that his

wrists weren't restrained. He seemed surprised. And cautious. He licked his lips, and Tar handed him the water cup that was close by, held the straw to Travis's lips, and Travis drank deeply. "Did he make you play Russian Roulette too?"

"Yeah, he did."

"But we didn't break." Travis gave a small smile and closed his eyes briefly.

Tar didn't press anything. Hell, just the mention of Russian Roulette was enough to make him panic, and he was pretty sure the entire room could hear the fast thrum of his heartbeat.

As if in response, Travis opened his eyes and motioned for Tar to come closer. When he did, Travis touched a finger to Tar's carotid pulse lightly. "Tar, take a breath."

Tar nodded woodenly, and suddenly, Travis was sitting up, murmuring in his ear and when had this become about him? He was supposed to be comforting Travis. But obviously no one had given Travis the memo.

"Just let me hold you," Travis murmured, and Tar leaned in and let him do so. Because he needed holding—probably had for a long time—and both Travis and Creed had homed in on that because they were as dangerous and damaged as he was.

Because like recognized like.

Travis was reassuring both of them, saying, "Not real" and "You're safe" and "He's not here and can't hurt you without your consent." Only after Tar's pulse returned to normal did Travis move away. But he didn't go far. "Where's Otto?"

"He's locked up."

"He shouldn't be. I don't think. He was always nice to me." Travis looked as confused as Tar felt.

"I don't think Creed saw it that way," Tar told him. "So for now, Otto stays put."

"I can talk to him?"

"From behind the glass, yes. If that's what you really want to do."

"We both knew him, didn't we? Creed and I?"

"Yes. Creed knew him, but Otto thought he was Travis... so it seems like he wanted to talk to you the most."

Travis's cheeks flushed. Tar wanted to press him, probably should have done so, but for the moment, he just handed Travis more water. There were several full bottles on the table by the bed, and he handed Travis one. He downed an entire bottle and half of a second before telling Tar, "I tricked Otto and escaped."

"Is that why he wants to talk to you?"

"Maybe." Travis shrugged. "He shouldn't know that he was the reason I was able to leave though."

"Because you grifted him somehow? Tricked him?"

"Something like that." Travis glanced around as if worried he'd get in trouble for admitting that.

"Otto was Snow's then? His soldier?"

Travis nodded. "Definitely. He was actually a lot higher up than he seemed. He told me that Snow wanted it that way. Made it easier for him to find out if anyone had any escape plans."

Shit. "And he told you because..."

Travis grimaced. "He thought I was in love with him. That I'd stay with him. That's why he trained me...to be like him."

"Do you think you're programmed?"

Travis gave a genuine smile. "No. I let them think I was really into it. I mean, I learned a lot of things I knew I'd need after I escaped. I couldn't count on Creed for everything. I didn't want to burden him all the time. I wanted to help. So I threw myself into training, and Snow gave up on training Creed. He said I was pliable. Compliant. Competent." He didn't look pleased by the compliments he recalled. "I hated when he touched me. Hated every fucking second of it."

Tar nodded, the familiar weight on his body returning. He wondered how quickly Otto would inform Travis about Loch and his connection to Snow.

And was that why Otto was waiting for Travis to show up, all this time? Would that prove to be Travis's trigger, even though he didn't think he had a trigger at all?

Tar hoped he was right.

"How's Loch?" Travis asked finally.

"He's...in rehab."

"How are you?"

"Worried about both of you." Travis worked his fingers in Tar's and put his head against his shoulder, admitting, "Creed's really mad at me."

"Why?"

"I'm scared to tell you. You've already felt his pain."

"I'm tough. I can handle things better than Creed. I've just never felt him like that."

"Wounded."

"That's a good way to put it."

Tar sighed. "Creed learned something about Loch. And he felt betrayed. I can understand it, but Loch's my best friend. I wouldn't be this close to him if he was anything like Snow."

"He's nothing like Snow."

If Travis was going to learn about this—if he was going to be triggered, this was the right place for it to happen. "Loch is Snow's nephew, Travis. That's when I met him."

Travis let his hand slide out of Tar's, but he didn't say anything.

Tar drew in a shaky breath before continuing. "Loch was coming in from boarding school the night Snow lit his compound on fire. I killed Loch's brother; he was Snow's right hand man and I hated him. Loch and I fought, but I realized fast that he'd been abused by Snow his entire life. Didn't know anything about what his uncle was doing."

Travis stared at him. "You helped him escape."

"We helped each other escape. And he's been working with me and Jasper ever since to help take Snow down."

"And Otto told Creed this?"

"Yes. And that's why.... you ended up here. Creed freaked out and you..."

"Rescued him from his pain," Travis added. "He didn't want me to. I forced my way out. I've never had to do that before. What do you think that means?"

CHAPTER TWENTY-SIX

CREED WOKE, but he didn't open his eyes—not right away. That was a trick he'd learned in the early days because the second you opened your eyes, you gave yourself away. So he'd learned to take several moments, keep his breathing deep and his face expressionless with no eyelid movement as he listened to who and what surrounded him.

In that pit, with the goddamn chain around his neck, he'd sworn he'd find a way out.

And he had.

That's how we ended up in the box.

"I had another boy who I built this for. I thought I'd never find another one who resisted the way you do. So this? There is no escape for you—not physically. And in time, not even from your own mind. You'll break," Snow promised.

Creed stared at him defiantly. "And the other boy? Did he break?" There was a small tell from Snow, and Creed swore that he wouldn't let the boy this box was built for down. He wouldn't fail.

Obviously, it could be done.

He just hadn't realized how high of a price he'd pay. And dammit, he'd paid.

He yanked himself out of those memories because the familiar buzz was there, and no, Travis didn't need to protect him again. Creed needed to figure out why Travis had come out again in the first place.

The smell was pleasant but industrial. A hospital? His head hurt, and the soft sounds of the television filtered through his brain. He heard someone moving around in the background—a woman, judging by the soft footsteps and the slight smell of perfume.

He slitted one eyelid and saw the lights—not harsh—and realized he didn't feel threatened as much as cautious. So he blinked and turned his head and saw a woman in scrubs—a nurse—coming gingerly towards him.

"Do you need anything? Advil for your head? You're due for more," she said calmly.

Would it really be Advil? He couldn't be sure so he shook his head.

"I'll get Tony LaSalle—that might make you more comfortable," she said.

"Tar," he murmured.

"I'll get Tar as well," she agreed and went to the phone. She didn't try to muffle her voice when she said, "Tony, can you come in and see—" She glanced at him, like she wasn't sure exactly who he was, and hell, that explained the memory lapse. "Your patient? He's awake...and he's asked for Tar specifically.... okay, I'll tell him."

She hung up and said, "They're both coming in now."

As if on cue, the door opened. Creed sat up slowly and put his back against the wall but remained seated on the bed as Tony and Tar approached him.

"You need something for your head—I can see the pain in your eyes," Tony told him. "Just Advil. I'll give you something stronger if you need it—but I'd rather not make you drowsy."

Yeah, that made both of them. He nodded, and she brought him Advil and a soda, and he downed the pills and the drink. And then he glanced over at Tar, who looked worried as fuck.

And then everything came back to him, and his fist crushed the soda can in response.

"Creed, take a breath," Tony warned.

"You take a fucking breath," Creed spat then turned his attention back to Tar. "And you? Why don't you tell me what you and Loch conveniently forgot to before now? I'm sure it just slipped your mind that Loch is related to Snow, right?"

"We were going to tell you..."

"Once I was here, right? So you could stop me from trying to kill Loch?" he asked, and Tar at least had the decency to nod. "Christ. And you wanted trust."

"You can trust me."

"You helped do this to me by not telling me that Loch was one of Snow's."

"No, he was never one of Snow's," Tar said fiercely. "He was born into the family that hurt you, yes. And that's not something he can ever take back. But he's tried to make things better—tried to fix what his uncle and his brother did."

"Where's his brother?"

"He's dead," Tar said flatly. "I killed him after I escaped... right before I tried to kill Loch."

Creed absorbed that. "Should've finished the job," he said, right before he lunged at Tar.

―――――――

Thankfully, Creed had been too weak to do much damage, and Tony must've sensed his agitation because he'd managed to inject Creed with a sedative as soon as Tar took him down.

Creed didn't pass out completely, but he was groggy—and pissed. "Get the fuck off me, Tar. Don't ever want you touching me again. Go away and leave me here."

Something broke inside of Tar, and he'd done as Creed asked, walked out of the room and out of the facility and ended up back at the hotel, although he didn't really remember driving there. His mind was a blur of emotions as he realized he'd lost Creed and Loch both to Snow within a twenty-four-hour period.

And after several hours, the familiar anger snaked up his spine...that other part of him might've unified, but it was still there, waiting for the right pressure, the right circumstance to break out.

And losing the two most important people in his life?

Yeah, that could do it.

"Tar, breathe." Jasper's hands were suddenly on either side of his head. "Come back to me. Please. I won't lose you—not like this."

He didn't question how Jasper found him, because that was Jasper...always several steps ahead. "It's hard."

"I know. But you're stronger. You're the strongest one and I need you. Creed needs you and Loch needs you. Please. Don't go back to the way you were."

"I don't want to, but..."

"But you're angry. So angry. But you can't use that anger against your best interests. That's letting Snow win. You're stronger than he is, and you always were."

"If I split again..."

"I'll take care of you. Tony and I will never abandon you —never stop trying to get you back. But you're still here, Tar. You—just you. So breathe, and stay with me. Because I need your help with Creed and Loch."

Jasper's eyes were guileless. The man had never lied to him. Never abandoned him. He never would. And so he breathed, closed his eyes and felt Jasper's hands on him, listened to his soothing words, and finally—*finally*—the bitter anger seemed to dissipate, leaving him wrung out but all him.

He opened his eyes and saw Jasper, who nodded. "Good, Tar. That's really good."

Tar smiled. "First time anyone's ever called me good."

"Not true—you just haven't been listening very carefully." Jasper handed him a soda, and Tar drank it down, felt the sugar begin to level him.

"I should've told Creed myself. And I should've been the one to tell Loch about Liam."

"Your gut told you it was too dangerous to do either of those things—and you were right. Stop second guessing yourself. You can't take the entire weight of the world on your shoulders."

Tar nodded, let Jasper's words guide him. "I need to see Loch. I need to know what's happening to him."

"I think you already know."

"I need to see it. He needs to see me."

"It might make things worse."

"It's got to get worse before it gets better."

Jasper drove Tar back to the facility and walked him up to Loch's floor. Tony was waiting for them in the hallway, looking as worn out as Tar felt.

"Are you okay?" Tony put a hand on his cheek, and Tar nodded. "No, you're not. But I can't expect you to be."

"He'll get through this. We all will," Jasper said.

Tony's gaze flicked over to his. "I always believe you when you say it."

Tar smiled at the open affection between the men. At sixteen, he'd been surprised by it, but now, he'd never been more grateful for the lack of pretense. "How bad is he?"

"He's been calm since the last time you were up here. He listened to reason when I talked to him, but he's still not right." Tony frowned. "I think I should go in with you."

"I think that's the worst idea ever," Tar told him. "Loch's already feeling cornered. I don't expect our meeting to be warm and fuzzy, but it'll go much worse if he feels the need to bring backup."

"Agreed." Jasper nodded. "But you'll get gassed and dragged out of there if things go bad—just know that."

"Wouldn't expect anything less," Tar agreed. And five minutes later, he was walking down the hallway of the empty wing—save for three security guards—and headed to the room at the end of the hall.

One of the guards wanded him for weapons before he unlocked the door, more for their own safety than Tar's, in case Loch overpowered him. "Want me to keep it unlocked?"

"No, for your safety, lock it behind me."

"And what about your safety?" the man asked, but Tar just walked inside.

Loch was sitting on the floor of the padded room wearing scrubs, his legs spread, arms balanced on his knees, and head lowered. He raised his head up slowly, narrowing his eyes as he gave Tar a head-to-toe once-over that chilled him to the bone.

Because something in Loch's eyes wasn't right.

You're imagining things. Panicking. Calm the fuck down and talk to him, he ordered himself. "I needed to see you."

Loch laughed, a hoarse, unrecognizable chuff that did little to ease Tar's fears. "Came to confess your sins, Tar? I hear that's good for the soul."

Tar took several steps forward—and closer—to his best friend. "I need to tell you..."

Loch pushed himself up off the floor and closed the distance between them. "About Liam? About Creed knowing Liam? Because Jasper and Tony already broke the news to me."

Tar braced for a punch, a push, but neither came. "I wanted to tell you."

"But you thought I was too weak to handle it. You thought I'd need a full support system."

Tar crossed his arms. "Yes. That's exactly what I thought."

Loch rolled his eyes. "Such bullshit, Tar. You always talk about *us* and *trust* and..."

"You're not doing this. You're not making this about me. It's not my fault. Liam was Snow's."

"Just because Creed says it, that makes it so?"

Fuck, Tar didn't like the look in Loch's eyes—the tone of his voice. He wasn't unsteady—detoxing—none of the things he usually was when he quit drinking. Tony was right...none of this was good. "Why would Creed lie?"

"Because he's Snow's."

"That wasn't what you were saying yesterday afternoon."

Loch smiled. "Just because you're easy to get into bed doesn't mean you should believe everything you hear."

Tar tried to tell himself that the barb was just Loch lashing out because detoxing was never easy. But this was different—it was like Loch was a different person. "Liam was Snow's. He was too fucking perfect."

"He was more perfect for me than you ever were," Loch said. "That's why you hated him."

Tar needed to back the fuck out, to walk away before he heard something he couldn't unhear.

Addicts could be mean—when they lashed out, they tried to hurt you because they felt you hurt them.

Tony's words.

"Now you've turned Creed against me too."

"I didn't—fuck. I didn't think he'd have that kind of reaction. Did you?"

Loch shook his head. "You've got me right where you want me. Just ironic because you and Creed are the ones who belong in the psych ward."

"Loch—don't." He put a hand up like that could physically stop Loch's spew of hatred. "Please—"

"You're so fucked up," Loch continued. "I told Tony that

—how you let Creed fuck you. How you're always looking for affection. Maybe you're the reason I drink. I watched you kill my brother. How can I ever think of you as anything but a psychotic, broken murderer? Because that's all you are, no matter how hard you try."

Loch lunged at him even as his words echoed in Tar's soul and he moved swiftly out of the way to avoid the blow. He'd never seen Loch like this, not when he'd been drinking, or even in the early days. Even that first night, when they'd fought for their lives, it hadn't been blood sport, not like this.

Not with Loch's hands around his throat.

CHAPTER TWENTY-SEVEN

TAR WOKE with a cough and a gasp.

"It's okay, Tar—you're out here with us." Jasper's voice. Tar blinked and saw Tony standing on the other side of the bed. "We gassed the room. No choice. You weren't fighting back."

Tar nodded. "He's..."

"I know," Tony finished for him. "I'm going in there to talk to him. I'm going to try to hypnotize him."

"Dangerous," Tar managed. He grabbed for the water and let Jasper help him sit up while he drank.

"The gas will wear off in a few minutes," Tony assured him. "And yes, it's dangerous. But I did it for you, and look how things turned out."

"You think this is more than just detox." It came out as a statement, not a question but Tony nodded anyway. "You can't go in alone."

"I went in with you alone. I'll be fine," Tony tried to assure him but Tar didn't feel any better about it.

"I've never seen him like this. Never," Tar emphasized, then turned to Jasper. "He shouldn't be alone with Loch."

"It's his job, Tar. And he's got a damned good success rate. And if we're seeing what we're all afraid to say out loud, then Tony's the only one who should be with Loch right now." Jasper's words burned through him and Tar conceded because he wasn't really being given a choice.

"I want to watch," he insisted.

"We can do that," Jasper promised. "Both of us."

And after Tar recovered fully from the gas, and Tony felt prepared enough, they turned the camera on in Loch's cell.

"After the gas, he woke up and went back into that position," Tony told him.

Loch was in the same exact position he'd been when Tar came into the room. "He didn't freak out or try to escape? Nothing?"

"Nothing. He's just calm," Tony said.

"Maybe I misread this. Maybe he's just angry about the Liam thing. Betrayed by him and by me," Tar started.

"Well then, it shouldn't be hard to find that out." Tony put a hand on Jasper's shoulder and then said, "I'll be fine," before he left the room...but Tar couldn't be sure which one of them he was trying to convince.

He stood shoulder to shoulder with Jasper and watched Tony walk into the room. The audio was on, as Tar imagined it was when he was in there. He swallowed, hard, as Loch's head lifted slowly.

"Hey, Tony. I was hoping you'd come back."

"Why's that? You want to talk about why you're so pissed at your best friend?" Tony asked calmly.

Loch laughed, but it sounded all wrong. "And you're my friend too, right?"

"I'm your doctor, but yes, I'm your friend too."

"Which one are you right now?"

"Both, Loch. I can't separate them —I've known you for too long," Tony said honestly. "Why don't you start by telling me how you feel?"

"How I feel? I'm angry."

"Part of that's the detox."

"I don't want a drink. That's the last thing on my mind."

Tar shook his head. "That's not right. At the cabin, he couldn't go longer than a few hours without drinking."

"Was that normal?" Jasper asked.

"No, that was different. The last time, he could go days... weeks, even, without drinking." Tar's heart pounded. "Tony needs to get out of there."

"So trying to hurt Tar...it's anger because of Liam?" Tony was asking Loch.

Loch shrugged. "Tar always hated Liam. Never gave him a chance. I think he was jealous of him."

"Maybe he was. Liam took a lot of your time. Came between you, didn't he?"

"I wanted him to come between us." Loch rubbed his hands together as if he was cold. Then he began to shiver. Rock back and forth. "Fuck. So fucking cold."

"Loch, what's going on?"

"I don't know. I'm freezing. Why's the air on?" Loch's teeth were chattering, and Tony moved closer to him, as Loch's eyes rolled back in his head.

Jasper was already dialing for a medic when it happened.

Loch, slammed Tony to the padded floor before leaping on top of him and pummeling him unrelentingly.

Loch, slamming Tony to the side. Tar watching it as if it was slow motion—a horrible movie.

His worst fucking nightmare.

It was supposed to be you.

Tony was strong—trained—but Loch was on an all-out assault, and he'd drawn first blood, no doubt breaking Tony's ribs and possibly puncturing his lung on the first move.

It was a move they'd both been taught to make. And still, Tar waited for Loch to go down—it was five seconds since the first attack...and nothing.

"The gas isn't working!" he heard Jasper yell, and he yanked himself away from the screen

Jasper wasn't waiting to figure out why—he was running down the hall, with Tar at his heels. The second they went through the double doors and found the guards passed out, they figured out where the gas went instead. This wasn't the time to figure out how Loch had accomplished that. Instead, Tar held his breath until he and Jasper got into the room, where Tony lay unconscious on the floor, and closed the doors behind them.

The window was wide open—Tar ran to it as Jasper went to Tony's side. He looked down on the sideway from the second floor and caught sight of Loch rolling out from the bushes he'd landed in.

"I see him," he told Jasper.

"I've got Tony. Go find Loch—bring him back. That's a goddamned order."

Creed heard the alarms and noticed the guards come in quietly—and no, this wasn't good. Not at all. He felt the danger in his bones, and for once, it wasn't him.

"What's happening?" he asked the nurse. "Is it Tar? Or Loch?"

The pure pain in his voice must've gotten through to her, because she mouthed, "Loch."

Shit. He stood, and the guards came toward him. "I have to go to him," he told the nurse. "I'm not going to hurt you or anyone else, but I have to be able to go to Loch. Because Tar's going to go to him and it's going to be bad. Please."

She looked unsure, and the guards were circling him. Then she sighed. "Stand down."

"Ma'am, we can't—" one of them started, but Creed took that opportunity to grab her keys and push out the emergency exit, ignoring the alarms that followed him. He waited right outside for the first guard—tripped him and grabbed a weapon, before knocking out the second and third guard.

The nurse came out into the hallway. "Check on them—they'll be okay," he called over his shoulder.

"One floor up," she told him. "And if you hurt any of them, I'll come after you myself."

CHAPTER TWENTY-EIGHT

TAR DIDN'T HESITATE—HE went out the window and dropped down to the ground, landing in the soft dirt behind the bushes that surrounded the building. He got to his feet quickly and found himself face to face with Loch, holding him at gunpoint.

"What the fuck are you doing, Loch?" He heard the confusion in his own voice, and for the briefest of seconds, Loch frowned, but it was quickly replaced by a neutral expression. And his eyes—dead like a goddamned shark's. It shook him to the core. "Loch, it's me."

"I know exactly who the fuck you are." Loch's voice still held the odd, guttural quality.

"You almost killed Tony." His voice broke on Tony's name, especially after he realized that Tony might actually be dead. "You killed the man who saved me. Us. Please, let me help you."

"I'm walking away. If you try to stop me, I'll kill you." Loch began backing away as a car pulled up to the curb closest to him.

Tar glanced at it and saw Liam behind the wheel. Liam, smiling at him. His body froze, like he had ice water in his veins, and it took everything he had not to run to the car, drag Liam out, and beat him to death on the sidewalk.

But Loch would kill him—Tar didn't doubt that. So instead of moving, Tar smiled back at Liam, who looked surprised.

I'm going to kill you, fucker...and I'm going to enjoy it.

He turned his gaze back to Loch, whose hand was on the door handle. "I'm coming to rescue you, Loch, if that's the last thing I do."

Loch stared at him for a beat longer before getting into the car with Liam. The car screeched away, and Tar turned to head to the parking lot and his truck. Halfway there, his own truck darted out and almost killed him. He slammed both hands on the hood and saw Creed in the driver's seat.

He went to the passenger's side, never happier to see a friendly face, and realized there was never a friendly face on the other side of a gun.

Tar ignored Creed's warnings and got into the truck anyway. Shooting Tar now wouldn't help anything, but Creed made him hand over his phone and handcuff himself to the door anyway. He wasn't taking any chances where Snow and his men were concerned.

"I'm not one of Snow's men—no more than you are," Tar said steadily as Creed headed toward the highway. "And how the fuck do you know where to go?"

"I was in the parking lot and saw Liam in the car, waiting. I planted a tracker."

"And you think he didn't see you?"

"I know he didn't—he stayed in the car the entire time—and it hasn't stopped moving." He showed Tar the screen on his phone. "You've known the entire time that Loch has DID too."

"No."

"Bullshit, Tar—you misread him. He's been working with Snow this entire time. You rescued another monster." Creed watched his accusation burn through him, wondered why he didn't feel more satisfaction at the devastation on Tar's face.

Finally, Tar ground out, "He doesn't have DID. And he's not working with Snow—not purposely. He's been programmed by Liam. It started with Liam. Loch is still Loch."

"Not for long." Creed glanced at him. "Is this going to bring out your inner killer?"

"Go fuck yourself, Creed. Use both fists."

"Is that a yes?" Creed persisted. "Are you still stable? What am I up against if your other persona comes out?"

"Put it this way—you won't live to talk about it."

"I didn't want this," Creed growled. "I was living a normal life until you found me."

Tar snorted. "A normal life? Who the fuck are you kidding?"

"It was fine until you and Loch got involved."

"You want Snow hurting innocent people?"

"Neither of us is innocent, Tar. Neither is Loch. And we haven't been for a long fucking time."

"Don't we do more good for people than we ever could with Snow? Don't you want to?"

"There's only one reason I'm going after Snow—because he deserves to die. So does anyone who's been helping him. Beyond that, I'm out. And unless I get that promise, I'll kill you before I kill Snow."

"Then kill me," Tar said evenly. "Go ahead—I'm an easy target."

No, Tar was anything but easy. He held up Tar's phone. "I'm calling Jasper. He's the one who'll make that decision."

He put it on speakerphone, and Jasper picked up with, "Tar, where are you?"

"I'm in my truck with Creed. He's kidnapped me," Tar said before Creed could speak.

"Creed, I'm not in the mood for this shit," Jasper growled and Creed swore he almost snapped to attention at the command in Jasper's voice. "You and Tar need to play nice—I don't give a shit how angry you are right now. Trust me, I'm angrier. But I need you two to find Loch and bring down Snow. This might be our only shot."

Tar broke in. "Liam took Loch away. Liam must've paid the guard off and redirected the gas." He paused. "How is Tony?"

"Going into surgery. Creed—release Tar and you two work together. You two bring me back Loch—and Snow and Liam's dead bodies." Jasper hung up.

Tar shrugged. "So much for telling him that you were done."

"Fuck you, Tar. And why is Tony having surgery?"

"Loch almost killed Tony. Liam made sure the gas didn't work in Loch's room—he gassed the guards instead, so Liam had ample time to do some real damage." Tar's voice trembled a little on the last word.

"What?" He slammed his palm against the steering wheel. "How will Jasper ever look at Loch again?"

"What do you care? You're leaving. You're on your way out."

"And if you try and stop me—"

"I know—you, or maybe Travis, will kill me. Christ, you've got to come up with a better threat. People have been threatening to kill me for a long time. Death doesn't worry me. It's living that scares the shit out of me."

He stared straight ahead and Creed knew he was serious...mainly because he also felt the same way. "This was never going to work out anyway."

"Us?" Tar asked, then forged ahead without waiting for him to agree. "I guess it'd be better to just walk away than try. Less risk."

"I'm not scared of risk."

"Where your heart is concerned? You are. I can't say I blame you." Tar leaned his head against the window. "Just get me to Loch."

Creed forced his concentration back on the highway he was barreling down. Liam's car was still moving fast, several miles up ahead of them. "I'm taking Snow out."

Tar bit out fiercely. "And Liam's mine."

Creed wouldn't take that away from him.

Loch rode in the car with Liam for over an hour before Liam pulled off road and followed a narrow dirt trail up a hill.

After the car rounded a corner, Liam slowed down as they approached a large house in the middle of nowhere.

"We made it. You're home, baby." Liam told him, and something inside Loch recoiled at his words. Liam must've noticed because he ran his hand through Loch's hair, close to his ear. "I know this must be confusing…"

"You left me." But as Liam's hand caressed him, it suddenly didn't matter that much anymore. Suddenly, a car careened around the corner and pulled up directly behind them. "Who's that?"

Liam glanced into the rear-view mirror. "We were expecting this company."

Loch turned in his seat and watched men come out of the surrounding woods, carrying rifles. The truck doors were opened and he saw Tar being pulled out…and another man. "Who's that?"

"He's one of Snow's newest. And he's done a great job. Come on, Loch—your uncle's waiting for you," Liam urged. "I'm sorry I had to trick you, baby. I was watching you mourn me. Ripped my heart out."

"You did what you had to." The words came out easily, but he felt wooden. Drugged. Flat.

He followed Liam inside the house where Tar was tied securely to a chair that looked bolted to the floor, a gun to his head. The other man who'd driven the truck stood near Loch's uncle, who smiled at Loch.

"Lochlan, my boy." His uncle came forward and rested a hand on his cheek. "I can't tell you how good it is to see you again." He looked to Liam. "Thank you for watching him for me—for bringing him back to me safely. We've got so much work to do, and it's time for Loch to take his place by my side."

Loch nodded, not sure of what he meant, but it evoked a reaction from Tar. Locking eyes with him, Loch felt his hot anger burn through him, and suddenly, he was angry too. He just wasn't sure why.

"Loch, what the fuck are you doing?" Tar asked him, and Loch had a sudden urge to tell him that he had no fucking idea, that he needed help, that Creed wasn't supposed to be holding a gun to his head.

"Loch? Look at me," Liam was telling him, a hand on his head like it was in the car. Then all of those other thoughts were muted in his mind and it felt...odd. "Don't worry about Tar."

"Does he need training?"

Training? Where did that come from? But Liam looked at him approvingly. "We've tried that, but it hadn't worked."

"Let me."

"No, Loch. It's a waste of time."

"You don't want me to prove myself." It was an old argument—Loch was sure of it, but Liam just shook his head and looked amused, and any discomfort fell away.

Liam's hand came off his head, and he and Snow began to talk in hushed tones. Loch's brain seemed to click like a slideshow that was going too fast—pictures of him with Liam, in bed, at dinner, laughing—but there were other pictures too that didn't include Liam, and they were important. He tried to grab onto those pictures and felt the memories fighting to emerge. But they remained frustratingly out of his grasp. He knew all of these men, but the hows and whys of Tar and Creed were hazy.

"What am I doing here?" he asked Liam, who turned from Loch's uncle.

"Do you remember when we were together?" Somehow, that was *all* he remembered, and he nodded. "Good. Just try to relax." He stroked a finger behind Loch's ear this time, and Loch leaned into it immediately, all the stress and worry dissolving. This was right. "Trust me."

"You'll walk me through this?"

"Of course."

"You just left me." Loch couldn't help that particular memory from returning, and he caught Tar's gaze on him, which made him hot and needy and uncomfortable. His eye caught Creed's, and the feeling intensified, and Loch suddenly wanted those two men far more than the man in front of him. But even as the finger stroked behind his ear, pulling him back to Liam, he managed to ask, "Why did you leave me? You let me think you were dead."

"We talked about why. I think you're just confused. Just kiss me, Loch."

Loch leaned in and kissed him, and it felt familiar, but not in a good way. He heard Tar's curses and pulled back to stare at him, and then at Creed, whose palm was wrapped around Tar's throat.

Loch's uncle came over and patted Creed's shoulder. "You've come a long way, Creed." Creed nodded, and both men looked at Tar. "And Tar? Nothing's changed, I see."

Tar refused to look Snow in the eye.

Loch wanted to know more, but simply asked Liam, "What're we doing with Tar?"

"I think he's more trouble than he's worth." Liam nuzzled his neck. "Maybe you can take care of him for us."

"You're not trying training."

"We've tried that, Loch," Snow told him. "Unfortunately, he couldn't be trusted. Not like Travis, who finally seems to have convinced Creed to play nice."

Loch processed that, even though the information seemed...wrong. But the pain that had been shooting through his head every time he tried to think things through was back. Still, he persisted. "Why did you wait so long to find me?"

His uncle looked at him with sympathy. "I never left you, Loch. Not completely. That's why I sent Liam in for you. Tar interfered, as always. Didn't you, Tar?"

Tar's eyes were angry but he wasn't fighting the bonds.

"What did he interfere with?" Loch asked.

Snow gave a satisfied smile. "You, Loch."

Tar flexed his wrists when Snow spoke to Loch.

Loch looked confused as fuck. "I still don't understand what Tar did."

Snow frowned, because he knew exactly what Tar did—and what Tar would do the second he could get loose and away from Creed. "Loch, Tar interfered with your entire life. Your legacy."

Legacy my ass. He glared up at Creed, who looked back at him impassively. The fact that Snow had also welcomed Creed back into the fold made Tar die a little inside.

Snow's voice might be graveled, and he definitely looked older but none the worse for wear. He'd been living well. And this was a full compound. He was training new men.

But Loch wasn't the same man he'd been when he'd

attacked Tar and Tony in the facility. That Loch was hardened and angry—the man in front of him was confused. Subservient.

"Now that Loch's back where he should be, we can finish what we started," Liam said firmly, never taking his eyes off Tar.

Tar—who'd just been able to free his wrists from the ropes that held his hands behind his back while everyone was otherwise occupied, flew toward Liam...

Only to be stopped by Loch. Fucker slammed him like a brick wall and took him to the floor, and that was fine because he knew how to fight Loch. If Creed would just kill that fucker Snow, then Tar could get his hands on Liam...

But Creed was suddenly on him too, helping to drag him up and chain him. He stared at Creed, betrayal ripping through him again.

"Just like the old days," Snow murmured to him. "Still fighting. Still refusing to break. I think that's going to change, Tar. I just wish it could've been different."

"I just wish you'd let me snap your neck," Tar shot back.

Snow looked at Creed. "You know where to put him. Loch and I don't have time for this. We've got important matters to discuss."

Creed put a hand on Tar's head and injected something into his neck. When Tar woke, it seemed like seconds later, but it was probably closer to an hour—it was the same dosing Snow used to use on him. Tar recognized the feeling—half drowsy, half floaty.

Just like the old days. Especially when he realized where he was.

The box. And Creed had drugged him and put him in

here. He closed his eyes and wondered how his instincts could've been so goddamned wrong. He'd missed the fact that Loch had been programmed, and the more he thought on it, the more he realized that Loch had most likely started drinking to stave off the urges from the programming. But had Creed been on Snow's side the entire time?

He opened his eyes because he didn't have the luxury of wallowing. Instead, he moved quietly and felt around the box. The familiar dimensions. The familiar carvings. But there was something else in here. Several somethings.

A knife. Two knives. A loaded Sig Sauer. A phone. Was this a trick too...or was Creed actually helping him? Jesus Christ, he was going to kill the man when this was all over.

He checked the phone and saw a message.

Lid's locked. They'll be coming for you. I'll give you warning.

He cursed under his breath, tried the lid gently, and felt it give easily. He let it back down quietly, so he could pop out like a demonic jack-in-the- box when necessary.

His hand went back to his side, and he felt something inside his pocket.

Matches. *Such a romantic.*

It pulled him out of the panic attack he'd been trying to stave off. This was revisiting a nightmare, but he was awake and in control.

You didn't break before. You won't this time. Never.

"Never," he whispered to himself before he took up one of the knives Creed left him and started to carve the new word above the old ones.

CHAPTER TWENTY-NINE

TRAVIS HADN'T COME out at all—not to see Liam or greet Snow or save Creed, and he didn't bother to try to unpack what that meant. He took it as a sign that this shit was up to him. That Travis knew what Creed had to do in order to free both of them.

Travis isn't programmed. You're not in danger of Snow pulling you back in.

Whether or not Snow fully believed his act, Creed couldn't be sure, but he'd keep playing his part. He stood in the center of the camp with Liam, Loch, and two guards, watching Liam whisper to Loch.

Finally, after ten minutes of whatever pep talk he was giving Loch, he turned to the two guards and said, "Get Tar—he's perfect to practice on."

Creed wondered how much they'd suffered because they both looked haunted, but they didn't hesitate to do Liam's bidding.

When Liam had ordered them, Creed had hit the button on his phone that he'd set to ping Tar's burner and then shut his phone off while it was still in his back pocket. When Liam stared at him, he pulled out the taser he'd put in his other back pocket.

Liam nodded his approval. And, less than a minute later, Creed watched as the men dragged Tar out. Creed had been half sure Tar would've taken the guards out and made an end run toward Liam. But no, Tar never did anything easy. Now, he was practically on his knees, his head bowed, mumbling.

"Out of practice, Tar? Too used to the good life?" Liam asked and lifted Tar's head by grabbing a hunk of his hair and yanking on it.

Tar squinted his eyes and spit in Liam's face. Creed winced as the back of Liam's hand—with its big ring—caught Tar on the cheek, slashing a line that wept blood. Creed's throat tightened with rage, and suddenly, any remaining anger he had toward Tar dissipated.

Stand down. Tar knows what to do. But Tar was mumbling brokenly, and maybe Creed had overestimated his ability to come back here into hell. Maybe his unification wasn't built to withstand this.

"Loch, it's time for you to show us what you can do." Liam turned to Loch, who was watching the entire scene in front of him dispassionately. He motioned for the men to tie Tar to the cemented pole, meant just for this purpose. They wrapped Tar's arms around it, face-first, his bare back exposed to the rest of them.

"I thought we weren't trying to train him," Loch said when Liam handed him the whip.

"We're not—we're showing everyone what happens to men who misbehave. You're going to flay his skin off, and he'll remain here, for everyone to see."

And he'll die here if left like that. Creed didn't flinch, just nodded at Liam as if he approved of the plan, and wondered why the hell Tar didn't take his chance when he had it.

The thwack of the whip echoed in Creed's ear as he watched it hit its mark on Tar's back, leaving an open cut in the flesh. Loch stood still as stone, staring at what he'd just done in horror.

Liam came up next to him and rubbed behind his ear, and Loch seemed to snap out of it. "Trust me—this is what your uncle needs done. He needs loyal men."

Suddenly, Tar gasped and seemed to simply go still on the pole. Liam frowned and walked around to see Tar's face. Creed moved as if to help, holding the taser up, and watched as Liam slapped Tar's cheek—the one that was already cut, causing blood to splatter in the air. He moved in closer and lifted one of Tar's eyelids. Tar's hand shot out and stabbed Liam in the carotid with a slim, silver object. Liam choked—tried to yell—but blood bubbled out of his mouth instead.

Tar had moved so fast that, if Creed hadn't seen it with his own eyes, he would've thought Liam just dropped dead out of nowhere. He moved in, but Tar was already free, so Creed turned and stabbed the first man who'd brought Creed out with a sedative he'd stolen from Snow's house. The second man put up slightly more of a fight, but the end result was the same. Creed didn't want to kill anyone who might have a shot at being saved, and for all of these men except for Snow, that remained TBD. He bound their hands and feet with zip ties and called in their coordinates to Jasper from Tar's phone after taking a picture of Liam's body.

We need backup. We've got Loch—we're going after Snow.

He took another picture of Tar holding Loch, then pocketed the phone and went to the two men. "Let's get you looked at."

Tar glanced at him—his cheek bled heavily, as did his back. "There's no time. Where's Snow?"

"Still at the main house."

"Tar, what's happening?" Loch asked, but he was touching behind his left ear, the way Liam had done to him earlier.

"I don't have time to explain it right now," Tar told him. "I promise, when this is all done—"

"You're done," Loch snarled...and suddenly the touch behind the ear made sense. Creed leaned in and used the sedation on him, catching Loch in his arms.

"Let's get into the cart." He carried Loch into the repurposed golf cart and lay him down in the back, buckling him in securely. "You need to hide," he told Tar. "I'm going to race up to Snow, like I need help with Loch. I'll pretend you escaped. Grab another cart and follow behind me."

Tar nodded. "If you hurt Loch—"

"I won't, Tar." He took off, up the hill Liam had driven them down. Snow was comfortable here—more so than he'd ever been. He had a guard with him, but he counted on Liam to keep him isolated and safe.

Creed beeped as he approached the house. The guard came out, and Creed yelled, "Liam's hurt—Tar sedated Loch and headed up this way!"

The guard came running and leaned over Loch, allowing Creed to stick the needle into his neck and knock him out. He pulled him off of Loch, where he'd collapsed, and gently lowered him to the ground before zip-tying his wrists together.

It was only then that he heard the scream—an ungodly sound that tore through him. It came from the front of the house and had him running, weapon in hand, ready to shoot anyone who got in his way.

The screams were coming from Snow. Creed had put him inside the box, but he'd broken off a piece of the lid so they could see Snow's face. Now he handed Creed the matches. "Get this done. Jasper's orders."

The helo flew overhead, as if just mentioning his name brought help. Creed stared down at the man who'd caused them all such pain. "Your life's work is nothing. No one's going to remember you. The public has no clue you exist, and neither does anyone in the CIA, save for two men. You're staying a secret. No one's going to talk about you."

And then he dropped the match onto the wooden box. He and Tar stood together, listening to Snow's screams of pain and terror as he slowly burned to death from his feet upwards, the fire consuming the man and the box.

Over soon.

CHAPTER THIRTY

JASPER HIMSELF CAME DOWN from the helo to assist. At first, Tar thought that maybe something had happened to Tony, but the first thing Jasper said to him was, "Tony's through surgery—he's going to be okay."

"There's an implant—behind Loch's left ear—that's how Liam controlled him. Get it out," Tar told him.

"First thing, Tar. First thing," Jasper promised.

Only then did Tar allow himself to sit down, fire and burning flesh the only thing he could smell. Once the adrenaline waned, he knew he'd be in a hell of a lot of pain, but for now, he waited until Creed carried Loch onto the helo. Several more men fast roped down from another helo that hovered, men who would handle the prisoners and the guards and bring them to the facility to be checked over.

"You did good, Tar," Jasper murmured as he pressed a cloth to Tar's cheek and motioned for the medic to come over. "Geary's going to take a look at your back here—easier to get a dressing on it while we're not moving."

"I need to get out of here," Tar said.

"I know. Just a few minutes."

But when Geary tried to touch his back, Tar tried to punch him. It wasn't until Creed came over to help hold him and talk him down with Jasper's help that Geary was able to clean and lightly bandage his wound. Then he did the same for his face, saying, "We've got to get him back to the surgeon ASAP."

"Let's go then." Jasper and Creed helped him into the helo, and from there, it was a blur. The ride was under twenty minutes, and they were all whisked away from each other upon landing. Tar was sedated for his stitches, but he knew the surgeon so he gave his consent.

When he woke, he was propped onto his side with his cheek and back bandaged and an IV in his arm.

"It's going to take a few days of rest for that back to heal. If you move too much, it's going to rip open again," the doctor warned. And hell, Tar didn't have anything better to do but sleep, so they kept him comfortable.

And one day, Tar woke up feeling much less drugged, and the doc took the bandage off his face to reveal a thin line that looked like it would heal well, if not completely disappear.

His back needed to stay bandaged for longer, but he could be up and about. One of the nurses helped him shower by holding a piece of plastic over his back so the water didn't touch it, and that helped Tar feel more human.

Now, it was time to find Tony and Jasper. He knew Creed and Loch were both here, but he wouldn't be allowed to see either of them. According to the nurse, Tony was thankfully recovering well—he had broken ribs, a broken arm, and a concussion, along with various cuts and scrapes and contusions.

Once Tar had been able to visit with him, Tony admitted that he would never acknowledge to Loch that he'd done it.

"Why? It wasn't him," Tony told him. "Why hurt him any further?"

"Just make sure he's okay, and I'll keep all your secrets," Tar promised. And then he had to go through the brutal task of reliving what had happened, working through anger and guilt and everything else that had been dredged up.

"You did it, kid." Tony's tone was gentle, but the look in his eyes held the fierceness he was so well known for. "This chapter of your life is officially closed."

"Except for all the men who've been hurt."

"You can't save them all, Tar. Not anymore than you already have. You've given them a chance—it's up to them to take themselves the rest of the way. You did it. So did Loch and Creed. Now, it's their turn."

He hadn't asked about Loch or Creed, which Tar was sure would go into Tony's notes.

After Tar had been cleared, both medically and by Tony who insisted, despite his injuries, Tar sat with Jasper on the leather couch for a SITREP of the events leading up to Snow and Liam's deaths at Jasper's big house.

"The device behind Loch's ear wasn't a tracker—it merely allowed Liam to alter Loch's thoughts. Very subtly when Liam wasn't close by. He needed to be with Loch in order for it to work fully—it was based on physical touches."

"Conditioning," Tar bit out.

"Yes, exactly. But there's no permanent damage or consequences from having it implanted."

"So those personality changes?"

"Part detox and part the implant. Loch would definitely notice something happening. Drinking was his way of trying to make whatever he was feeling stop." Jasper shook his head. "With his history of addiction, I didn't think that it could be anything more nefarious. And Loch must've felt the same way."

"So was Liam following us?"

"Not at all. Otto got in touch with him, and he had certain privileges, since he wasn't deemed a threat. He could send letters to family members. Phone calls. All of them were monitored but nothing he'd said or sent threw up any red flags."

"How's that possible, Jasper?" Tar asked, trying not to be angry at his friend and mentor and failing miserably.

"Because there were never any. He was writing to Liam the entire time—pretending he was a family member. Calling him too. The only difference was the way he said goodbye this last time. He made the call the day Creed ended up in the infirmary."

"So Otto really was Snow's this entire time."

"Otto's family was a part of Marin Snow's cult."

"Shit."

"He was young, but Snow took him out of foster care when he was able to. That's where a lot of the kids came from. Some of them too young to even remember." Jasper stared at him.

"I don't want to hear anymore." Tar had never asked about where he'd been before Snow's—like Creed, he'd always figured that wherever he'd come from was probably not worth investigating.

"Tough shit." Jasper's voice wasn't harsh, but Tar knew there wasn't any escaping what he was about to learn. "Tar, Otto knows you from the cult. Marin Snow's cult. You were so young when you were taken out of there...and you were put into foster care."

"What do you want me to say, Jasper? That my life was fucked from day one?"

"I'm sorry, Tar. But I think knowing helps. You might not think so, but in the end, it does."

"Oh fuck that. Helps how? To know that Snow used the CIA in order to track down all those foster kids like me? To know that, whoever gave birth to me was too fucked up by Marin Snow to care?" He wanted to curl up in a goddamned ball.

"None of the adults we captured were fit in any way, shape, or form to be parents," Jasper said gently.

"And let me guess—none of them fought very hard to keep their kids," he added, unable to keep the bitterness from his voice.

"Many of them killed themselves after they were deprogrammed. Guilt at what they'd done."

Tar gnawed on his bottom lip. "Mine?"

"Yes, Tar. Both of yours. I'm sorry."

Something settled inside of Tar, and hell, maybe Jasper was right. Maybe knowing this was important, would take away any of those *what ifs* that attempted to break through every now and again. "How bad was this cult, Jasper?"

"I think you've been through too much to know."

Tar didn't argue—his imagination could take care of the rest. "What happens to Otto now?"

"He'll stay here. We'll keep trying. It's all we can do."

While Tony healed, he worked with Creed. The only concession made was that Jasper was right next door, watching everything on his computer. No audio, but that didn't matter. Creed also knew there was gas ready to be pumped in.

Tony refused a gun during the sessions, and Creed did everything in his power to not make Tony nervous. But it was hard to stay still because so much of these sessions were triggering on so many different levels.

Creed's unification was far simpler, mainly because he chose not to have one. Travis was still there, calm beneath the surface. Creed worked on controlling Travis, calming him and making sure that he didn't need to invite Travis to cover for him.

Because Travis was dangerous in his own right—but only to those who threatened Creed.

"He's still here. He's a part of me," Creed told Tony during their tenth session in as many days.

"I suspect he always will be," Tony agreed. "And in your case, that's not a bad thing. He didn't try to come out at all around Snow?"

"I thought it would happen, but no—he let me handle all of it."

"And you did," Tony said quietly. "And after a few more sessions—and an agreement to check in regularly for the next five years—you'll be done here."

Creed's gut tightened at the mention of that. "Is Tar okay?"

"Yes."

"What about Loch?"

Tony sighed. "You don't have skin in that game anymore, Creed. Not with Tar, either. Just concentrate on you. You're getting what you asked for—exactly what you told Tar."

"I can't know anything?"

"It's classified, Creed. You may not know a lot about how the agency operates, but you know that. You don't want to be a part of this life, and Jasper agreed. We're grateful to you, and you'll be compensated. But there needs to be a clean break...it's better for all of you that way."

Creed whirled around from the window. "How can you forgive him? After what he did to you—how can you just let it go?"

Tony gave him a tired smile. "Are you talking about me—or you?" Creed opened his mouth and then closed it. "That's what I thought." Tony shifted in the bed and winced. "I can forgive Loch because I know he loves me. I know how much he's sacrificed."

"He's related to that psychopath. Just because you reprogrammed him this time—"

"Loch's nothing like his uncle—I think you know that. And Snow's dead. Liam's dead." Tony closed his eyes. "You're safe, Creed."

Yes, Creed was safe...and soon? He'd be all alone. And that didn't bother him so much because he could handle alone. It was the memories of Loch and Tar, the ones he thought would help him so much to have.

Now, he realized how much worse they made everything.

Loch woke after what seemed like a deep dive under water and found himself chained to a bed in a padded room. Alone.

At least you're not gagged. But he did have a pounding headache and he had no memory of how he got here. Maybe this was some new alcohol awareness program?

He stared at the ceiling for a few minutes. There had to be a camera in here noting he was awake, so he waited to see who'd come through the door.

Instead, the television turned on. A video—of him. Lashing out at...Jasper. Tar. Creed. Asking where Snow was.

"Because I'm one of his. We're blood, dammit," he heard himself shout as his body went cold. "Snow's my blood. I'm getting him a lawyer."

The look in his eyes on that video...

You were turned. By Liam. And that's why he couldn't remember anything. "What day is it?" he asked now. "What fucking day is it?"

Two men in white coats came in. "It's Friday," one of them said. "You've been out for seven days. Before that, you escaped and went to Snow's compound with Liam. Willingly."

Panic rose inside of him. "And I hurt people?"

"You did, yes," the second orderly said. "Dr. LaSalle wants to see you. But we need to prep you first."

Loch closed his eyes. "Go for it. I'm not going to fight this."

Not yet, anyway. But he had a feeling something not all that deeply buried inside of him would.

After both Jasper and Tony signed off on Loch no longer being a threat, and his surgical cut had healed to the doctor's satisfaction, Loch went to Jasper's house, where Tar had been staying.

Tony and Jasper were both there for the first reunion, and when Loch walked into Tar's room, Tar just sat and watched him, slightly wary but fighting a smile.

"Hey, Tar. You saved my life."

"It's becoming a habit. Maybe we could take a break from it?" Tar asked. For a long moment, neither of them moved and then suddenly, they both were, meeting in the middle of the room. Hugging.

When they broke apart, they were alone.

"You all right?" Tar asked.

"I'm sorry, Tar," Loch told him in response. "You were right not to tell me about Liam at the cabin—"

"That wasn't you talking. It hasn't been you for years. I should've...I should've known."

"Yeah, well, that makes two of us." Loch shook his head. "Liam made sure he was my trigger."

"He definitely made me want to kill," Tar muttered.

Loch snorted softly. "I guess I never had a chance with him. Programming me without my knowledge is the perfect punishment—the perfect humiliation."

"You weren't the only one hurt by him. He was a monster. Creed said he was a favorite of Snow's. Liam used to torture him."

"That's why Travis didn't say anything to me—because Creed took the brunt of those punishments." Loch walked around Tar and lifted up the back of his shirt to look at the long, healing wound that had sliced through the middle of Tar's tattoo. "And you and Tony took the brunt of mine."

"Don't try to push me away because of this. No more excuses."

"I want you, Tar. I love you," Loch said firmly, and Tar turned fast to look at him, surprised. "I love you."

Tar just moved into his arms as Loch repeated the words. Loch hugged him, mindful of his back. "Love you, Loch. So glad you're here."

"Me too."

"Creed's gone. He wanted out."

"Because of me."

"We both kept the truth from him." Tar pulled back and shrugged.

"Maybe Tony and Jasper can get a message to him. I'll work to prove I'm safe, for both of you." He shook his head. "All this goddamned time I stayed away because I was bringing you trouble. Turns out, I was the fucking trouble."

Tar tilted his head and smiled. "I've never had a problem courting trouble, Loch. Why stop now?"

CHAPTER THIRTY-ONE

Five months later

CREED KNEW he was courting trouble by hanging at the docks where Sergei's men did their dirty business, but he really didn't give a fuck.

He guessed some things never changed.

Still, in deference to not dying, he'd grown out his hair, dyed it, and wore a goatee. He'd always moved differently than Travis did, so he didn't have to try to change his gait— he'd been told that by Jasper and Tony... and the two other men he couldn't think about without making his throat uncomfortably tight.

Dodge told him he was running with the devil by doing this... but he'd noticed Dodge never came right out and told him to stop. No, most nights, Dodge came down here with him.

When Creed asked why, Dodge told him, "I always appreciate learning a new skill set."

Hell, Dodge had moved back here with him—and some

of his other acolytes had followed him. They helped when they could, but Creed didn't want to put any of them in danger.

During the past months, Creed'd infiltrated shipments and freed innocents, sometimes by calling in police and then disappearing, sometimes by doing it on his own. He'd become the ghost in the night—the thorn in the Russian mob's side on this particular dock. They talked about him in hushed terms because the other crimes that Travis had committed had never been solved. Of course, they believed the same man was causing all the problems.

They were right.

But even with the Russians spooked, the job was still like trying to empty a river one cup at a time.

Creed recognized a few of the men only from the brief prison ride he'd taken with them. Travis had been the one doing the grifting and the fucking during that time, and he'd kept Creed completely protected. Creed had only come out after Travis had been threatened with a prison cell.

Creed had always handled the cage better.

Sergei had helped him plan his escape from the marshals by acting as a go-between with Dodge. When Creed had disappeared, the feds hadn't had enough evidence to hold Sergei, so Creed had been pretty certain he'd catch sight of him again.

It hadn't happened yet because Sergei? He was just *gone.* Disappeared. He'd heard the men discuss his disappearance in whispered tones.

At first, Creed wondered if Travis had come out, and he missed it, but he was pretty sure that didn't happen. He hadn't felt Travis's brain buzz in months, and weirdly, he'd never felt closer to someone he'd never actually met.

Now, it was close to midnight. The docks had been quiet tonight, so he ambled away from where the Russians usually congregated and headed toward his truck. Halfway there, the full moon caught his attention—big and beautiful and bright, so he turned to stare up at the sky.

"Planning something?"

Creed didn't turn around as the familiar voice washed over him like a warm rain.

"Creed? You okay?"

His throat tightened at the second voice. He hadn't realized how much he'd missed both men until this moment. He'd been lying to himself—and he'd been okay with that.

Until now.

He still didn't turn around but managed, "Shouldn't be talking here."

"Then come with us—we're at a hotel down the block. Just...to talk. Please." Loch's voice was hoarse, and Creed couldn't say no, even if he wanted to—not when he heard the hurt in Loch's voice.

He'd walked to the docks, so he got into the backseat of Tar's truck, and it was all so familiar. So right.

You don't know why they're here. They might just be checking up on you. Reminding you that you have to go to the institute for random checks.

The car ride was quick—less than five minutes, and they were riding up the elevator and walking into Loch and Tar's room.

They were always meant to be together.

Creed walked to the sliding glass doors that looked out on

the docks and wondered how long they'd been here, watching him. "Why'd you guys come here?"

"For you," Tar said simply.

"To check up on me?" Creed finally turned around to face them and immediately realized it had been a mistake. "Because I'm fine." He bit the lie out. It tasted bitter as fuck on his tongue.

Loch stood silently while Tar stuck his hands in his pockets. "You're working?"

"I'm keeping busy. Now that Snow's taken care of..."

"You and Travis are going back to killing traffickers?" Loch finished for him.

"I think it's just me. And no, I'm not killing them, although it's really hard not to. I'm just helping the victims." It was Creed's turn to shove his hands into his pockets and realized how fucking lonely he'd been. How he'd been dying a little inside every day since he'd made the choice to leave them behind. Because that's what he'd done—he'd abandoned them. Not the other way around.

"Creed?" Loch pressed gently.

His words tumbled out in a rush before he could stop them. "I tried to find out how both of you were. Jasper and Tony said I couldn't know."

"Because you wanted to be done with the program," Tar reminded him, but there wasn't any judgment in his tone.

Creed lowered his head because it was suddenly hard to speak, surrounded by the men who'd given him back everything. For once, he hadn't felt broken or different.

But the past months of being cut off from them and floating aimlessly? Not so great.

"Creed, we understand why you needed to get away. We

really do," Tar started tentatively. "Cutting you off was for your own safety, not ours."

"Safety?" Creed bit out, then shook his head to stop him from saying anything else.

Loch changed the subject. "Jasper told us that you went and talked to Dodge."

"Didn't want him to worry," Creed admitted. "He helped Travis a lot."

Tar nodded. "Does he know about..."

"Travis and me? He said he suspected something was up because of the personality changes, but he likes us both." Creed had been staying with him, but these men probably knew that too.

"You're still pissed," Loch murmured.

"I'm pissed at everything."

Tar chuckled before running a hand behind his neck. "C'mon, Creed—look at us. Please."

Creed finally raised his head and really looked at them this time. He stared first into Tar's blue eyes, which were warm. And then he dragged his gaze to Loch's dark ones. Still haunted, but this was Loch, not the confused man he'd last seen at Snow's. "You didn't start out with Creed."

"You came into the picture pretty quickly," Loch reminded him. As if he needed reminding.

"You were into Travis." It came out as part accusation, but Loch didn't take it as such.

Instead, he simply nodded in agreement. "Travis is a big part of you. He always will be, in one form or another."

Creed couldn't disagree with that. "So what are you guys doing now that Snow's dead?"

"You've got a job offer for us?" Loch asked.

"I mean, you'd both need some training but..." Creed smirked, and Loch pulled him close.

"I'm sorry my family was responsible for your pain." Loch's hands went to both sides of his head. "I'm sorry."

Creed whispered, "I know. I thought you two were ultimately better off without me."

"We're not," Tar said firmly.

"Not at all," Loch echoed, before bringing his mouth down on Creed's, a soft kiss that immediately went nuclear on both their parts. Creed's mouth opened, and his tongue tangled with Loch's, Loch's hands fisting in his hair.

Tar's mouth went to his neck—he kissed and sucked and marked while Loch ravaged his mouth. And when Loch pulled away, his eyes were bright, his smile wide. "Missed you."

Creed could only nod and let himself be tugged over to the bed. He let Loch and Tar alternate between kissing him and stripping him. Their hands on his body, their mouths on his skin, their names on his lips. They settled into the bed, rutting against one another.

"Missed this," Creed managed.

"Missed you," Loch emphasized, his palm wrapping around Creed's cock, fisting it, stroking it. It didn't take long before Creed was begging *Loch* and *please* and *more*.

"You like that, baby?" Tar murmured, his fingers running down the seam of Creed's ass before one blunt finger pressed inside of him.

"Fuck," Creed barked, unable to tear his gaze from Loch's, who'd now moved down his body and licked his cock from root to tip. "Please don't make me wait. Been too long."

Loch smiled, and then Creed's cock was engulfed in the

wet heat and suction of his mouth while Tar worked three fingers inside of him, brushing his gland as Loch deepthroated him...and it didn't take long before he was shooting down Loch's throat.

Tar tugged at his shoulder, and Creed moved to his back, Tar's fingers still inside of him. Loch leaned in and sucked one of Tar's nipples, hard enough to make him cry out, and then he kissed Tar. And Creed watched them kiss while Tar opened him mercilessly.

When they broke the kiss, all their focus turned back to him. Loch played with his nipples while Tar spread Creed's thighs.

"Do I need a condom?" he asked, in a tone that held zero judgement. "It's okay if—"

"There's been no one since you two," Creed admitted. "If you don't believe me..."

"Of course we believe you," Loch told him. "It's the answer we were hoping for."

Tar wasted no time and pushed inside of him. "So tight, baby."

"Don't stop," Creed urged. "Please—make it hurt. I want it to."

Tar smiled because he understood. He grabbed Creed's hips and sank fully inside of him with one long stroke, and then he groaned. "So good...you have no idea."

Creed did—because he started to move, wanting the friction. Needing it. Tar complied while Loch's hand went to Creed's cock, his mouth on Creed's, on Tar's, urging them both while he stroked his own cock.

He came on Creed, rubbed his come into his belly like he was marking him, while Creed was still being fucked by Tar, fucked and held. Maybe even cherished, if the way Loch looked at him was any indicator.

He wanted to stay here forever...but he had no idea if that was in any of their futures.

"We're not done, Creed," Loch whispered, as if reading his mind. "Not by a long shot."

When his orgasm hit, a blinding streak of white behind his eyelids, none of it mattered but the feel of his own pleasure at their hands.

The hours had passed quickly, and the sun was just coming up as Creed lay between Loch and Tar, too comfortable to even think about moving.

Of course, being tied to the headboard had something to do with that, but he wasn't complaining. At all.

Instead, he tugged at the handcuffs. "You planned on coming here and tying me to the bed?"

"They're stronger cuffs than the last time," Tar told him seriously.

Creed shifted, and the cuffs fell off.

"C'mon—I had those specially made." Tar frowned.

Creed laughed and shifted, but immediately both men moved so they were still touching him, like they were afraid he'd disappear if they didn't have skin-on-skin contact. "Was I that easy to find?"

Tar smirked. "Let's just say we understand how you think."

"So does Jasper," Loch added.

Creed smiled. "I think I'd be pissed if he didn't."

"You've been careful?" Tar asked.

"Trying to. I figured I'd have to avoid Sergei, but he seems to be..." He trailed off as he caught the not-so-innocent look on both men's faces. "You two had something to do with his disappearance, didn't you?"

"Us?" Tar shrugged. "So suspicious. Look, if he's gone, he's gone. It's a good thing, right?"

"And the feds are going to leave you alone too," Loch promised him. "Whether or not you accept our offer."

Creed's gut tightened. "What offer?"

"Come back. Work for Jasper—with us. We can still focus on trafficking. But this way, the feds will be off your back because you'll be one of them. Not exactly, but you know what I mean." Tar's gaze held him as surely as an embrace. "Dodge can come. And his...associates too."

"There's no such thing as coincidence," Loch told him firmly. "This was meant to be."

Tar gave him a half smile. "It's over now, Creed. Time to come home."

At his words, Creed moved into Tar's arms, and Loch immediately closed in so he was surrounded by the men who'd saved him... by the men he'd helped to save, bound by a shared past and a collective pain, but together by choice.

It's over now. And he'd finally found home.

ACKNOWLEDGMENTS

As I always say, it takes a village, and this one's no different. Special thanks on this one to Jill Corley for her amazing beta read, and to M.A. Hinkle of LesCourt Author Services for the proofreading. Thanks to Garrett Leigh for the amazing cover and to Frauke from Croco Designs for the formatting—and literally everything else, not limited to but especially my website and newsletters and helping my online world run smoothly.

To SE's Dirty Deeds, because you guys are always there for a laugh or a cheer or a cry—thanks for all your support! And for all my readers, because your emails and DMs reviews all keep me going.

And, last but never least, to Zoo, Lily, Chance and Gin—love you guys!

NEWSLETTER

Sign up for the newsletter of SE Jakes and her alter-ego Stephanie Tyler!

Be among the first to learn not only about new and upcoming books but also appearances and signings as well as special promotions and giveaways!

http://stephanietyler.com/newsletter/

BOUND BY HONOR

MEN OF HONOR, BOOK 1

A promise forces two men to bare themselves...completely.

One year ago on a mission gone wrong, Tanner James failed to save the life of Jesse, his Army Ranger teammate. Before dying in that South American jungle, Jesse extracted a promise that won't let Tanner rest until it's fulfilled—no matter what it costs him.

Damon Price loved Jesse, but problems in their relationship had come to a head right before Jesse left on his final mission. Now a reluctant Dom and a man still in mourning, he's not happy when Tanner appears at his BDSM club. And even less happy with Jesse's last request—that Tanner sub for him for one night.

After a rough start, Damon realizes that the tough soldier, despite his protests, aches for someone to take control. And Tanner senses a hesitance, an insecurity in Damon that makes him wonder if he's simply a placeholder for Jesse, or if their tentative connection could grow into something more.

For Jesse's sake, they agree to try one weekend together. Then duty calls, and a series of attacks that have been happening near the club hits too close to home, making both men wonder if giving their hearts is a maneuver fraught with too much risk...

Warning: Contains rough language, rougher sex and warriors who fall hard for each other.

CHAPTER ONE

TANNER JAMES HAD BEEN to hell and back more times than he could count over the course of his twenty- six years and was always pretty sure he'd live to make the trip again. But this time, even as adrenaline raced through his body and every muscle tensed for battle, hell beckoned with a one-way ticket and without a goddamned firefight in sight.

No, that would've been easier, *much* easier than this slow crawl to the door of Crave—a BDSM club with the reputation of being both accessible and safe—the week before Christmas.

He looked up at the dark sign with white lettering at the entrance and thought about turning back and going home.

If he hadn't promised Jesse that he'd do this, that he'd look up Jesse's former boyfriend, he'd be home right now, having just returned from a month-long mission, not about to offer himself up like some bondage sacrifice.

This wasn't his scene. Not really. He was all about rough sex, was bisexual with a definite preference to men for as long as he could remember, used to having to *don't ask, don't tell,* thanks to his military career—but this? Having to go in and greet the owner with a message from his dead lover? Well, that was fucking weird and could get him thrown out on his ass.

Jesus Christ, this was going to suck.

The man checking patrons who entered was dressed in bright, loud colors. Tight black leather pants. Guyliner. And he flirted in an over-the-top manner with anyone he deemed hot enough.

Tanner knew he'd be the subject of the man's flirtation. Although he'd shrugged it off his entire life, the looks and stares and come-ons he'd been on the receiving end of forever told him he was handsome.

He was more interested in being the best Army Ranger he could, spent most days knee-deep in jungle crap with paint on his face and men who only cared that he could shoot an M-14 with dizzying accuracy.

"Hey."

"Hello, gorgeous. Please tell me you're alone." The man peeked behind Tanner, saw no one and clapped his hands. "Alone. There is a God."

"I'm looking for Damon Price."

"I'll bet you are," the man said with a shake of his head. "Shame, really, that they all want what they can't have."

"I just need to talk to him."

The man erupted into peals of girlish laughter and Tanner rolled his eyes. He'd never been into queens and this was why. If he was going to fuck a man, he was going to fuck a man. "Tell him I've got a message from Jesse."

The man stopped, nearly choked, but before he could answer, he was elbowed out of the way by a much taller blond man—ruggedly handsome although unsmiling, and Tanner wondered if he was face to face with Damon himself.

But rather than introduce himself, he asked, "What did you say about Jesse?"

"You heard me," Tanner bit out.

The man nodded slowly. "I heard you. I just don't know how Damon's going to feel about this." He paused. "Are you sure you want to go there?"

Tanner reacted before he could stop himself. "Why the *fuck* would you care where I want to go?"

The man raised a brow and held up a finger, indicating for Tanner to wait a minute, before disappearing down a back hallway.

Last chance to head for the hills. And despite the ease with which he could do so, Tanner remained rooted in place.

He couldn't see very far into the club at all from where he stood—it was designed purposely to let the incoming patrons hear the familiar sounds of sex occasionally rising over the music. The smell of sex was also unmistakable, partially hidden and mixed with whiskey and smoke. It was meant to beckon, to lead men astray...and Tanner didn't bother to hide his hard-on.

A few minutes later, Tanner was being led by the blond man who introduced himself as LC back to a private office with a big *Do Not Disturb* sign on the door.

No doubt, *this* counted as disturbing Damon, but it had been eating away at Tanner for a year now. He had to rid himself of this burden, do what Jesse asked and then go home and pretend none of it ever happened.

Before going in, he glanced at his watch. Just after midnight. Exactly the way Jesse had wanted it.

A hard growl of a voice called, "Come in."

LC stared at him, and Tanner, in turn, stared at the floor for a long moment. And then he opened the door and realized he'd been anything but prepared for Damon Price. Tanner was big and broad and strong, stood six foot three and turned heads wherever he went. But Damon—he was well over six foot five, with jet black hair and chiseled features. He stood, hands at his sides in a deceptively casual stance, dressed in full black leather and looking like a fucking badass.

Tanner nearly hyperventilated, because Jesse hadn't mentioned this part.

"He's my boyfriend and he owns a club," was all Jesse said. *"He's strong—reminds me of you. He's a Dom."*

"I'm not a Dom."

"No. But you could probably use one. It would be the only kind of man who could handle you."

Jesse had closed his eyes then before Tanner could tell him he had no interest in being anyone's bottom boy. Because Jesse had been talking to him about boyfriends and Doms when he'd been dying, slowly and painfully in the middle of a jungle in South America where he and his Ranger team had been on a mission, and Tanner had been fucking helpless to stop it.

Fuck.

He shoved his hands in his pockets so Damon wouldn't see the fists he couldn't uncurl and hoped the pain didn't show in his eyes.

This was supposed to bring closure—to both Damon and Tanner. There was no way to break a promise to a dead man.

Damon studied him for a few minutes. Tanner wasn't the type to squirm and he wasn't about to start now. Finally, the man said, "I hear you have a message from Jesse. And I swear to Christ, if you're fucking with me, I'll put your head through the wall."

Tanner snorted in spite of himself. "Okay, sure. I'd like to see you try."

Damon pushed away from the desk and stood toe-to-toe with him. "Talk."

Talk. Yeah, like it was that easy. "Jesse told me to come here—to ask for you. To tell you that..." Fuck. He shifted, aware that the proximity of Damon was freaking him out. If he hadn't been Jesse's, Tanner might've made a move without a second thought.

As if he knew what he was thinking, Damon arched an eyebrow at him, his lip curled into a half sneer.

Fuck it all. "I'm supposed to tell you to have a session with me. Jesse wanted it that way." "A session?" Damon repeated.

"Yeah. I'm supposed to let you Dom me. It was Jesse's dying wish."

Damon paled, took a step back from Tanner, and then another. "Is this a sick joke?"

"Do I look like I'm joking?"

"You little fuck." Damon had Tanner's shirt bunched in his fists, was slamming him against the office wall hard. "You sick bastard. You think you can ingratiate yourself to me by using Jesse?"

Tanner ground his teeth together hard and tamped back his anger. He'd known Damon wouldn't take this well. If Tanner had been in the same position, he doubted he would either. "He asked me to wait a year before I came here. He died after midnight."

"How do you know that?" Damon demanded. "Even I don't know that."

No, he wouldn't. The mission was deemed classified—and Jesse's time of death a closely guarded secret. "I was with him when he died."

Damon let out a long, hissing breath and let go of Tanner's shirt.

"I'm sorry—I didn't know how else to tell you. Jesse made me promise—"

"Stop saying his name," Damon growled hoarsely.

"He made me promise I'd wait the year. Said you wouldn't be ready before that. That you'd need to be dragged back into the land of the living, kicking and screaming. He said to tell you...to use the skull- and-crossbones collar with the broken latch." He spoke fast, stopped to catch his breath at the end. Gauged Damon's reaction.

The man hadn't moved a muscle during Tanner's speech. Simply stared, and Tanner tensed more, wondering if he was going to have to fight tonight.

Fighting and fucking were definitely two of his favorite things to do, sometimes all in the same night—or hour—or hell, the same time, but he had a feeling that he'd be pushing his luck taking on this guy.

He was in way over his head. And he couldn't remember the last time—if ever—he'd felt that way.

Damon's features relaxed slightly. He sat back on the top of the desk, folded his arms and stared Tanner up and down. A hard, assessing stare that was enough to make Tanner hard with desire and anticipation.

He wasn't sure why the sudden thought of Damon taking him got him hot, but that was short-lived, because he saw the tension in Damon's stance, the pain in his eyes. Tanner wanted to apologize, but he wasn't sure what for. Wanted to tell Damon that he was scared to fucking death that the Domming would actually happen—and also scared that it wouldn't.

He was so fucked up he could barely see straight.

Damon finally spoke. "I wouldn't touch you. You're not man enough to handle me."

Jesse's words echoed in Tanner's ear. *It would be the only kind of man who could handle you.*

Tanner hadn't been able to handle a relationship—or being touched, really, since what happened to Jesse last year. And so he nodded and he said, "You're right about that. This was a mistake."

The failure hanging on him heavily, he pushed out the door, went through the club and headed for the parking lot.

Jesse.

Damon had mourned over that man, cried over him, beat his fists against the wall, up until three months earlier. Things had eased, but he still wore the cloak of grief that sometimes threatened to choke him.

Now was one of those times. He'd waited until the gorgeous man left his office before he fell apart and tried his best not to hyperventilate.

Use the skull-and-crossbones collar with the broken latch.

The boy who'd just left his office would have no way of knowing that—wouldn't have known that Damon kept that collar in his loft, had fixed the latch right after Jesse died because it was one of the only things he could do.

Damon wouldn't be able to use the damned collar on this boy—Jesse knew that collaring meant something—that it didn't happen on a first night together.

You don't even know the boy's name.

He shuddered involuntarily that he'd thought of him as *the boy*. Because that's what he'd called Jesse—and only Jesse.

Jesse had been the first to ever thaw what Damon had considered a heart of ice. First, and the *only*.

But something tugged at his gut.

He could've been lying. This could be part of an elaborate scam.

The only thing was, the man had definitely been military. A Ranger, like Jesse, or so he said. Damon didn't doubt it, had a nose for those things, having been in special forces himself what seemed like a lifetime ago. And the timing was exactly right. Jesse had died a year ago, nearly to the hour, although he'd lied to the boy about not having that information.

Fuck.

He called through the open office door, "LC, grab that guy who just left."

"I'm not your bitch," LC drawled, and no, LC was no one's bitch...not since Styx left. "And he's already in the lot."

"Dammit."

LC held his gaze for a second and then called to one of the bodyguards. "Renn—grab the guy in the brown leather jacket who just left. And bring a few guys—he won't come willingly."

LC didn't say anything more, didn't have to, and just headed to the front of the club to supervise. And Damon waited in his office, trying not to pace. Trying not to picture what the boy would look like, bound and spread for him.

Trying to pretend he wasn't hard at the thought of it.

He shifted but could do nothing to hide the erection in the pants he wore, and when LC barged back into the office, it was the first thing he noticed.

Thankfully, he didn't comment on it, just said, "They've got him and he's not happy."

"Makes two of us."

"Did he really know Jesse?"

Damon nodded. "He says that Jesse sent him here—wanted him to have a session with me."

LC's eyes widened, but wisely his mouth remained closed. He was part owner of Crave, working mainly behind the scenes. He was also Damon's best friend—the only person Damon confided everything in. The only one he trusted enough to let him run the business in those months after Jesse died, when Damon couldn't get out of bed most days. LC had finally gotten him up and functioning.

Just then, the boy was dragged back in by three men—he was pissed for sure, but not fighting as hard as he could. Damon knew that, and whether it was grief or curiosity or both, he couldn't tell yet.

"Let him go," Damon commanded, and the men dropped him and left the room with LC, the office door shutting behind them as the boy stumbled forward until Damon caught him, held him hard by the biceps and stared at him again.

He was handsome as hell—all-American-looking, a blond haired, blue-eyed devil, even with his lips twisted into an angry grimace.

"What the fuck do you think you're doing?" The boy jerked out of his grasp and yes, he was strong. Damon had suspected as much. Earlier, when Damon had him by the shirt, backed against the wall, he hadn't flinched. It was the calm of a man who knew how to fight—who knew how to kill.

"What's your name?"

A jut of a chin, a glint of wild eyes and he ground out, "Tanner."

"Why did you come here?"

"Because I made a promise to Jesse when he was dying. I don't break promises like that."

"And you're willing to follow through on what he wanted."

Tanner pressed his lips together—he wanted to say no, that much Damon knew. For some reason, this handsome, strong, brave man wanted nothing to do with being Dommed, and it didn't appear to be for the usual reasons.

No, he wasn't uncomfortable, either in this club or with Damon and his leathers. But something was most definitely wrong with him.

"I'll do what Jesse wanted, yes."

"But you don't think you're man enough."

He waited for Tanner to snap an answer back, but none came. Instead, he shrugged.

"Well then, there's no time like the present. But no collar." He motioned for Tanner to follow him, out the door of the office, down a small hallway and into a room marked Room Four.

Once inside, Damon pressed a few buttons to bring the lights up and to remove the shading from the plate-glass divider that separated the room from the rest of the club.

As soon as he did so, the bar began to cheer. Damon activated the two-way speakers as well, so the sounds went from muffled to completely clear.

Tanner's eyes widened. "We're doing this here—where everyone can see?"

"Yes. That's what Jesse would've wanted."

Tanner couldn't have known that was the furthest thing from the truth—that Jesse understood the value of privacy at the start of a D/s relationship.

That Jesse would hate him for this.

Well, Damon hated Jesse for dying and leaving him. For refusing to quit the military and let Damon take care of him for the rest of his life.

For recognizing that Damon had been slowly dying inside during the last year of their relationship and continuing to satisfy his own needs instead.

Tanner swallowed hard and then he nodded.

Yes, let's see if this man is for real.

If you have enjoyed this excerpt, you can find the rest of *Bound by Honor* here:

http://www.sejakes.com/books/bound-by-honor/

BOUND BY LAW

MEN OF HONOR, BOOK 2

The one man he can't forget is the one whose memories could destroy them all.

After the one man he trusted disappeared, it took Law Connor ten years to take a chance on another relationship. Trouble is, right about the time he's finally ready to let go of the past, the past stages a hostile takeover.

Back when they were teens, Styx was the boy with no memory. He and Law had each other's backs until he was forced to leave to keep Law safe. Now a CIA agent, he's finally discovered who he is, and why he's a hunted man.

Detective Paulo McMannus has almost succeeded in helping Law forget his lost love when Styx comes plowing back into their lives. No way is Paulo giving up his lover without a fight.

Suddenly Law finds himself on the run with Styx, the man who can still bring him to his knees...and with Paulo, the man who brought him back to life. The worst part? He can't choose between them. And it's getting harder to remember why he should.

Warning: Contains rough language, rougher sex and warriors who fall hard for one another.

PROLOGUE

HE'D BEEN Styx for literally as long as he could remember.

If there was a birth certificate that proved otherwise, he'd yet to stumble on it. His reissued one gave a date of birth that seemed reasonable, since his old hospital records were simply gone—it was as if he'd materialized out of nowhere. Having absolutely no memory of his youth before the age of sixteen didn't help matters any. His first centered on waking up on a bench in Central Park, wandering into a gay club where he ended up crashing on a cot in the back for a while, until the owner invited him home.

The owner was Greg, who'd figured Styx for underage and had given him a refuge and a new life. The one who'd helped him get the new birth certificate and ID. At first, Styx had waited for the catch, assumed Greg wanted something from him. As it turned out, Greg did. He wanted Styx to grow up safe and sound, was paying it forward, the way a man had done for him years earlier.

Law had already been there about two years when Greg took Damon in, followed in swift succession by Styx. None of them were formally adopted by any means—CPS wouldn't have looked kindly on a forty-year-old gay man taking in underage gay boys, but it had been aboveboard from the start, a light in all three men's lives that ultimately saved them—from outside forces as well as themselves. It had been a real home—and Styx owed the man everything.

All three had been straddling the line between boy and man and had been drawn to Greg as if he were some sort of Guardian Angel. Styx had never changed his opinion of that.

Greg had never asked for a penny. He'd died about sixteen years ago and Styx still missed the hell out of him. Missed the other men as well. Styx had left them when he was almost twenty without so much as a note in the middle of the night when a threat from his past came out of the blue, and he turned himself in to the CIA a year later, when the burden of his past got too much to bear alone. For the past sixteen years, he'd lived like the spook he was.

He'd kept up with Law and Damon—both had gone the way of the military, and they remained friends, running clubs together up until a few months ago. He'd only allowed himself to visit Law three times, and although he'd never come right out and told Law or Damon what he was, both men had spent enough time around elite forces to be able to sniff out the fact that he was a spook.

It was what he did—who he was. And lately, it had him missing Law, the love of his damned life and the man he left behind, to the point where he was driving himself crazy.

But the past...it was coming for him again. Although he knew why, he still had yet to remember it for himself. And now, he had a chance to find out the full, fleshed-out version, and he was driving to reach the place where it would be delivered to him.

And so Styx walked up the stairs and closed the door, and he waited for the knock that would change his life.

LC slammed out of Crave, the BDSM club he used to be part owner of and where he never should've gone back to in the first place, got into his Porsche, and let it coast along the deserted streets. He willed himself to relax, let the music pound through him, but he knew that wouldn't work.

No, he needed to fuck. He'd already fought, slamming the shit out of some asshole who'd tried to throw his weight around at the club. And LC, already primed for action, had taken over, ignoring Damon telling him to stand down.

Damon, his friend and other former owner of the club, had yanked him off the man and hadn't said another word, and LC had left before he did or said something he'd regret.

He was so damned tired of regrets. Tired of being alone and thrashing around at night, dreaming of two different men —one he loved and one he was falling for.

Thing was, the past few weeks, the dreams had been... different. And it was time to start listening to where his subconscious was pushing him.

The houses flew by him and he knew where he had to go, the destination calling him like a beacon.

He headed up the walk and let himself in the main door, a skill he'd used widely and well for years, almost long forgotten, and it made him smile when he remembered it easily. The lock clicked open and he went up the three flights with stealth and thought about doing the same to the apartment door.

But he knocked instead, two hard bangs, and he heard movement inside. He hoped the man was alone, wanted him to be—needed him to be, even though he had no right to ask or expect that at all.

Where the hell have you been? was written all over his face, and the man refused to let LC in at first. But LC persisted and Paulo relented, and finally LC barreled in, grabbing and kissing the man until he stopped resisting and twined his hands in LC's hair and moaned into his mouth.

He practically carried the man back inside the apartment, kicked the door closed behind him before they tumbled to the floor, clothes ripping off, grunting, grabbing.

Then he pulled back. "I've been thinking about you. Dreaming about you...can't stop."

"About time," was all the other man said before LC covered his mouth again with a kiss.

The knock startled him, although it shouldn't have. Styx hesitated before opening the door—a highly trained, gun-carrying, wet-work assassin hesitated opening the damn door to his own apartment and yeah, maybe it was time to think about getting the hell out of Dodge.

But he opened it, the door to his past, took the envelope from the man's hands and didn't look him in the eye. His hands shook, making the fat envelope flutter in his fingers, the only sound in the otherwise silent room.

The world was silent at three in the morning, and typically, he liked that. Now, he longed for sounds, any sound but the tearing of the envelope and the unraveling of a life long buried by necessity.

He held that life in his hands, and the responsibility, the revelations, all threatened to crush him if he wasn't careful.

For the first time in a long time he realized he no longer wanted to be careful.

CHAPTER ONE

PAULO WASN'T TAKING no for an answer, so LC had no choice but to concede to having dinner with the man. They were getting past the anonymous fucking stage and Paulo knew that, took advantage of him when he was weak from orgasms. Hence, the fancy goddamned dinner at an expensive restaurant where the detective obviously knew the staff. They got a private table in the back and appetizers began arriving without them having to place any orders. Paulo kept pouring the wine and LC got looser with each glass, and he knew he'd be going home with Paulo again that night for sure. Or maybe he'd take Paulo back to his new apartment for the first time, a new place, a fresh start...the same guy more than once, and that was a fucking record that had remained unbroken for ten years.

"Tell me what LC stands for," Paulo murmured now. "Or I'll tie you down and fuck it out of you."

"That's incentive to tell you?" LC asked as he scanned his menu for the main courses, not wanting to let Paulo see how turned on he got when Paulo spoke like that. Because he did so easily, his eyes hot, and LC remembered how good his body had felt against the younger man's.

Before last night, it had been about three months since he'd seen him last. Paulo had come to visit LC in the hospital after he'd thwarted an attacker who'd been hurting men outside Crave. Before that, Paulo had given him a gift—a gift certificate, to be exact, for a tattoo, which LC hadn't used yet. Paulo's torso was close to being covered with them, intricate designs that swirled over muscles in his back and arms and made him that much goddamned harder to resist.

LC loved looking at them, loved tracing them with his tongue, his fingers, watching the way they moved when LC was pounding him, the way he had last night.

"I was glad you came over," Paulo said after they'd finished the appetizers and waited on the next course.

LC had been surprised, too. He'd been restless for months and prowling the club scene no longer held his interest. Crave was sold and things were moving forward.

Everyone was moving forward and he'd been standing still. At first, there had been a lot to do with the sale of the club and the lofts and the construction of the new apartments he and Damon bought, along with the rest of the building. They were now living on opposite ends of the top floor, and the plan was to renovate and rent the rest of the apartments.

There was still a hell of a lot to do, but LC didn't feel like handling any of it, especially not last night. No, he'd wanted to handle someone, and his car had pointed in the direction of Paulo's place almost as if he'd had no control.

But LC knew that was bullshit.

Paulo had barely been able to get out a hello before LC had him pinned, telling Paulo he'd been dreaming about him before he could stop himself. After that, it was a blur of hands and tongues and *oh yeah*s, and then LC was agreeing to dinner, because he'd just taken the man without so much as a this-is-where-I've-been-for-the-past-few-months explanation.

He'd stayed through until the sun came up and straggled back to his new place, and now he was here, next to this man in this dark restaurant, and he'd been turned on from the time Paulo had picked him up.

If he was honest with himself, Paulo was handling him and LC really fucking liked it.

Paulo hadn't asked him any more about the dreams LC had about him, and for that, LC was grateful. Because this, the tug in the stomach when Paulo looked at him, was new... the first time since Styx, and he knew this man could make him happy, if he allowed it.

He downed the rest of his wine and stood before he told Paulo that. "Headed to the restroom—I'll be back."

"I'd join you, but I have a reputation in this place," Paulo said with a sly smile.

"I'm sure." LC threaded his way through the back hallway, found the men's room. He pissed and washed up in the private restroom, wiped his hands on a paper towel, and it was all normal. So normal.

Until the lights went out and shots rang out inside the restaurant and an arm came up across his body, a hand over his mouth, and his natural instinct to fight like hell was quelled with a single breath.

Styx. He'd recognize the man's scent—his touch—blindfolded. Many a time he'd actually done so, but this situation was a thousand percent different.

"Not a word." Styx's voice, rough like gravel. Rougher

when he was angry or aroused. His breath was warm and minty—Altoids. The man had always been addicted to them.

Damn, you remembered the oddest things when your ass was on the line. And speaking of asses, his was pressed hard to Styx's groin...and the man's arousal was unmistakable. Nice to know he wasn't the only one affected by the close proximity.

He moved his head and Styx took his hand away.

"Paulo," he said, and Styx answered, "Your friend's safe—my associate has him."

Good, that was good, but Jesus, what was going on here?

He heard the slight snick of a gun's safety being released and then heavy footsteps. Whoever was coming wasn't interested in stealth.

Not good.

"Whatever happens, stay put in here. I'll take care of everything." Styx barely mouthed the words but LC heard them loud and clear. And then he was left alone in the dark, and yeah, that was the story of his goddamned life with and without Styx, and he listened and waited.

No more shots, but someone had been killed. LC had been around stealth and death long enough in the Army to the point where he could taste the violence. He'd been on the receiving end of it since birth.

Goddammit, LC, shake that shit off.

And then Styx was back, tugging at him, and LC resisted. "I'm not going anywhere until you tell me what the hell's going on out there."

"There's trouble. Now shut up and do what I say."

"I'm so beyond listening to you."

"You have no idea who and what you're up against.

Come with me," Styx said, and LC reluctantly followed him into the restaurant's storeroom, close to the parking lot. And even though it was dark as night inside the restaurant's back room, LC would know the man, could practically see the dark blond hair, longer than it had been, eyes that never failed to mesmerize him, the hard body and even harder cock that had probed him earlier.

LC knew what he was up against—and he was powerless to stop it. And when he started to edge past Styx, Styx let him go at first and then pushed him hard against the wall by the door.

"Are you with that guy?" he whispered into LC's neck, and he wanted to tell Styx not to do that.

Instead, he ground out, "His name is Paulo. And now you're worried about my dating habits?"

"I'm always worried about you."

"The not calling or writing is a great way to show that."

"It's the way it has to be."

Has to be...not using the past tense meant that's what would happen after Styx did whatever it was he needed to here. "What, exactly, is happening out there to get the CIA involved?"

"Can't tell you."

"Right. I don't have the clearance to be involved in any part of your life." Never did. Never would. "Let fucking go of me."

"You can't leave now."

"Then you'll have to arrest me."

With that, Styx reached up and yanked LC's arms down and behind his back, and when the cuffs snicked on his wrists, he cursed bitterly. "Where's Paulo?"

"Safe."

"Not what I asked."

"Are you two serious?"

"Why don't you tell me? You've been spying on me for God knows how long."

"I call it keeping you safe."

"Get. The fuck. Off me."

Styx didn't listen. Never did, which was why the military hadn't been for him. "You bottom for him?"

"I'm trying to figure out why the hell you would care if I did."

"Guess I have my answer. And you know why."

"Not anymore, Styx. Too much time's passed."

He felt Styx's body stiffen, thought the man would release him. And then...

And then Styx's hand went to his cock as he sucked on the back of LC's neck along the spot—*that spot*—he'd discovered drove LC wild.

The only one who'd ever found it, and oh God, he was going to come in his fucking pants if Styx didn't stop.

And Styx would not stop.

"Like that, baby?" Styx whispered after licking the spot where LC knew there'd be a red mark that would stay there for days, then used his tongue and teeth and hands, slipped into LC's half unzipped jeans to work his magic.

"Fuck...please...don't, Styx." But he was saying *don't* and meant *don't stop*. And it was something he wanted—needed —too much to struggle more.

He'd always been a goddamned whore for this man—that would never change.

"Styx." The name, moaned into the dark, and if the man called him by his nickname, he'd lose it in his pants.

A few minutes and then a husky whisper answered, "Yeah, come right now, Law."

Law.

Law had no choice. His body always deferred to Styx's wishes. *Always.*

Styx wiped the man's stomach with some hastily grabbed napkins—he'd pulled Law's shirt up before he came so at least there wasn't a huge mess, and it had taken everything to not get on his knees and let Law come down his throat.

He threw the used napkins aside and fixed Law's clothes as the man remained silent, his breathing calming from the riot it had been moments earlier, when he'd come and cried out Styx's name.

God, he'd been dreaming about that for fucking ever.

"How long have you been checking up on me?" Law asked finally, his voice hoarse.

"Since the second I left your side."

"Right, and that was your damned choice." Law was furious. He slammed Styx off him and Styx hit the wall hard, and he tried to stumble forward.

Too late. Law had him pinned. Law, who had elite training and had gotten the handcuffs off like they'd been paper. Now, his body ground against Styx's. "You're a goddamned coward, running from me. From us."

"You don't understand."

"Then make me," Law demanded. When Styx said nothing, Law brought his mouth on Styx's in a punishing kiss meant to torment him with memories. His tongue forced itself into Styx's mouth, his cock pressed against Styx's as their groins ground together and finally, Styx brought his hand up to twist in Law's hair, keeping him from breaking the kiss. He tasted like Styx and mint and God, he'd missed this more than he even knew.

This was why he'd stayed away completely. For him, Law was like a drug—addicting and intoxicating, and he was in so much trouble.

He didn't care. Not when Law's hand reached between them and unzipped Styx's jeans so his hard cock slapped unfettered into Law's hand.

Styx groaned against his mouth at the contact, felt Law smile and then his hand stroked his cock in a way that Styx remembered, played with his Prince Albert piercing in a way that made Styx want to scream and fuck him immediately.

Law had always been talented. Now, more so and Styx wanted nothing more than to let him take over completely, to admit everything to him and beg for forgiveness.

He was this close to doing so, especially when Law stroked harder and fast and Styx's balls tightened and his orgasm loomed imminently.

"Fuck...Law." He threw his head back as his hips bucked uncontrollably.

Law could always make him come like this, could always make him lose control...and love it. Styx wondered if Law felt the same or if the loss of control would make Law angry and retreat back into his shell once the orgasm faded and he regained his senses.

Law didn't clean him or zip him, left Styx to do it himself

and when he was done, the lights came up—Tomcat's signal for the all-clear. For now, at least.

The man's real name was Clint, but he hadn't used that in the year and a half he'd been on the sting inside the motorcycle gang's operation. Better that Styx and everyone else used the call sign. Better...and safer.

Law was staring at him, sizing him up. Goddamn, Law looked good. Rugged, sensual...age had done him well. "Law, you've got to let me explain."

"I know what you want. You want control over me. You don't want me, but you've made sure I can't be with anyone else." Law was furious, ten years of pent-up anger tearing into Styx's soul.

He couldn't admit to Law that he'd done it enough to himself. Oftentimes it made him seek escape in whiskey and men until he couldn't see straight. And it never goddamned helped worth a damn.

He reached out to pull Law close, to admit something when they heard more shots. And Styx did grab Law, but only to stop him from running through the restaurant to check on his friend. "Wait—stop," he told the man, and Law consented for a second as Styx called Tomcat.

Tomcat told him, "There's another assassin—get the hell out of there."

"It's okay—everyone's all right," he lied to Law. "We've got to get out of here."

Law leveled him with a gaze, his voice as dangerous as Styx had ever heard when he stated, "Not without Paulo."

. . .

When Paulo first heard the shots that rang out from the kitchen, he sprang into action. ID'd himself as a cop, told everyone in the restaurant to get down and stay down under tables or behind the bar and then he pulled his gun and snaked his way through the hallway toward the kitchen. Prayed that LC hadn't gotten caught in the crossfire.

He remained flat against the wall, ready to check the bathroom for LC when he caught sight of a tall man coming down the corridor, toting a gun and flashing his badge. CIA. He motioned for Paulo to duck into the small break room to his right, and he did.

"What's going on?" he asked the agent.

"We have it under control."

"My friend was in the bathroom—"

The agent held up his finger and spoke into the mic on his wrist, then asked, "You Paulo?"

"Yes."

"He's all right. He knows you're okay." He put his arm down and extended his hand. "Call me Tomcat. Nice work keeping everyone calm out there."

"Do you need me to call the precinct?"

"I'm sure they're coming—right now, we'd prefer to keep this quiet."

Yeah, that was how the feds did things, but Paulo couldn't shake the feeling that the danger hadn't passed. That Tomcat was actually shielding him from something.

Was this man protecting him? "I don't need a bodyguard."

Tomcat simply grinned a little and murmured into the mic on his wrist again. The man was at least six foot-five, with dark hair, tattooed arms and a fierce-looking sawed-off shotgun. Looked like some kind of rogue agent. "You're gonna stay with me anyway."

Paulo didn't answer, and the men remained silent for what seemed like a hell of a long time. Then more shots rang out and he and Tomcat immediately went guns up against either side of the door.

"I'm going—you stay," Tomcat told him.

"Fuck that. What about all the people in the restaurant?"

"You're my concern."

Paulo nodded as if he conceded, because it was faster. Left the room a minute after Tomcat and went in the opposite direction toward the main part of the restaurant. He checked on the patrons, assuring them that he would protect them, making sure no one needed medical attention, because some of them looked like they were in shock.

And then he stilled, because it was too quiet and not at all like a typical aftermath. Whether or not Tomcat was after someone in the kitchen, there was more than one assailant here.

Paulo checked the windows of the restaurant—it was all quiet on the street front, but that wasn't odd. It was a dead-end, out-of-the-way place and the restaurant was the only destination. The parking lot was in the back and there was only one front entrance from the street.

But there was another doorway to the right—no doubt to a back staircase. Paulo saw the knob turn and then a man came barreling out from where he'd been lying in wait.

And he was staring right at Paulo. Gunning for him.

Paulo didn't wait to ask how long he'd been there, aimed and pulled the trigger twice, took the bastard down without hesitation.

He'd learned his lesson once, the hard way—hesitation cost you—and, if you were lucky, it was only your pride.

"It's okay," he told the patrons, went to the downed man with his gun still drawn, kicked the gun away from the body and knelt to take a pulse.

There was none. Paulo felt for his ID and pulled out a couple of photographs instead.

The first was a picture of him leaving the hospital, dated three months earlier, according to the back. The next showed LC in the hospital, sleeping in his bed, and a piece of paper had the name of the restaurant and the time of their reservation on it.

This had been an ordered hit.

The thought that he and LC were being targeted churned his stomach, and he continued to roust the dead man until Tomcat was hauling him to his feet and sirens sounded in the background.

"Jesus, but you don't listen."

Paulo jerked out of his grasp and checked his cell phone, pulled out the battery and found no bugs, but that didn't matter—they could've triangulated the signal some other way. He turned it off just in case it was sending out a signal as Tomcat checked out the dead man on the floor.

"Please, help my husband."

Paulo turned immediately to help the older gentleman who was having trouble breathing. The air smelled like gunpowder and was thick with fear, and Paulo got the man flat with his feet up as his wife gave him his heart meds under his tongue.

In a minute, the man's color came back and Paulo allowed Tomcat to move him away.

"Where's LC?" he demanded as Tomcat waved the paramedics in to help. Two men in suits—more obvious agents than Tomcat—came in behind them, presumably to smooth over the situation.

"You're a pain in the goddamned ass," Tomcat muttered to him as they walked toward the kitchen. Paulo saw the blood spatter but he wanted to see LC for himself and that was more important than investigating right at the moment.

"Listen, cop—"

"Detective."

Tomcat stopped in the middle of the hallway. "Whatever. Look, this is a bad situation."

"That guy was an assassin," Paulo said, and Tomcat stared at him as Paulo shoved the pictures into his hands. "He was gunning for me before I'd even turned around. My picture was in his goddamned pocket. Mine and LC's. So don't goddamned bullshit me anymore."

Tomcat put his hands up as if in surrender, told him, "I'm going to put you in the kitchen with your friend and another agent. Think you can stay put and stop being a hero long enough to get an explanation?"

Paulo stared at him, trying to determine if that was sarcasm, and saw nothing but respect in the man's eyes. It might make things easier, but this was far from over.

After Law refused to leave, there were two more shots that practically had him clawing at the door. He'd even tried to take Styx's gun to go out there but Styx held him back and listened on the mic as Tomcat kept him up to date.

Apparently, the cop was suddenly a hero—and completely fucked at the same time. He'd discovered the hit out on him and Law...the only thing he didn't know was that Styx was the main target.

If Styx had his way, no one beyond him and Tomcat would ever know that part. But it was far too late to keep the secret that his father was also after Law, and Paulo now, by default. The only one he would keep was the fact that his father didn't want him back into the fold this time—no, the man wanted him dead.

"Where's Paulo? I want to see him," Law demanded.

"Fine." Styx gritted his teeth and muttered to Tomcat using the mic on his wrist. "Bring him in here."

It only took a minute before Tomcat was ushering Paulo in, the towheaded man looking more handsome than Styx remembered.

Paulo looked more than pissed, glared at Styx as he went to Law who was barreling toward him too. "You all right?"

The complete concern on both their parts was impossible to miss and threatened to overwhelm him, and he almost turned away when Law tugged Paulo into his arms, murmured, "Jesus, I'm fine. Heard the shots."

"Good." Paulo looked over Law's shoulder at Styx, his eyes held questions but he didn't say anything else.

"Can we get out of here and go home?" Law turned to ask Styx.

"No." Styx glanced at Tomcat who then slipped out of the room, no doubt to get the safe house directive in order, because what would happen next would not be pleasant for any of them. "These men are dangerous."

"And they're after us?" Law asked.

"They're after you because of me. They followed me to your hospital room and they've been tailing you ever since," Styx admitted.

"Why?" Law demanded, ignoring the part about the hospital visit, which made Styx's gut tighten. What had he expected, Law to run into his arms with that admission?

"Because they know that the best way to get to me is through someone I love."

Paulo stared between the two of them as he remained in Law's arms—because Law was holding on to him tightly. "You're the one who left him for years."

"You're the one who'll leave before the year's out, if your stay-in-one-place-for-two-years-or-less pattern holds. Or is Law the love of your life? The one who'll make you stay, even if it means trouble?"

Paulo turned back to Law. "At least now I know your first name. But that doesn't mean I don't get to tie you down."

Paulo almost smiled at the growl the blond man named Styx emitted after his comment about tying LC down.

Law. Granted, Paulo had known LC's real name was Lawrence Connor because he'd investigated his past—he'd just been waiting for LC to tell Paulo himself and it had killed him not to be able to use it. And that asshole CIA guy was probably the only one LC let call him that. So yeah, the pleasure at the zing was short-lived because he was the one getting screwed in this situation.

Law. It suited the handsome man whose hair was a darker blond than both his and Styx's.

He wasn't even touching Styx's comment regarding his past. Styx, who was glaring between him and Law, even as Law gave him a small grin. "It's a deal."

"I hate to interrupt this magic moment," Styx started, and Paulo broke away from Law, fisted his hands and went toe-to-toe with Styx. The agent was a few inches taller than he was, but Paulo had taken on bigger and badder in his time, and he wasn't going to let this motherfucker think Paulo would kowtow to him.

"Then don't."

"Got yourself a bodyguard, Law?" Styx asked with a grin Paulo itched to punch off his face.

Law stepped in between them, his hand on Paulo's shoulder, tugging him back even as Paulo demanded, "Why aren't we getting the hell out of here if it's so dangerous?"

"Look, cop—"

Paulo knew it was time to push Styx. "If I don't start hearing an explanation now, I'm calling my precinct."

"Try it," Styx told him through gritted teeth.

"Come on, Paulo. We'll figure it out," Law told him, and Paulo turned from Styx back to him. He was grateful Law was safe and in one piece, and wasn't ready to tell him about the photos in the assassin's pocket. Styx would have to let them both in on everything soon enough, and Law already looked wrecked.

"There's nothing to figure out—you'll listen to me and do what I say," Styx persisted, and Paulo didn't have to worry about punching the shit out of Styx, because Law was mad enough for both of them.

"What the hell are we supposed to do now? Hide out in some shithole until you catch whoever's shooting at us?" Law demanded, no doubt partly to distract him from the pissing contest he appeared to be in with Paulo.

Styx eyed him coolly. "Yes. Tell the cop to give me his phone. And then I'm taking both of you into protective custody."

Law shook his head. "You've got to be kidding me. What —now we're going into witness protection for reasons unknown? Bullshit."

"I know the reasons." Styx's eyes met Paulo's and the two men came to a silent agreement. "Like I said, I've been trying to avoid this for months."

"Why's it taken that long? Oh, wait, that's SOP for the CIA," Law muttered. "Who got killed here tonight?"

"You don't have the clearance for that intel," Styx told him, and Paulo watched the fireworks between these men with great interest. The tension there was extreme—sexual and otherwise, and Paulo couldn't believe he was stuck in the middle of them.

"So let me get this straight—the three of us have to hole up together so we don't get killed?" Paulo asked, and Styx nodded, looking as grim at that prospect as Paulo felt. "For how long?"

"As long as it takes."

"I am going to need way more of an explanation than that, Styx." Law ran a hand through his hair, his irritation mounting as evidenced by the tension in his shoulders. Paulo put a hand on one of them, because no matter what, Law was safe for now.

"We can't hang around here to discuss this," Styx told him. "I'll tell you more when we get someplace a little less public, all right?"

"You weren't worried about that earlier," Law growled, and Paulo made a mental note to find out what that was all about, but first he put his hand on Law's arm.

"There was an assassin I shot. He had pictures of us in his pocket," he told Law, who stared between him and Styx.

Paulo actually felt bad for the agent, because Styx looked at Law the way Paulo felt...and why would you stay away from someone you loved so damned much?

None of this made sense, but it appeared he'd have nothing but time on his hands to unravel it.

If you have enjoyed this excerpt, you can find the rest of *Bound by Law* here:

http://www.sejakes.com/books/bound-by-law/

HOLD THE LINE

INKED, BOOK 1

Holding on loosely has never been such a challenge...

What happens when a tattoo artist and a Delta Force soldier keep a promise and take a cross-country trip together? Quinn and Con are about to finally meet and find out.

Quinn thinks he's the responsible one, but he quickly learns that he needs to loosen up if he's got any shot of holding onto Con.

(This novella is now available as a standalone, but was previously published in the Danger Zone *Anthology, with all proceeds going to* Hope For the Warrior.*)*

CHAPTER ONE

QUINN MCKENNA GLANCED down at the stack of paper that had arrived certified mail just hours before, care of his younger brother, and then back up at the man hanging out by the pool table.

He didn't have a picture of Conlan "Con" Jenkins in his packet—just a basic description—but he realized now he'd have known the tall, handsome Delta Force soldier anywhere. There was something in his bearing that Quinn picked out easily. Maybe it was because Quinn's father and brothers had been Delta too, so he was in tune with the way they operated. Most of the Special Forces soldiers he'd come in contact with in his younger days, including his father and his brothers, appeared so outwardly casual to the rest of the world, blending in when they needed to. But Quinn knew that Con was consistently on alert, and that, if asked, he'd be able to give a description of every single person in the place tonight.

Bet you'll find him playing pool, Scott had also offered next to the name of the bar/restaurant picked for the initial meet-up, then added, *He'll be the one winning, with a lot of pissed-off guys around him.*

So yes, Quinn'd picked Con almost from the start, but remained at his table, casually scoping the soldier out while he ate dinner. He noted both he and Con were early for their meet-up, and wondered if they'd both been trying to outmaneuver the other. Not that there was any reason for that kind of thing—this was supposed to be a fun trip, not a competition. A trip ordered by Scott, and something neither Quinn nor Con could—or would—refuse.

Quinn could hear that phone conversation echoing in his ears.

"Bring my best friend to me," Scott had ordered him three weeks ago on the phone, and in Con's paperwork, Quinn now saw that Scott had written, *Bring my brother home to me.*

When they'd spoken on the phone weeks earlier, Scott had also explained, "Con's dangerous with too much time on his hands."

Quinn remembered wanting to bang his head against the wall but had asked instead, "How dangerous?"

"You'll travel with him for a couple of weeks—you tell me."

Quinn immediately understood just what his brother meant, because Con was obviously well versed at hustling pool. The guys he'd been playing had gone from friendly to very disgruntled, and Con either noticed and didn't give a shit or else he was oblivious.

Quinn was betting on the former.

Then again, Con had refused the bets at least six times, had told the men asking that it wouldn't be fair, and not in a cocky, assholeish way. But the men weren't listening and Quinn knew there was a fight in Con's future. And that meant there'd be a fight in Quinn's as well.

There was still time to bail. He glanced at his watch, noting he was still early enough that Con wouldn't miss him if he left. Unless Con had pegged him from the moment he'd walked in.

Scott wants this, he reminded himself. And he wouldn't refuse his brother, no matter how badly he wanted to.

And he really wanted to. But Scott couldn't make this trip this year, not like he'd planned, and so he'd asked Quinn and Con to do it in his stead. They'd start here, outside of L.A. and end up in the Catskills, and ultimately, Scott's wedding, by way of the strange and varied path Scott had created for them.

By rights, Scott should've been here, a buffer between them, the glue that would bond them. Con and Scott had served together. Sat on the bus together to Basic, and from that point forward they'd been inseparable. Con did come home with Scott for some holidays, but Quinn hadn't been there for any of those. He was the older brother, off sowing his wild oats, which was true. But during that time, he'd also become a licensed tattoo artist. He'd also been featured on a few of those ink shows on reality TV, but he had no real aspirations to be a regular, even though his boss wanted him to be. Mainly because the producers also wanted to include more about his personal life, thinking that would make for great TV.

But this wasn't TV—this was his motherfucking life, as he'd pointed out. His private life was private for a reason, although he'd never made any bones about his sexual orientation, or his bent toward BDSM. The writers of the show offered to find him love, especially if they could follow him into the club scene.

His boss at the tattoo shop told him he'd cave sooner than later. Right before he'd given Quinn the time off to make this road trip. And if that was a bribe, it was a pretty effective one. So he'd pushed back appointments. But really, Scott did the rest of the work, from the big things like booking hotels and restaurants to the mundane of actually planning the route ("*Con will tend to ramble and he doesn't like to use maps—says he doesn't need them*")—and yeah, that was so *not* how Quinn operated.

But hell, he couldn't deny how handsome Con was. Not pretty boy, no. He was rugged looking, lanky with a swagger that probably made most guys want to be him or fall to their knees and beg to be fucked by him.

It made Quinn want to push Con to his knees and force his cock in between those full lips, watch them swell from sucking as his eyes glazed with pleasure.

You're supposed to be keeping an eye on him, not fucking him.

Did Scott even know if Con was gay, or bi? Did it matter?

What mattered was that this would be the longest trip of Quinn's life.

———

As soon as Con saw the pool table, he'd known he was fucked. Because he was nervous. Jumpy. And as much as playing pool always got him in shitloads of trouble, it also calmed him.

He'd come back to California forty-eight hours earlier after eight months OUTCONUS. He'd routed through his home post for seventy-two hours and then he'd literally come straight to this bar in Normalsville, USA.

He wasn't ready in any way, shape or form to be around civilians. Scott knew that—it was probably why he'd given Con a chaperone, in the form of Quinn McKenna.

Quinn'd arrived ten minutes after Con. Situational awareness was his job, and a guy like Quinn caught his attention easily. He'd seen pictures, but none had done Quinn justice. He'd walked in like he owned the place.

And he's bossy as fuck, Scott had told him often. And the way Quinn'd marched in, like he was planning on taking and conquering, made Con smile. Mainly because he didn't play by bossy rules. But looking at Quinn...maybe he should start.

Still, Con had been ignoring him for the better part of an hour, in favor of racking up. The pool cue, the chalk, the sharp snick of the balls as they snapped smartly together all drew him in, especially because of the way they mixed with the smell of beer and tobacco and cologne, all the bar chatter and music. The familiar sounds of his childhood.

And the people...he could group them easily, had been born and bred to group them in the most advantageous way possible. The monied set. The good ole boys. The cowards. The troublemakers.

Where Quinn fit in, Con had some idea, but he was open to really finding out. After a few games. And so he'd shot several, fucking up the first break the way he always did. His dad thought that Con had just perfected the art of the scam easily. Con had let him think it.

What was the alternative? *No, Dad. I really didn't fuck up my games on purpose—I let my nerves get the best of me...*

"You had a clear shot. Blind man could've made it."

Con didn't bother glancing up at the sound of the voice. Guaranteed, it was a plaid-shirted guy who'd been sitting at four o'clock, trying to pin him down for a so-called friendly game of pool.

Right now, Con screamed "easy betting money." But Con didn't want to bet on pool, hadn't planned on hustling tonight. The pressure had started from Plaid Shirt and then a few of his friends, and Con suggested they keep it friendly, play for beers. But the guys thought he was chicken. Goaded him.

Finally, because he needed to play pool and make them shut the fuck up, he took the bet. He figured he'd given them enough of an out that he didn't have to feel guilty. Now, an hour later, he was up two grand and up against three pissed-off regulars who would no doubt try to roll him in the parking lot when he left. At this point, they were in the "refusing to let him leave" stage of bargaining. The "just one more game" bullshit, like they'd suddenly get lucky.

Ain't happenin', boys.

Finally, Quinn'd sidled up to the table, looking like just another guy checking out the action. But he wasn't just another guy—he was big and tall and handsome...and he turned a lot of heads. He could probably fight well. But really, Con wouldn't have any problem taking on these guys the way he took their money. He'd told them not to—he'd been truthful, so that absolved him of any guilt he might've had.

Hell, he had enough guilt already—needed a fucking U-Haul for it—and wasn't looking to add more weight to pull.

Instead, he took a drink of the seltzer water that'd been fueling him most of the night and finally made eye contact with Quinn. The two of them were standing slightly away from the pool table, watching Plaid Shirt rack up—again—with the others watching him like they were afraid he'd just disappear into thin air.

Con could definitely do that, but it was more smoke and mirrors than anything. All of this was. So he stared at the big man who looked at him, disapproval written all over his face. It was literally going to be like being watched by Big Brother. Although he looked nothing like Scott, Scott had shared family pictures ad nauseam.

Con had none. In return for warm fuzzy family pictures and their accompanying stories (that Con had actually liked but would never come right out and admit to), Con taught Scott to hustle pool. Well, to assist. Hustling was a skill best learned young and used regularly, especially when someone was depending on it for survival. He'd learned early on that if he didn't hustle, he didn't eat. That's how he'd grown up.

"You're good," Quinn said in a low, deep voice.

"I know," he said irritably as Quinn's dark eyes locked him in place. He swallowed, forced himself to look away.

"How long are you going to keep this up?"

"I've been trying to get out of here for an hour."

"So go."

"Gotta give them a chance to make their money back. Wouldn't be fair otherwise," Con pointed out.

"Since when's what you do fair?"

Con smirked. "Since now. And you have no idea what I do."

"Hustler with a conscience. Interesting."

Yeah, it was interesting all right. "I'll meet you two exits down the highway."

Quinn raised a brow but didn't say anything.

Con wanted to be annoyed, but he was too busy noticing the tattoos that snaked out from under Quinn's pushed-up shirtsleeves, and one that twined elegantly along the side of Quinn's neck. "Seriously. Don't wait here for me. I'll be fine. Trust me."

Quinn looked between Con and the pool table and gave a soft snort in retort.

Quinn didn't listen to Con's orders, mainly because he didn't take them, not that he didn't believe Con could handle himself. When Con readied to leave, Quinn saw three of the men follow him out. Quinn brought up the rear, walked out onto the dark sidewalk in time to see Con smoothly dispatching the three men, doing barely any damage, but enough to make the men go back inside the bar.

For reinforcements, Quinn figured.

"Ready?" Con called as he got on his Harley, which was parked two spaces over from Quinn's big truck.

"Do we have a choice?" Quinn asked as he started his truck.

Con laughed, a sound that carried over the roar of his

own bike. "Unless you want to deal with more of them. I'm happy to do it."

Fuck. Not especially. Was it going to be like this for the entire trip, getting Con's ass out of scrapes?

"You weren't supposed to wait," Con called to him, right before he pulled out into the road. Quinn followed close behind, the two vehicles taking off smoothly into the night and disappearing without anyone following them.

They'd gotten lucky. Quinn knew that. He could only imagine the amount of times a trail of cars had followed Con.

Finally, he pulled off the exit, behind Con, as planned. They parked along the side of the rest stop where they'd have a good view if anyone drove in. It was mainly truckers stopping here this time of night anyway.

Con got off the bike and strolled up to Quinn's truck. Quinn opened the door and slid down to meet him. "What would you do if I wasn't here?"

Con laughed, sounding slightly crazy "What? You think I need you to bodyguard me? Newsflash—I don't."

"Fine. So we ride together and go our separate ways at night. You can hustle pool and defend your own honor."

"While you rest your old man bones? Sounds good."

"Let's leave my bone out of it," Quinn growled. Con looked right between his legs, letting his gaze linger, then slowly let it drift up to Quinn's face.

God, this fucker needed to be taught a lesson and Quinn was itching to do that, wanted to take him over his lap and...

Con grinned, like he knew what Quinn was thinking. Which wasn't possible. He was military, not psychic.

"We're not doing that every night," Quinn informed him.

"Last I looked, this wasn't a military base and you aren't in charge of me," Con told him.

Quinn raised a brow. "You're looking for someone to take charge?"

Con hesitated for only the briefest second. "Did I say that?"

Well, he might as well have, because dammit, Con was screaming for someone—the right someone—to hold him down and fuck him.

But he was supposed to simply be taking a road trip to see Scott. With Con. "Escorting him," was how Scott termed it. As he put it, "Without you, Con would eventually make it here, probably with a police car in tow."

Quinn glanced at Con. "Doesn't the military have rules?"

"Lots of them. Be specific."

"Moral ones? Propriety."

Con snorted. Motioned to himself. "Not in uniform, right? And I don't see any MPs around. Dude, I'm free. And you're killing my buzz."

Quinn's buzz was nonexistent, unless he counted the low-level buzz in his head that made him want to strangle Con and take him in hand in equal parts, and *fuck*, that wasn't good.

Instead, he went back to the truck, grabbed the itinerary that was Con's and handed it to him.

Con began to flip through it, standing under the lights of the Arby's in back of him. "Looks like our tour guide/travel agent took care of everything."

"Yeah, these came this morning." Quinn had glanced through the itinerary briefly. "It's got both weeks planned, down to the hotels he's reserved and paid for."

Con sighed and stuffed the folder in his bag. "Are we set for tonight?"

"Hotel's an hour away."

"We're starting tonight?"

"According to Mr. Control Freak, yes." He glanced at Con's bike. "Want to stow this? I've got a cover for it."

"You ride?"

"S'why I bought this truck." He opened the flatbed and pulled the ramp down. Con wheeled the bike up easily, chained it in and covered it up.

Then he joined Quinn in the cab, sliding into the passenger's side and dumping his camouflage duffel behind the seat. "She ride well?"

"Not bad. Better since I played with her."

"Gearheads," Con muttered, but he nodded with a smile when Quinn started the motor and it rumbled to life with a resounding roar.

Neither one of them was very talkative. They were both wound up from that last minute burst of adrenaline, and Quinn just wanted to get to the hotel before he lost that charge. With the radio pulsing some old school heavy metal—music Con didn't object to—Quinn tried to figure out the suddenly compliant soldier sitting next to him.

Scott'd never mentioned Con being gay or bi and it was obviously possible that he'd had no idea. Between DADT—because repealed or not it'd still been a part of Con's military life at one point—and the fact that these men were in one of the most gay-unfriendly professions, Quinn couldn't blame Con for not discussing his personal life.

Con didn't seem like he was the type to hide what he was, though. At least not off-base. While he could easily pass for straight, Quinn noted that, at least tonight, Con had made sure to catch as many men's eyes as he could.

Granted, Quinn had never come out and told Scott he was gay. He figured his family hadn't been able to handle the fact that he wasn't enlisting, and being gay would throw them over the edge. It wasn't a reveal he deemed necessary.

And the Dom part? Yeah, no fucking way.

Maybe he'd read Con's vibe wrong but, but...yeah, no. Especially not when Con had given him that smile and boldly looked him up and down.

Hell, had Scott known about him and told Con? Was this some kind of weird set-up?

Granted, if it was, Con had seemed as clueless about it as Quinn'd been. At some point, Con had started looking through the itinerary again. "Christ, he turned this into a military op."

"That he did."

"Well, this is what he wanted. Can't not comply with his wishes now," Con pointed out.

Two weeks. "Think we can make it in one?"

"And hit all the hotspots he highlighted?" Con shook his head. "What's the rush? I'm making the most of this—I plan to have fun in as many states as I can."

Jesus. Quinn rubbed his forehead. Nothing about this trip was fun, especially the endpoint. There was still time to say "fuck it," to get on a plane and show up, and hell, what was Scott going to do? Send him back to gather up Con? The guy was a grown fucking man in the Army, for Christsakes— he could get himself across the country.

And if he couldn't? Well, then maybe Con had bigger problems than Quinn should be expected to handle.

By the time Quinn pulled the truck into the hotel's lot, it was close to three in the morning. Con let him check them in, take the keys, sign for the room, and then Con followed him into the elevator.

The room was a two-bedroom suite. Con walked toward the room to the left immediately.

"We'll sleep in today and travel through late afternoon. We'll get to the next stop before nine tomorrow night and we'll be back on Scott's schedule," Quinn said firmly. Con grunted, went through the connecting doors ("Without shared suites you'll never keep track of him," were Scott's instructions) and left the door open.

Quinn glanced into Con's room and saw the man's clothes in a trail leading to the bed. And Con was only under the sheet—really, only partially under—and very obviously naked.

And there was no ink on his body at all—at least from what Quinn could see, which was three quarters of a solid body. That was a shame, because Con really had the perfect contours.

Stop thinking about his contours, Quinn.

But he couldn't stop. These next weeks would no doubt be a crash course in everything Con. And what an education it would be, if tonight was any indication.

And since his mind was racing, he did what he always did when he needed to calm the fuck down—he sketched.

He'd been born with art in his blood, and he'd been sketching from the time he could hold a pencil. He'd also liked giving orders. "Bossy as fuck," his father would say. "He'll make a good general."

He glanced back and forth between the bed and the

paper in front of him, drawing freehand...and feeling oddly freer than he had in a long damned time.

If you have enjoyed this excerpt, you can find the rest of *Hold the Line* here:
https://sejakes.com/books/hold-the-line-2/

ALSO BY SE JAKES

Men of Honor Series

Bound By Honor

Bound By Law

Ties That Bind

Bound By Danger

Bound For Keeps

Bound To Break

Phoenix, Inc. Series

No Boundaries

Inked Series

Hold The Line

Thirds

EE LTD. Universe

Free Falling

Hell or High Water Series

Catch A Ghost

Long Time Gone

Daylight Again

Not Fade Away

If I Ever

Dirty Deeds Series

Dirty Deeds

Havoc MC Series

Running Wild

Running Blind

Running on Empty (April 29, 2019)

WRITING AS STEPHANIE TYLER

Shelter Series

Shelter Me

Pieces of Me (*forthcoming*)

Mirror Series

Mirror Me

Rule Of Thirds

Walk In My Shadow

Double Blind (coming soon)

Skulls Creek MC Series

Vipers Run

Vipers Rule

Section 8 Series

Surrender

Unbreakable

Fragmented

Defiance Series

Defiance

Redemption

Salvation

The Defiance Series Collection

(Defiance, Redemption & Salvation)

Temperance

Dire Wolves Series

Dire Warning (prequel novella)

Dire Needs

Dire Wants

Dire Desires

Shadow Force Series

Lie With Me

Promises In The Dark

In The Air Tonight

Night Moves

Lonely Is The Night

Hold Series

Hard To Hold

Too Hot To Hold

Hold On Tight

Holding On (novella)

Hot Nights, Dark Desires Anthology

Night Vision (novella)

Harlequin Blaze

Coming Undone

Risking It All

Beyond His Control

WRITING AS SYDNEY CROFT

ACRO Series

Riding The Storm

Unleashing The Storm

Seduced By The Storm

Taming The Fire

Tempting The Fire

Taken By Fire

Three The Hard Way (novella)

Hot Nights, Dark Desires Anthology

Shadow Play (novella)

ABOUT THE AUTHOR

Stephanie Tyler is the *New York Times* bestselling author of romance novels spanning multiple genres, including Romantic Suspense, New Adult, Paranormal Romance and Contemporary Romance. She's a hybrid author who writes for multiple publishers, including Random House, NAL/Penguin, Harlequin, Carina Press, Mammoth Books, Belle Books and Samhain Publishing, as well as Riptide (as SE Jakes) and indie publishing. Her books have been translated into half a dozen languages, nominated for an RT Readers' Choice Award and garnered top picks from *RT Books Magazine* as well as starred reviews from *Publishers Weekly*. She's a frequent workshop presenter and has contributed stories for anthologies for charities, including *SEAL of My Dreams*, which has raised over 150K for the Veterans Medical Association.

Visit Stephanie Tyler at www.stephanietyler.com.

SE Jakes is the pen name for *New York Times* bestselling author Stephanie Tyler, and half the co-writing team of Sydney Croft. First published in 2011, SE Jakes has quickly risen to be a bestselling author in the LGBT romance genre, as well as a fan favorite. Her books are frequently highlighted in *USA Today* and have been reviewed by *Library Journal* and *RT Books Magazine*. She's been nominated by several sites for Favorite M/M author and has finaled in the Goodreads M/M Romance Readers Choice Awards in 7 categories. She's a hybrid author who writes for Riptide Publishing and Samhain Publishing, and she indie publishes as well.

Visit SE Jakes at www.sejakes.com.

Sydney Croft is the alter ego of Stephanie Tyler and Larissa Ione, two *New York Times* bestselling authors who blend their very different writing interests into adventurous tales of erotic paranormal fiction. Together, they developed a world where people with extraordinary abilities, like the power to control storms, could live and work with others like them. The series has been described as "Erotica meets the X-Men," and is unique in its own "erotic superhero romance" niche. Larissa and Stephanie live in different states and communicate almost entirely through email, though they often get together for conferences and book signings.

Visit Sydney Croft at www.sydneycroft.com.

For more information:
www.stephanietyler.com
stephanie@stephanietyler.com